"Imagine a story that has all the character of York, then fill it with all the ghosts from there too ... and whilst you're at it make it QUEER. Perfect if you like books like *Cemetery Boys*, *Ninth House*, *The Fell of Dark* and *The Taking of Jake Livingstone*"
Rory Michaelson, author of *Lesser Known Monsters*

"*Sixteen Souls* is a boundlessly clever, heartfelt queer take on the story of a sensitive young man who sees dead people. Talbot has a crafted something chillingly delightful! Perfect for any ghoul-lover's shelf"
Adam Sass, award-winning author of *Surrender Your Sons* and *The 99 Boyfriends of Micah Summers*

"*Sixteen Souls* was ridiculously easy to fall in love with. Victorian ghosts, a delectable mystery, a luscious York setting, and an irresistible queer friendship and romance, *Sixteen Souls* is a perfect read for fans of Gaiman and Stroud. I wish I could read it for the first time again!"
Dawn Kurtagich, author of *The Dead House*

"*Sixteen Souls* transported me so entirely, I feel as if I have walked the streets of York and seen the ghosts myself. An outstanding debut, this thrilling adventure perfectly mixes spookiness with mystery, sadness with love, and is filled with gorgeous characters you won't want to say goodbye to"
Bex Hogan, author of *Isles of Storm and Sorrow* series

"A deliciously dark debut from Rosie Talbot. I dare you not to fall in love with Charlie and his ghosts in the heart of haunted York"
Cynthia Murphy, author of *Last One to Die* and *Win Lose Kill Die*

Sixteen Souls uses British English conventions, spelling and grammar, as well as British colloquialisms.

Please be aware that some of the material in this story contains themes or events of death/dying, body horror, physical torture, violence and mentions of suicide, self-harm and murder. For a full list of content warning, please visit **www.rosietalbot.co.uk**

SIXTEEN SOULS

ROSIE TALBOT

SCHOLASTIC

Published in the UK by Scholastic, 2022
1 London Bridge, London, SE1 9BA
Scholastic Ireland, 89E Lagan Road, Dublin Industrial Estate, Glasnevin,
Dublin, D11 HP5F

Text and Map © Rosie Talbot, 2022
Illustrations by Andrew Davis © Rosie Talbot, 2022
Internal design by Becka Moor

The right of Rosie Talbot to be identified
as the author of this work has been asserted by her under
the Copyright, Designs and Patents Act 1988.

ISBN 978 0702 32532 8

A CIP catalogue record for this book is available from the British Library.

Printed by CPI Group (UK) Ltd, Croydon, CR0 4YY
Paper made from wood grown in sustainable forests and other controlled
sources.

1 3 5 7 9 10 8 6 4 2

www.scholastic.co.uk

For the living
(please read this book out loud for the dead)

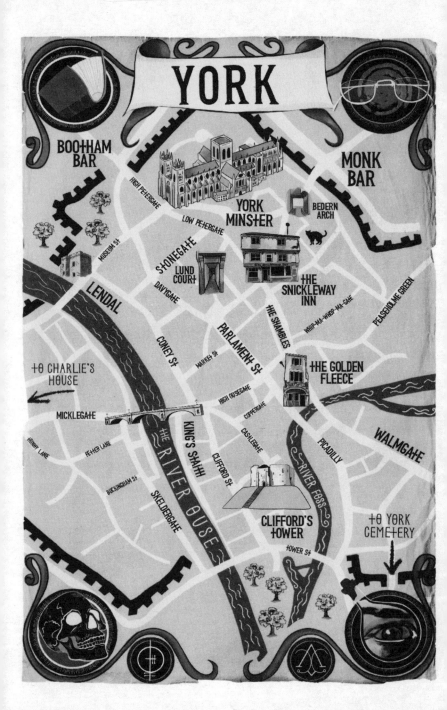

I

✝HE HAUN✝ING OF CHARLIE FRI✝H

It's the recently deceased that trouble me the most. Older ghosts aren't so bad. They're always dressed in jerkin and hose or corsets and wide skirts, so they're easily avoided – eyes down, earbuds in and they've no idea I can see them. But the newly dead look just like everybody else, and that's what makes them so dangerous.

I don't go rambling about the old part of York more than I have to, and never on my own. Today, Heather walks beside me as I move carefully down The Shambles, her stethoscope tangling in the yellow lanyard that holds her hospital ID. In the six years since her death she's not changed: same messy plait, pretty plump face, grey high-waisted slacks and a wrinkled shirt, her sleeves rolled up no matter the weather. She's nattering away in that honeyed voice of hers and I'm not really listening, but I let her words wash over me and keep walking, trying to disguise the slight limp that's been nagging me since the bus.

My prostheses have started to rub. I should have double socked, but then my sockets get too tight and I'm sore and aching by the end of the day. There's nothing I can do about it now. I never take my lower legs off in public, especially since the twins got at them with Mum's glittery varnishes. Now I've got pink and purple sparkles all over the covers.

We move along the cobbles. The old timber-framed buildings overhang, as if competing for daylight. It feels like each side of the row is leaning into one another, the jewellery shop longing to whisper a secret to the fudge makers opposite. Nothing is level here, not the walls or jambs to the squat doors, not the panes of glass in their quaint Victorian shop-front windows. Some have metal signs shaped like pies or shields hanging above them, with ornate metal brackets to fix them to walls of brick, cob and wood, walls that haven't really been clean for hundreds of years.

History hangs in the air like a stink I can't escape. Guy Fawkes was born here, they strung-up Dick Turpin here and Saint Margaret Clitherow was pressed to death beneath her own front door. So, it's no surprise that the ghosts are almost as numerous as the tourists.

I'm often told I'm an old soul for a lad of sixteen, but they've got it wrong. I'm no Old Soul. Actually, I do my best to avoid them.

I have to side-step around a ghost in a fur-trimmed cloak by feigning sudden interest in a window display of bunting and babygrows. Next, I twist back like I heard someone calling my name, all so a woman in a ruff doesn't bump into me. Unlike the other living people on the street, I'd be as solid to her as she is to me.

That's the price of seeing the dead. They can vanish through walls, pass right through regular people, but me, I'm flesh and bone to them. They can touch me. They can hurt me. The dead can be very demanding, not to mention dangerous if they get too keen and I can't leg it before they draw blood.

Sod that.

I'd have preferred to get the bus out to Monk's Gate shopping park where the floors are smoother and the ghosts fewer, but there is a shop here Heather insists we visit.

"What do you think about themed bookends?" She follows half a step behind me, acting like she's a confused ghost desperately trying to communicate with the living. The dead haunt people as often as places. I mean, there's nothing much for them to do except hang around and complain, even if no one but me can hear them.

I don't answer Heather's question, talking to a ghost on a street this haunted would be daft. She goes on some more, reeling off a list of gift ideas, and I go on pretending I've no idea she's there until she cuts off mid-sentence. I can't help following her line of sight to a boy propped against the door frame of a nearby shop. He's a child of the slums, frostbitten fingers, no shoes, stinking rags draped over a flickering, skeletal body.

There is no sixth sense, no gentle tapping on the inside of

my skull or uncanny sensation that something otherworldly lurks nearby. Feelings like that are for books and movies. The child looks as real to me as anyone living, but then boots and trainers march through him and he half fades from view.

A wash of cold fear weighs on me. Heather blocks my view of the kid and talks me down until I can't hear my heartbeat any more.

Of the three kinds of ghosts: free, tethered and looped, the looped ones are the worst. Trapped in the memory of their death, they're unaware they're even deceased, existing beyond our time and place in a bubble of their own. But sometimes their personal reality bleeds into our world, and that's very bad news for me.

I turn away, guilt tightening my chest.

I have to preserve my sense of what's real.

My foot catches the edge of the pavement and I trip. Heather lunges and grabs my arm, supporting me in an impossible stumble down into the cobbled gully. I scan the narrow thoroughfare, hoping no one saw me cheat gravity. When there's no sudden onslaught of eager dead I release my breath.

"All right?" Heather asks. I nod, as subtly as I can. She lets go of me but her lips are pressed thin with worry.

We need to be more careful.

Adjusting my weight, I catch my reflection in the darkened window of a gift shop closed for redecoration. Heather is beside me but I'm standing alone. The dead don't have reflections. I look like the kind of lad that might cause trouble

– square face, snub nose, broad frame with muscle on big bones – like my dad.

We set off slowly. I know the shop as soon as I see the book and quill sign above the door. Despite my unease I crack a grin.

Inside, the green walls and cabinets are stuffed with everything from tabletop games and fancy stationery, to collectable replicas of The One Ring and Harley Quinn's baseball bat. It's full and cramped but Heather knows how to move in a crowd without being walked through. We take our time browsing but half my attention is always on remembering not to give myself away. It's all too easy to forget no one else can see or hear her.

"Charlie, do not turn around." The voice is female, but it's not Heather's. The accent is so clipped it sounds deliberately posh, almost fake. "You've picked up a tail."

I pivot slowly, proud of my self-control, to face the blonde woman in her mid-thirties standing amongst the robed mannequins in the centre of the shop. From the string of natural pearls at her throat to the cut of her skirt suit and neatly pinned curls, Audrey Nightingale is straight out of a 1940s photograph. Picture perfect.

Her lips tighten. "I said *don't* turn."

"What are you doing here, Nightingale?" Heather asks, crossing her arms.

"Looking out for our boy, of course." Stepping around a young couple taking selfies, Audrey focuses her hawk-like gaze on me again and reaches for the three-headed toy dog

I've picked up. I quickly look away. Like all ghosts, her hand goes right through solid objects. Seeing it always gives me the shivers.

Although Audrey hates my rules, she usually follows them, so she must be in a pissy mood today. "Do you want me to leave, or do you want to know who's following you?" My expression must say it all, because she continues. "Outside, with the dark hair and the green jacket."

Heather pretends to be studying a display of replica swords to get a look at our tail. "You sure?"

"Oh, I'm sure. He *thinks* he's being subtle."

Sharp spring light catches the edge of his face through the windowpane. I turn away at the same time he does. My age, maybe a year or so younger, but dressed like he's trying to look older in chinos and a cable-knit jumper under a new waxed jacket.

I don't doubt that he's following me. Audrey rarely makes mistakes. I look back. He risks another glance at the three of us, his gaze lingering on Audrey, then he strides into the shop opposite.

If he can see Heather and Audrey then he's dead – recently, judging by his clothes. Maybe he wants me to contact his relatives and deliver a message, something I'd *never* do. I'm not an errand boy for the dead.

Experience tells me I'm wrong. First off, he doesn't look desperately relieved that someone can see him. Secondly, there's something in Audrey's expression that chills me – a tendon standing out in her neck, a taut alertness in her eyes.

She glances at the street. "We need to get you out of here."

There it is again, that flash of fear. She's trying to hide it, but she's afraid and she's not the type to scare easily. Likely then that he's a Hungry One, a spirit who believes a taste of my special ghost-seer flesh and blood will restore him to life.

God. I don't need this.

"He's seen us together." Heather's voice is higher than usual. "We should split up."

"Meet me back at the bus stop, yeah?" I mutter.

With a reluctant nod at me and a firm glower at Audrey, Heather squeezes my hand and slips away. A shop assistant gives me an odd look, which is rich coming from someone dressed up in Dothraki leathers. I move towards the till, grabbing some wrapping paper from a nearby stand on my way, then hurry to pay for the toy dog.

How am I going to leave without Waxed-Jacket following me?

"We'll go out the back," Audrey whispers, giving me directions to the storeroom. "The code is 4531Y."

"How'd you even know that?"

"Know what?" the bloke at the till asks, assuming I'm talking to him.

"Oh—" I can feel the heat in my cheeks. "Nothing."

I stuff the toy in my backpack. The shop assistant rolls the wrapping paper into a tube for me. I hold it like a sword as I head to the back of the shop and the staff-only door marked, NO ADMITTANCE, EXCEPT ON PARTY BUSINESS.

Sweat makes my hands slippery, but I manage to key in the

code and open the door without turning to double check I'm getting away with it.

Audrey waits for me on the other side.

"Move quickly," she says, "but not *too* quickly. Head up, like you're meant to be here."

Hurrying past simple shelves stacked with products, I catch my breath when a voice carries out of the little kitchenette off to the side. Although I brace myself for an angry confrontation with an employee demanding to know what I'm doing here, I reach the fire exit without meeting anyone.

"It's alarmed," says Audrey.

I grimace, place my hands on the bar and press down hard.

A heartbeat later I'm hurrying through the food market, ears still ringing. It takes me fifteen minutes to circle around the city centre, heading north under the shadow of York Minster because there are too many restless dead around Clifford's Tower. Mad Alice isn't in her alley so I slip through Lund Court on to Swinegate, narrowly avoiding a collision with a top-hat-wearing tour guide and his congregation of eager ghost hunters.

I'm limping by the time I cross the river at the Memorial Gardens and head along the old city wall towards the train station. When I finally pause for breath, Audrey is gone. I'm alone. No one is following me. I chew on some gum to get the taste of fear off my tongue.

Heather is leaning against the bus stop when I arrive, looking on as I check through the pockets of my puffer for my ticket. My left stump is stinging. I'll have to take my prostheses off as soon as I get in. To ease the ache, I sit on the metal bench and settle back against the glass shelter. Heather sits beside me and because there's no one else around, I allow myself to lean in to her a little.

My thoughts go back to the lad dying in the cold over and over again. I wish I could help him, but last time—

No. I can't think about last time.

Tucking the roll of paper under my arm, I pull the toy from my bag, suddenly worried that I've not made a proper choice at all.

I turn it for Heather to assess. "Think he'll like it?"

"He'll love it." There's an edge to her voice, something left unspoken, but I've no energy to pry.

Our bus appears, only half full, meaning we can ride home together. Relief lifts me up. We stand. The bus pulls in and as we step on board I flash my ticket at the dull-eyed driver. He barely looks at it, but he brightens when he sees the toy dog.

"Got my lad one of 'em for Christmas. Guardian of the underworld that."

I nod and smile.

Heather and me sit by the window near the front so I can stretch out. As the bus pulls away I notice a figure watching from where the old city wall runs opposite the station. Wax-Jacket is bold as anything, standing in full sun like he wants me to know he's there. Heather hasn't spotted him. Good, she'll only worry.

A sudden, ice-sharp thought sends me sitting upright.

He didn't follow me; Audrey would've marked him. So, he

knew where I was going. He got here first and waited.

The jolt I feel has nothing to do with the rumble and whine of the engine as the bus follows Queen Street and turns on to Blossom. No, there's no such thing as sixth sense, but my bones feel heavier and there is a pulse in my skull like I'm holding out against answers to a question I never wanted asked.

For the first time in a long time I feel haunted.

2

FRIENDLY NEIGHBOURHOOD GHOS✝S

There are far fewer ghosts out where we live, but they're still about – wandering the aisles of the local B&Q, standing in line at the chippy for old times' sake, or pacing the top of our cul-de-sac lamenting the state of their prize roses.

"They don't care, lad," Mr Broomwood calls, the tail of his dressing gown cord trailing as he crosses the street towards us. His face is all eyebrows and frown lines above a sloping mouth. "Simple soap and water would do for 'em aphids but they do now't, and they leave the bins out for days after the van comes round. Days. It were my home for forty years, they've no respect these tenants David put in, none at all. A letter would do, anonymous like—"

"It's not my business, Mr Broomwood," I protest, as I have almost every day since his death last October.

19

"Then whose is it, eh?" The old man puffs himself up, finger out and wagging at me like I'm a naughty puppy, or one of those men from the council. "If you can do summat about a wrongdoing then you've a duty."

I stuff my hands in my pockets. It's spring, but there's a nip to the air. "I'd look like a right weirdo."

"What does that matter? You always were an odd lad."

"Well, what do your roses matter?"

Lace twitches in the bungalow opposite. Mrs Ginty is probably wondering why the Frith lad is out on the pavement arguing with himself again.

"He said no, now let him alone." Heather takes my arm and we leave Mr Broomwood to his pacing.

I haven't always seen them. My early childhood was blissfully spectre-free until I got sick aged nine. The meningitis was swift and savage, taking both my legs below the knee. Then it killed me. Somehow the doctors brought me back – "God's own miracle" according to my Nan.

The world I came back to is a lot more crowded than the one I left.

Dad's taxi isn't in our bungalow driveway. The lights are on and I breathe in the comfort of home. Boots and coats by the door; scuffs in the hallway from wheelchair versus Henry Hoover jousting; a stain on the ceiling where a pipe burst and Dad tried to patch it himself; blue carpet worn down the middle but still thick at the skirting.

Mum bellows that my tea is keeping warm in the oven. The telly is on and I can hear a staged argument reaching its dramatic crescendo, the kettle wailing in time for the ad-break brew.

I shout "Ta!" and I make for my room.

Dante the ghost collie's ears go up as soon as I get in the door. I give him a quick scratch. His happy whine is almost enough to make me glad I can touch ghosts.

A skinny red-haired kid is sitting cross-legged on my bed. When we met we looked about the same age. Now, I'm growing up and Ollie will be eleven forever. Our very own Peter Pan.

He motions to the photocopies blue-tacked to the walls. "Where you been? I've read this twice over."

"You'll see, old man," says Heather.

I want to give him his gift right away, but I need to transfer to my chair. It's like swapping shoes that pinch for comfortable slippers. Rolling up my trackie bottoms, I unclip the pin keeping the silicone liner and socket together and slip off my prostheses one by one, then the liners and socks. Ollie sucks his breath and Heather grimaces. Patches of skin have rubbed raw at the top edge of the liners. I've sweated a fair bit and it stings.

I slide into my wheelchair – ultra light frame, low backrest and no push handles. This room used to be Nan's and has a roomy bathroom. It takes me a few minutes to clean and wrap the sores in gauze, then scrub the liners and hang them to dry.

When I roll back to the bedroom Ollie is chatting with Heather about the latest wall comic. I photocopied *Hellboy: The Right Hand of Doom* at the library and pinned it out like a storyboard so he has something to read while I'm out, though he probably spent most of the day haunting the university's lecture halls. Ollie didn't have much chance at schooling when he was alive so he's making up for it now that he's dead.

Most of my bedroom is dedicated to his geekery. The shelves above the desk are a shrine to our favourite Avengers: Thor for Ollie and Spider-Man for me. Heather refuses to choose but we're both pretty sure she's got a thing for Scarlet Witch. Any free space on the walls is used for the ever-changing collages of graphic novels, comics and books we're reading.

Ollie's been getting into what he calls "the ancient classics": Homer, Euripides and Ovid. The ladies at the local library think I'm well intellectual. Mum says for the number of books I'm taking out each week I should get grades a damn sight better than I do. I used to do really well, back when Ollie was coming to class with me and whispering the answers into my ear. Teachers put my sudden drop in academic prowess down to trauma, and I let them think it. Truth is, without Ollie I'm just an average lad. I like stories well enough, but I'm a slow reader and if he didn't need me to turn the pages for him I'd never have finished any of the books he asks me to bring home.

I pull our gift from my bag and hold it out to him. I'm well chuffed with the wrapping job, especially considering I did it on the bus.

"Happy death-day, old man."

Ollie grins. "You didn't have to get me anything."

"We wanted to do something," says Heather.

Ollie was too sick to remember much about the day he died, only that it was cold for spring. Last year I had a look in the records and I found him: Oliver John Shuttleworth, died April 11th of influenza. I decided then and there we should celebrate every year.

I'd do the same for Heather, but she'd rather forget what happened to her.

Ollie looks about ready to burst. "Open it up then."

Carefully, I tear the paper where he tells me to, the corner first, then along the seams. When the wrapping is off and I'm holding up the three-headed-dog, Ollie's face splits into a wide, toothy grin. "Cerberus! Mate, that's wicked, thanks. Did you know Hesiod gave him fifty heads instead of three?"

Suddenly going into The Shambles, the ache of my raw skin, even being spotted by that Hungry One, is all worth it.

Dante nuzzles my hand, reminding me he wants to go out for a good bark at the local squirrels.

"I'll take him," says Heather.

Probably best. I don't have a decent excuse to go wandering the neighbourhood tonight.

Heather needs me to open the doors or they'll have to go through the wall and that's one of my rules.

Rule One: no moving through solid objects, walls or hedges when I'm looking.

Rule Two: no floating or otherwise breaking the laws of gravity.

Rule Three: no disappearing or reappearing.

On my way to let Heather and Dante out, I pop my head round the twins' door. Poppy, snug beneath her Queen Elsa duvet, offers me a drowsy wave. Lorna looks up from her book for long enough to tell me I smell like a cheesy fart. She's sharing her bed with our cousin Danielle. The boys, Anton and Jamie, are stretched out on the trundle. They greet me with fart noises and I feel marooned by the ten-year age gap between me and all the other kids in our family.

If the terrible trio are here for a sleepover on a school night it means Aunt Chrissie's suffering after her chemo. Everyone around here likes to lament at our family misfortune, saying we're cursed – my meningitis, then Nan going suddenly like she did, and now Chrissie getting sick. But they say all kinds of stupid things like "everything happens for a reason" and "at least if you're going to get cancer this is the one to get, eh?" Like there's an answer to that.

I let Heather and Dante out of the front door, quiet like. When I come back in Mum's watching me with the daft, soppy look she reserves for people she loves.

"You're back late."

I don't like to look at Mum when I lie to her, so I open the oven and take out my tea: shepherd's pie, peas and carrots. "Was at the library."

"Good to know you're taking your exams seriously." She passes me some cutlery and I manoeuvre my chair to the table. I know she's spotted my fresh bandages when she says, "Use your chair out and about if they're rubbing."

I say I will, though I won't. My chair is comfortable and

manoeuvrable and I'm lucky to have it, but I got sick of people staring, ignoring me outright, or asking whoever I'm with what's wrong with me, as if I'm not able to speak for myself. My prostheses help me to blend in, but I can't wear them for long without them rubbing. Five days until my next clinic and a new set of sockets. Let's hope that takes care of it, though I'm not holding my breath.

Mum leans against the counter and natters whilst I eat my tea. The beige linoleum, yellow walls and light fittings are the same as when Nan was alive. When we moved in I wondered if her ghost would be waiting for me, but the house was silent.

Ollie's in the doorway, listening to Mum's salon gossip. I catch his eye and smile. Mum pales a little and glances over, but she doesn't say anything.

Stupid. Careless. She sees the cracks, no matter how much I try to hide them. I've got to hide them, especially from her. At the salon she plays her part well – big hair, painted nails, smiles and laughter. Really, she has three kids at home, a sick sister and not enough time or money to cope.

After tea I offer to take out the rubbish, earning a call of thanks from Mum who is back in front of the telly with a mountain of ironing.

Sticking the bin-bag into the wheelie bin, I scan our cul-de-sac, looking for Waxed-Jacket. Mr Broomwood has retreated, probably to haunt his grandson's unsuitable tenants.

"He's not here."

I spin my chair, nerves tensing. But it's just Audrey skulking by the side of the house. "I've checked the neighbourhood. He didn't follow you home."

"Good. Who is he?"

"Someone you need to stay away from."

"A Hungry One, then?"

Audrey hesitates. "I'll keep him off you, just be careful."

Her fear is still there, buried deep, but she taught me to read faces too well for me to miss it.

"You're afraid of him."

Her gaze turns frosty. "Make sure Ollie stays with you tonight."

"What are you not telling me?"

"You're not ready."

"I am," I say on instinct, rather than because I believe it.

"You see, but you don't *want* to see."

Anger prickles my cheeks. "Er, yeah! Because it's fucked up my life."

Her response is a sad smile. It's really patronising, like if I were better at handling all this then she'd share amazing ghostly secrets with me. Maybe if she did, I could stop being afraid of the dead. Maybe I'd be more afraid. I don't know.

I wish I could pull that lad on The Shambles out of the deathloop he's trapped in. Most likely it would just drag me in and I'd find myself alone and freezing to death on a snowy street. I want to help him, I do, but I can't.

It would be better if I couldn't see ghosts at all.

Dante comes charging past, disappearing through the hedge and back out again, his tongue lolling. I turn around. Heather is standing there, chewing on her lip.

"All right?" I say for the sake of saying something, already embarrassed about my outburst. When I spin back to face Audrey the driveway is empty.

She's *always* breaking rule number three.

"She'll take care of it, Charlie. Try and get some sleep." Heather gives me a regretful half-smile and walks away. I call goodnight, wishing she'd stay. I'd feel better if she was close by, but she has her routine.

Back inside, I set up the hammock for Ollie, stuffing it with pillows to fill out his shape so it's easier to trick my brain into thinking he's lying in it rather than floating in mid-air. When I slip under my covers Dante settles beside me. I wish he were a better guard dog, but he's as likely to roll over for a belly rub from a strange ghost as he is to bark and wake me up. We lie there and I pretend to sleep. I can't help my thoughts turning to Waxed-Jacket.

He didn't look desperate, he looked determined.

That scares me more.

Clearing my throat, I prop myself up. "Ollie, you haven't seen any new faces hanging about, have you? Only, I got followed in town today. Probably nothing, but…" I let my words dangle like bait for a fish.

Ollie bites. "I'll keep watch in case they show. What's this ghostie look like then?"

I describe the curl of Waxed-Jacket's hair, the slope of his shoulders, how his hands were always in his pockets. Ollie's curiosity mingles with my dread and everything feels at odds.

"Wake me if anyone dead shows up, yeah? Not just him." I try to keep my tone casual and Ollie, to his credit, laughs and pretends I'm not scared.

3

†HE HANGED MAN

Monday I'm jittery as hell. Classes, revision sessions, one moment leading to the next, seconds to hours, and still I can't shake the feeling I'm waiting for something. It's like when a beefed-up older lad swears he'll get you. Maybe he will, or maybe he'll go back to chugging lager and smashing up bus stops and forget all about you. Either way it's a promise you don't forget in a hurry.

My school is a cluster of low grey brick buildings patch-worked together and dumped beside a car park, playing fields and a big sports hall. I don't know every student, but they seem to know me. Having a reputation for arguing with thin air gets you noticed.

"Oi, Olympics!" Mitch hollers from the end of the corridor. He's lanky but broad-shouldered with light skin, a pretty mouth and blonde hair flipped into a wave. He's got one arm

29

around his girlfriend, Leonie. They've attracted a cloud of hangers-on, mostly former friends of mine. At Mitch's shout, heads swivel my way.

I do my best not to groan because it's right daft thinking every kid missing a leg or two is going to don blades and zip about like Johnny Peacock, but people seem to expect me to become some sporting legend. Wishful thinking that one day they'll be able to say, *"Yeah, I went to school with Charlie Frith. He was an odd lad even then, used to natter away to himself and on a school trip he lost it completely and slashed himself up."*

I could ignore Mitch. I usually do, even when he's pretending he still likes me. He's invited me to sit with him and his mates at lunch before, but he was there when it happened and so was Leonie. I remember the fear on their faces and how they whispered about me.

And then there was that kiss.

Maybe he's forgotten, or forgiven.

Or maybe he's setting me up for a fall. My social standing can't take the hit. So, I pretend I don't hear him, getting out my phone instead. He jogs down the corridor and turns his easy smile on me. I envy the way he holds himself, like he knows everyone loves him. And they do. They always have, even when we were in primary school.

"Oi … Charlie." He says my name softly. "Some new lad was asking after you this morning."

Some new lad – who'd start this close to the end of the school year? And who'd know me? I went to a support group

30

for young amputees for a while and I was in Scouts for a couple of years. I try to remember the names of the other kids but come up blank.

Then I wonder why Mitch would go out of his way to tell me about it, like we're mates when we're not. Not anymore. So maybe there's a trick here I'm missing.

"Hiya, Charlie." Leonie has drifted down the hallway with the rest of their pack. Her springy curls are piled high on her head, the sides decorated with a chevron of bobby pins, a style all the girls will be copying within the week.

Mitch drapes a possessive arm over her shoulder, reassuring himself he's worthy, which I'm pretty sure he's not. Every lass at school wants to be Leonie's best mate and every lad – except me – wants to snog her. I get it, though, she's well beautiful – round cheeked, petite and curvy, with dark brown skin and long lashes. She's a prefect and top in every STEM class. She'll probably get a job working for a billionaire and set up a colony on Mars or something. Hell, she'll be the billionaire one day.

He's nothing special.

So why does his arm around her make me feel like I'm being torn apart?

"Right, yeah," I say quickly. "Thanks for letting me know."

And then I look up, past the hangers-on to the figure watching me from a stretch of bright corridor.

I don't so much freeze as falter. Leonie says my name and a question, but I'm not listening. I mumble something about being late and hurry away.

31

Ghosts move silently. I won't hear him following.

As I shove open the double doors and stumble into the car park, I risk a glance over my shoulder. Leonie is watching me like I'm a curiosity in a museum. Mitch just looks confused.

Hurrying up behind them is Waxed-Jacket. He's clocked me, and now he's coming for me.

The north wind gives chase, sending a chill through my school jumper. I don't know where I'm going – away, out, wherever *he* isn't. The bell rings. No one stops me as I leg it around the science block as fast as I can.

My prostheses aren't built for speed. The feet don't have the necessary flex for running. Forced to slow, I head off the path around the back of the classrooms where the planting has escaped all control. No way out, but I feel safer enveloped by the smell of fresh leaves and damp earth. Closing my eyes, I count my breaths.

Audrey would know how to give him the slip, but it's just me and I can't think.

I can't go home. Dad's not working until later. If I stride in early he'll pitch a fit. I've a study period now, meaning I won't be missed for an hour. If I can't run, I need to hide and in a better spot than this.

When the bell rings I head for the playing field. There's an old pavilion by the south boundary that's used to store sports equipment. It's far enough from the main building that I don't risk being spotted striding across open ground, or be seen from the classrooms, and dry enough I won't catch a cold. I can wait it out and slip back into class later. The door is ajar and I'm about to pull it open when I hesitate.

If Waxed-Jacket catches me in here there'll be no way out. *I* can't walk through walls. Instead I go around the back to where countless feet have eroded the turf to a strip of mud littered with fag ends.

Smokers come here, and couples stealing a snog between lessons. If things had been different, if I'd listened to Heather and not gone on that sodding school trip to Saint-Lô in Normandy, I might come here all the time for a bit of snogging.

But then all that started in France too, didn't it, so maybe not.

Mitch and me haven't ever spoken about it, not the kiss, not what happened to me the next day, or what he told everyone. We probably never will. I remember how he looked at me before we kissed. Now that's how he looks at Leonie.

Fine by me.

A dull thump sounds inside the pavilion. Is someone in there? I back up, my eyes fixed on the little window. Above me the great chestnut creaks and shudders. Something hits the back of my head. A boot caked in dirt, brown corduroy trousers, no socks—

The man's face is bloated, his swollen tongue sticking through grimacing lips. His body sways in the air, a rope tight on his neck. The stink of his bowels hits me. Blood racing, I stagger away.

He isn't supposed to be here.

School is safe. Heather checked the grounds top to bottom. Not a whiff of a tethered ghost let alone a deathloop. This man is like the boy in the snow. He doesn't know he's dead and he's reliving his last moments over and over. Any minute now his memories might catch me. I need to leave.

The man's bloodshot eyes snap open.

The school fades away and I'm faced with a wall of white tiles criss-crossed by strange, rusty symbols. Several candles sit in shallow clay dishes around the large room. I smell stale air and mouldering food. A pair of half-moon spectacles sits on a long table. I'm underground, a basement maybe? There's some old lab equipment, coils of rubber tubing, and two globe-like bottles on mounts with something fleshy swirling inside them.

I have to get *out*. I have to get out before—

The man steps from a stairwell midway down the chamber, a coil of rope in his arms. He's white, middle-aged, with close-cropped hair. Tears stream from his swollen eyes. He lights a fire in the deep sink and sends piles of hand-scribbled pages into the flames, helped along by a bottle of whisky. An old black and white photograph of a man and young girl burn last. I don't get a good enough look before the image bubbles and curls in the heat.

I'm too terrified to move. Even if I could, there's nowhere to go but back and forward in an endless loop. I feel the pull and try to fight it, but I'm as weak as I was at fourteen. The man opens his mouth to speak in a voice like air pushed through a broken bellows and I'm enveloped by the smell of sweat and chemicals and a grief so deep I can't stand it.

Rachel.

Something shifts.

The rope is rough against my palm. Resignation makes my bones heavy. I prepare the noose. I climb on the table. Step up. The chair wobbles. I kick it away.

Down.

Stomach plummeting, heart rushing. Pain. But my neck didn't snap. I feel momentary hope, then clenching tightness. My fingers claw at my throat. An agonizing pressure rises in my chest. The man is below me, watching. Darkness gnaws at the edges of my vision. My lungs scream for air.

We will do this again and again until my body dies and my ghost joins his for eternity.

Something smacks into me. Arms wrap around my chest and pull down. The noose tightens, and then slides off. What breath I have left in me bursts from my lungs as I slam into damp turf. Weight crushes my ribs then rolls off.

My pulse is weak, my thoughts sticky slow. I drag myself on to my elbows and hack into the grass. Each gasp of air is the sweetest breath I've ever taken. Waxed-Jacket is beside me, his hand on my arm.

"That was either very brave or very stupid." His accent sounds like those plummy blokes off the BBC.

I've no strength left to run.

"Oi, lads! What's going on?" We both look up to see the

Deputy Head striding towards us. Mr Farrell likes to poke his head behind the sports pavilion to catch smokers having a cheeky fag. I knew that. I knew and I forgot because I never come out here.

Waxed-Jacket doesn't wait around, he's up and sprinting, and I can see Mr Farrell in two minds about whether to go after him. He obviously realizes I'm the easier mark because moments later he's standing over me spouting questions.

Bile burns in my throat and I chuck up my lunch on to Mr Farrell's shoes.

And then it hits me. Mr Farrell said "lads", meaning he could see both of us, and under that waxed jacket the ghost was wearing our uniform – the same crumpled grey jumper, striped tie, and trousers that looked too long for him, like he'd raided lost property.

Which means … he's no ghost at all.

4

VANISHINGS

At some point I pissed myself. It happens with a hanging. Now I'm sitting outside The Head's office, a towel over the stain on my groin. My throat feels like I've been sucker-punched in the windpipe by the Hulk. They ask me questions, but my voice is just a thin wheeze.

Good. I don't want to talk: they'd not believe me anyway. They reckon me and Waxed-Jacket were fighting, having it out over some lass, or whatever they assume lads scrap about. No one knows who he is and I can't give them a name. When I managed to croak out that he's the new lad, they said there weren't any new students, meaning he might as well be a ghost for all the hope I have of tracking him down. If I wanted to find him again. Which I don't.

Except, if he's not a ghost, then he's a seer.

As a kid, I'd thought there must be loads of people who

can see the dead, right? Wrong. Still, I always hoped a doctor would sit my folks down and explain that their lad sees ghosts now, just a lesser known after-effect of meningitis, nothing to worry about.

Never happened of course, because it's not about how I died, it's about why I came back. And I don't remember any of that.

There's a blanket over me, but I'm still cold. The chill seeped into my marrow and I can't shake it. For a moment I'm back in the tiled room. I smell the smoke from the flaming papers in the sink, feel rough rope and then—

The bell rings, releasing a flow of students into the corridors. Large windows separate the administration suite from the main hallway. Curious faces peer through the glass like I'm some zoo animal. Leonie and Mitch are just beyond the swing doors. I don't want Mitch to see me like this. All I can do is duck down and put my head in my hands to hide my shame.

Anger fills its place. Audrey basically lied to me. If I'd known Waxed-Jacket wasn't a ghost then I wouldn't have run, wouldn't have hidden behind the blasted sports pavilion, wouldn't have got tangled up in a deathloop.

The swing door squeaks as Leonie strides in. She's surprisingly imposing for someone so short. I squirm in my seat. If she comes any closer she'll smell my piss and sweat. God, I bet I stink. Mitch is still on the other side of the glass, staring at me like he wants to pummel something, and he'd be all right with that something being me.

"Charlie," says Leonie, voice soft. "What happened?"

I keep staring at my feet. They're never going to let me forget this. I'm probably already the talk of the school. *"He did it again, yeah, just like the Normandy trip, well I wasn't there but Alyssa said... blah blah."* Sod off!

I'm shaking and I can't stop. Then, to my relief, the paramedics arrive at the same time as Dad and the commotion sweeps Leonie and Mitch away before they can torment me with whatever part of the past they'd planned to dredge up.

Dad squats to look into my face, grey eyes meeting mine. He's a big bloke, barrel-chested and thick-limbed, his hair retreating at his temples to the thin patch atop his head. He presses a hand to my shoulder and mutters something reassuring before Mrs Prabakar, the Headmistress, and Mr Farrell steal him away for a private chat. I'm prodded and poked by the two paramedics, hooked up to portable monitors for blood pressure or something. When Dad re-emerges from the office, his face looks harrowed.

I want to say sorry for putting him through this.

I want to know why Audrey didn't tell me Waxed-Jacket's a seer.

I want to check in with Ollie and Heather, because that deathloop isn't supposed to be there.

Falling inside it like that – tortured ghost, aching fear, helpless panic – it all happened like before. Our class went on a trip to Normandy as part of our World War Two module and toured battlefields, museums and memorials. Somehow, I managed to avoid any deathloops until the last day. I got overconfident, didn't see it coming. Two years on I'm still as weak and useless as I was then. If Audrey hadn't pulled me out…

What if something's changed and *all* of the loops in York have moved? The streets will be like a sodding minefield.

My vision goes watery. The cold is paralysing. One of the paramedics asks me a question but shaking my head is all I can manage.

"His blood pressure's plummeting."

I open my mouth to tell them I'm all right, really, and then the room twists, the air is sucked away and my brain goes quiet.

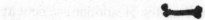

When I wake, Waxed-Jacket is sitting in the chair beside my hospital bed scribbling away in a leather-bound notebook. I scramble to sit up, buzzing with resentment. And he doesn't even get it. He just sits there, dressed like a prat in muted red chinos and a grandpa jumper. His shoes are old man shoes made of worn brown leather with patterns punched in them.

At least he's not wearing tasselled loafers. Nan always said not to trust a bloke with tassels on his loafers.

"What are you doing here?" My voice emerges fractured and sore.

"Visiting."

"It's family only." I've been in for loads of surgeries to release scar tissue so that I could wear prostheses. I know the rules.

He snaps his notebook shut. "I told the nurses I'm your secret boyfriend so they'd let me in."

"You *what*?"

"Relax, emphasis on secret. Your mum just left by the way."

"You didn't tell her I'm gay—"

"You are? Oh. No, no of course I didn't tell her. I pretended we were friends; she seemed delighted to meet me, said to stay as long as I like."

"They think you attacked me," I say.

"Really?" He raises his brow, like we're conspiring. "Because I heard from the nurses it was a student at York Secondary, and I go to St Matthews, so it's nothing to do with me." He's right chuffed with himself.

Smug git.

The duty nurse bustles in, exclaims his joy at my being awake, checks my vitals and explains the doctor will be along shortly. When he leaves, he glances meaningfully at Waxed-Jacket, winks, and pulls the privacy curtains closed.

I've spent the past few days seeing this lad's face every time I close my eyes, but he's different in the flesh, less sinister, irritating rather than intimidating. He's slender, with light tan skin, a long straight nose and dimpled chin. There's a shock of white amongst the bronze curls above his left temple, like he was struck by lightning.

I realize I'm staring. But he's staring back, taking my measure as if he's never seen me before. There's something

41

in that look I hate – curiosity, certainly – but pity too. I'm tempted to throw him out, but I need to know what he wants: because I'm bloody sure he wants something from me.

I'm not the only seer.

"Who are you?" I ask.

"Samuel Harrow, but you can call me Sam."

"Why are you following me, Harrow?"

His lips tighten and he leans forward, hands clasped. For the first time he doesn't look like this is all just a game to him. "Six months ago, shortly before we moved up here, I … there was an accident and I died … for forty-five minutes. Then, somehow, I came back. Now I can see ghosts. Like you."

For a moment I'm stunned. I knew it, but hearing him say it … I could laugh right now if my swollen throat would let me, and tearfully tell him how thankful I am that I'm not alone.

And then I think I'd like to punch him.

Does he have any idea what he just put me through? Nope, he thinks he can do what he likes, tail me in town, show up at school, pretend to be my boyfriend. Yeah right, like I'd ever—

I duck my head. Not my type. No way.

Harrow ploughs on. "I have so many questions about how and why, but that's not important right now. I'm here because I need your help with the vanishings."

"The what?"

He blinks rapidly, like I'm being daft. "The vanishings."

"Eh? What you on about?"

A crinkle appears between his eyes as they narrow. "Charlie, the ghosts of York are going missing."

I shake my head. He's lost the plot.

Harrow taps his notebook. "I'm doing my own local survey and I swear they've started disappearing." He counts the missing on his fingers. "Reid the Piper vanished a fortnight ago, a girl called Millie has gone too and there's been no sign of Mad Alice for over a week now. I've tried to investigate, but the ghosts around here won't talk to me, they either run scared or…" He points to a patch of nasty pink flesh on his palm. "They bite."

The dead are dangerous.

"What can I do?" I'm not offering, I'm just asking.

"You're a local; your experience outstrips mine and you're friendly with some of them. I was hoping you could help me solve the mystery."

I could say yes. For a heartbeat I want to because he's like me and I'm not alone anymore. But Audrey tried to stop us from meeting. Why? Because Sam Harrow can't be trusted? It's a risk I can't take, not until I've asked her.

"See that?" I twist my arms, showing him the thick scars on the inside of each forearm. "I've kept myself hidden for good reason."

Sam's face falls. "But … you went into that spirit memory."

He must mean the deathloop.

"By accident," I say.

"You weren't there to free him?"

"You can't *free* a ghost from a deathloop. Look, I didn't see it was there, fell in and got stuck."

His lips twitch. "So, I saved your life."

"No—" Yeah. He did, and maybe I owe him, but if he thinks I'm going to announce myself to the ghosts of York and go on some crusade that could get me killed, then he's flipped.

"Aren't you curious?" He leans in closer. "We died. We should have stayed dead, but we came back and we came back changed. There has to be a reason,"

"Nah, there doesn't." I try not to think about the frozen lad on The Shambles, or the sorrow of the Hanged Man. I can't help them. "Sometimes shite just happens to people; meningitis, cancer, life, death. It just happens." My voice cracks. "How did you even find me?"

For the first time he drops his gaze. I stare him down. He doesn't get to show up and make demands if he won't answer my questions.

"I did some research and found several accounts by Victorian mediums claiming their abilities began after a near-death experience, like mine. So, I started to look for people who'd had similar experiences. No luck, sadly." Sam pauses. He's nervous. "But after we moved here I found an old stack of the *York Herald*. There was an article on a club for young amputees. It talked about your sudden illness, how they'd declared you dead at one point. It called you a miracle. There was a group picture, and you were looking up, smiling at someone, but there was no one there. So, I … er, tracked you down."

I remember that article. Mum still has the clipping at home in one of her memory boxes. It came out a month after Heather introduced me to Ollie. He'd stood next to me for the photo, but ghosts don't show up on camera.

"And how exactly did you track me down?"

Sam rubs the back of his neck. "My friend Miri is really good with computers. She did her magic, got me your name, address and school. I think she accessed the records of the charity that funded your wheelchair."

He stands as I throw back my covers, determined to get away from him, but there's no wheelchair and my prostheses aren't here either.

"Get out." My voice is shaking. He had no right. Medical stuff, that's private for a reason. I could call the nurse but I'm not willing to make a scene, especially because, thanks to him, they'll think this is some kind of lover's tiff.

I expect him to stare at my stumps now they're on show beneath my hospital gown; most people can't stop themselves. But he's looking at my face, expression pleading. He probably thinks he can charm me because he's beautiful. Like Mitch, those good looks probably get him whatever he wants.

"I'm sorry," he says, like an apology changes anything.

How did I ever mistake him for a ghost? This lad is more alive than anyone I've ever met. His face dances with little expressions, chin shaking where he's trying to hold in emotion. He's grasping for meaning, like this affliction of ours is some kind of mission statement. This is the kind of person who'd be self-serving enough to knock on front doors and sit in living rooms nibbling at biscuits with grieving widows and say, "I've a message from your husband," and expect it to go well.

I was like him once. I thought I could fix everyone and, in the end, I almost broke myself.

"We don't owe the dead anything," I say. "And you don't go messing with people's lives."

He nods slowly. "You're right. I overstepped and I'm sorry, but I believe gifts are meant to be used."

I don't answer. I can't.

"Charlie?"

I hate the way he says my name, like it's his to use. If I close my eyes I can still feel the noose against my throat and the shameful ache of my fear.

"Just piss off," I say.

For a second, I think he's going to argue, then he grabs his posh journal and rips back the privacy curtain. "What if one of your friends goes missing? Would you care then?"

He walks away without waiting for an answer.

I curl into a ball. That parting remark smarts. It's a challenge; he knows I'm a hypocrite. Of course I'd look for Ollie or Heather if something happened to them, they're my best mates. I'd even search for Audrey because, despite ignoring my rules half the time, she saved my life in Normandy. I'll always owe her.

But I also promised Heather I'd stop trying to help the dead. It's too dangerous.

Harrow's not asking me to enter a deathloop, though, just talk to a few ghosts.

But then what? Endless hounding for favours, spirits showing up at my school or at my house looking for me, attacks by the hungry dead longing for resurrection? I'd be throwing away any chance I have of being normal.

As I lie listening to the sounds of the ward, a pale woman with sad eyes kisses the forehead of the girl sleeping opposite. The nurse walks over to check her chart and leans right though the pale woman. I shudder and close my eyes.

Normal is something I left behind a long time ago.

5

A DISTURBANCE IN THE FORCE

Dad arrives a few hours later, but I have to suffer examinations and questioning by three different doctors before they'll discharge me. I'm desperate to get home and talk to Ollie and Heather about the deathloop and meeting Sam Harrow, but with everything that's happened I forgot I'm booked to get my new sockets today. After the interviews and second opinions we're running late.

Even though we're in a rush, I pause at the memorial in the lobby. Photos of Heather are pinned among handwritten messages from family, colleagues and patients. Six years on they haven't taken it down. She was loved. She still is.

Dad squeezes my shoulder. He says he remembers her but he was panicked and exhausted and she was only one of many junior doctors, nurses and paediatricians to see me when I was admitted. I was the last patient Heather saw before her shift ended. A man attacked her not five hundred steps from the hospital. She made it into the operating theatre next to mine, but bled out before her colleagues could save her life.

We died at the same time.

Hers was the first face I saw when I came around in the children's ward, confused and sore – not yet realizing that one of my lower legs was gone, the other so mottled with clots it would also have to be amputated, or that I'd died for a while.

My first ghost. She's stuck with me ever since.

There's a new face on reception today, a friendly woman in a purple hijab, who brings up my details and tells us it might be a long wait. Once I'm signed in and settled, Dad heads to the café to grab a coffee.

As I take a quick piss, I see my reflection in the bathroom mirror. A blood vessel has burst in my right eye and there is a blotchy bruise around my throat where the rope pulled taught. I look like hell. I look like the dead should look: grey and tired and lost.

Let's see if Sam Harrow still thinks what we can do is a gift when he falls into a deathloop or when he loses all of his friends because they catch him having a nice long natter with a patch of air. If he's been poking around York asking after missing ghosts then it won't be long before the Mouldy Oldies get wind of him.

He has no idea what he's facing.

And I told him to deal with it alone.

Gripping the sink, I breathe out nice and slow. I've got a dislocated deathloop to worry about and final exams next month. I'm in enough shite as it is. Sam Harrow isn't my problem.

What about the missing ghosts?

He's probably making it up just to mess with me. Or he's plain wrong and Reid the Piper and Mad Alice have just wandered off someplace.

Back in the waiting room, I settle into the quietest corner and check my phone. I've no new messages because all my mates are dead. Harrow doesn't have Twitter or TikTok, but I find him on Instagram. His page is private. There's not much to see – an arty shot for a profile pic above a short bio, with his age (seventeen), a blue and pink trans flag emoji followed by his pronouns (he/him) and some snobby quote. I don't send a follow request, just sit staring at the screen a while, wishing I was brave enough to put my pride flag on my profile.

The local news, set on mute, fills the large screen on the opposite wall. They're interviewing an old man who could rival Mr Broomwood for the title of York's Grumpiest Bastard. The lagging subtitles spell out something about local vandals. There's a shot of police tape over a broken gravestone and graffiti on the grass, then back to the bloke talking about the *"desecration of a place of rest"* and how it's *"such a shock to all the volunteers."*

A familiar skinny kid with messy red hair tails a family through the reception doors, clocks me, and bounds over.

"You look like shite." Ollie flops into the empty chair beside me. "Fair warning, your mam is freaking out. It'll be the full inquisition when we get home. You didn't really get into a fight, did you?"

I grimace. "Deathloop."

Ollie's grin slides right off his face. "Where?"

"School playing field." I'm mumbling but I still earn an odd look from the prim couple sitting opposite.

I open ColorNote on my phone and type.

Male. Hanging. Tiled room. Underground? Early-mid 20th century?

I tilt the screen for Ollie to read.

"A hanging? Odd place for it."

The old part of York is packed with ghosts. There are fewer hauntings out in the suburbs and surrounding parishes. Tyburn and The Knavesmire are exceptions. Both areas are choked with clusters of loops, all hangings.

Not execution. Suicide.

But there's something off about it. In my experience deathloops linger where the person died. I'm pretty sure the land around school was farmland before York expanded, so what happened to the underground room? I type out the question for Ollie who reads it and shrugs.

"Farmers have cellars."

It doesn't feel right. Closing my eyes, I try to remember what the room was like. Strange science equipment, the smell of chemicals, not earth or manure, and dim electric lights.

"A disturbance in the force, then?" asks Ollie.

It's his name for a phenomenon we discovered last year. Three deathloops shifted from the train station to Gale Lane, nearly catching me out. Turns out major building work, or other disruptions, can shunt a loop to a new, more stable location.

"No one is digging holes around school," I whisper behind my hand. "So, if it did shift from somewhere else, what triggered the move and where'd it come from?"

"Dunno." Ollie scrunches up his nose. "Look up where they're redoing the roads, see if any of the loops match."

The council website lists local works. They're replacing water pipes at Monk Gate, but the only deathloop I remember there is a cyclist struck by a lorry. There's also works on Todcaster Road, which looks promising because the closest loops are all hangings. But they were Tyburn executions, a gallows end in the open air with a roaring crowd baying for blood, not a lonely death in an underground room.

We burn more data looking up hangings in York. They're all ghost stories we know, mostly dreamed up nonsense or historical executions that predate my hanged man by a century. His clothing was like something the gardeners might wear on one of those historical dramas Mum and Aunt Chrissie love. I need records of local suicides from the turn of the century to, like, the fifties. Not something I can find easily online.

I'm Googling newspaper archives when Heather strides in. Everywhere else her lanyard and stethoscope look out of place, but here she could pick up a clipboard and go straight back to work. I know she misses her job. She regularly comes back to check in on old colleagues. I offered to try and speak to them for her – my way of paying her back for saving me more times than I can count – but she won't let me. It's like she doesn't feel she deserves any favours. I've often wondered what's keeping her tethered within the city limits. I'd ask, but it's on the list of "things-Heather-won't-talk-about".

She gives me a pained smile. "What happened?"

Ollie fills her in. Then, using my phone, I type out how Waxed-Jacket is really called Sam Harrow and isn't dead at all. He followed me at school, visited me in hospital, stalked me online and accessed my private records.

"Another seer?" Heather looks stunned. "You're sure?"

"Bloody sure," I say. "And he's a prick."

The prim couple quickly move to the other side of the waiting room.

Head down, I type.

Harrow is dangerous.

"He saved your skin, though." Ollie seems impressed, and that winds me up more.

"I just assumed he was a soul because seers are so rare," says Heather.

Audrey warned me to stay away from him. Why? And why not tell me he's a seer?

Heather frowns. "You know her, this is probably some weird test to get you to develop your abilities or something."

She's scared.

Her expression tightens. "Of some lad? Seer or not, I doubt it."

I'm about to explain about the missing ghosts, but I don't. I couldn't say why not; I was planning to. Except I know Ollie will make a big deal about it and want to investigate, and Heather will likely say I was right to tell Sam to sod off because it's not my responsibility. But part of me worries that it is. It's not that I want to see Sam again, he could be – and probably is – lying about all this. But Mad Alice wasn't haunting her ginnel last time I passed that way. At the time I'd been relieved I didn't have to go the long way around, but now that I think on it, it's unusual.

"Audrey's got her own agenda," says Heather.

True, but Audrey let me think I was running from a Hungry One rather than risk me meeting Sam. Why? Maybe she doesn't want me to know about the missing ghosts, or she knows he's chatting bollocks and doesn't think I need the stress. Or is it because he's a seer too? I can't work out why that would bother her.

Audrey taught me how to read a face. She thought it might help me recognize who's dead and who's not. I'm not always spot on, but I don't doubt what I saw in her expression. Something about Sam Harrow terrifies her.

Heather doesn't want to hear it. The two of them don't get along. Heather can't forgive Audrey for what happened in Normandy, even though it's only thanks to Audrey that I made it out. And Audrey insists Heather coddles me by following my rules, rules that Audrey thinks are keeping me from my potential as a seer.

Heather rubs her face and sighs. Although she looks the same, I sense her weariness. "I'm going to take a look at that deathloop and see if I can work out where it came from."

It's only after she strides away that I realize we have an audience: Dad, clutching a takeaway cardboard cup and staring at me like I've lost my mind.

Dad's taxi smells like cherry air freshener and new leather. Rather than go through town and get stuck in the traffic around the station we turn on to Water End where the houses suddenly break for the churning river and the green flood plain. He clears his throat a couple of times, but it takes another minute of uncomfortable silence before he says, "What was all that about, then?"

"What was what all about?" I look into the rear-view mirror, wanting to catch Ollie's eye, but of course he's not in the reflection. I must be tired.

"You talking to yourself in the waiting room."

Ah, bollocks.

"You still hearing them?" asks Dad.

I wish I could just blurt out the truth and know it would go down well.

Hey, Dad, I can see and talk to the dead. Some of them are trapped by their own memories and can rough me up if I get too close. Yeah, pretty shitty, and while we're on big reveals, I just thought I'd mention that I fancy lads.

I shuffle closer to the window, pulling my sleeves down and gripping the cuffs. "I didn't do this to myself."

"No one is sayin' that."

I'm hoping that's the end of it, but I'm not known for my luck.

"We hear you chatting in your room a fair bit. I told your mam it's just how you learn. I was the same as a lad, liked to read things out, helps them sink in, doesn't it? I know you struggle with focus, but if you're having trouble knowing what's real and what's not, then we should go back to—"

"Bloody hell, Dad, I'm just on the phone to a mate."

"Which mate?"

"Harrow. Sam Harrow." My pulse races with the lie. "Mum met him at the hospital."

"Oh, right … yeah." Something in his tone bothers me. Did Mum hear Sam tell the nurses that he's my secret boyfriend? I'll have to tell my parents I'm gay sometime, and I will. Probably way before I tell them about the ghost thing, but only because I'm never going to tell them about the ghost thing.

Dad goes quiet, milling it over. His lot are Yorkshire born and bred back to the dawn of time. This city is steeped in ghost stories but he's a practical man, the kind of bloke who just-gets-on-with-it no matter what is thrown his way. If he knew the truth about my abilities, that's exactly what he'd do, get on with it. And if he can't see it, he won't believe it, and then he'll do what he thinks is right for me, which means doctors and pills. That will make everything so much worse.

There's worry etched in his brow. I reckon he's thinking back to when I was fourteen. The doctors thought the straight, deliberate cuts to my forearms were self-inflicted because that's what Mitch, Leonie and the other kids told everyone. After the Normandy trip I had to see a psychiatrist and have regular meetings with the school. Mum cried all the time. I felt like a stranger in my own family.

I don't want to go back to that.

We turn into our close, my anxiety eased by the sight of familiar hedges and lawns, and the slant of light on our squat bungalow. Mr Broomwood is stomping around his front garden. Everything is as it should be.

As we pull into our drive, I have to turn my gasp of shock into a hacking cough. Dad looks at me, confused as to why I'm trembling at the sight of our own home.

He can't see the dead girl standing on our doorstep.

6

UNINVITED

Dad switches off the headlights and the ghost becomes just another shape in the growing shadows. "Don't look," Ollie warns me as we get out of the car. But I can't help a quick glance, just in time to see Dad walking through her as he heads inside.

"You coming?" he calls.

The girl is in my way, but I grunt something that sounds like a yes. Her yellow-brown skin is almost glowing in the fading day. Scrawny with limp hair, she's dressed in a filthy blouse and a colourless pinafore. It's sad that.

Looped ghosts are always marked by their deaths, but free or tethered spirits, like Heather, Ollie and this girl, look how they remember themselves looking. Ollie would have died in bed, probably in pyjamas or something, but he remembers himself fully dressed in trousers, shirt, braces and cap. This girl probably can't think of a time when she was healthy, or maybe she never wore better clothes than those rags.

I take a small step forward. Her head snaps up, eyes widening in alarm and then ... she vanishes.

"What was *she* doing all the way out here?" asks Ollie.

"You know her?"

"Not by name. She's a Ragged."

Bloody hell, I hope not. Even the idea of them creeps me out.

Dad pops his head out to see what's keeping me. Shaken, I head inside. Lorna gives me a hug. Normally she's gobby as anything so I know she's been worrying. Poppy asks what made my eye so red and creepy. Mum pulls me close and gives me a tearful kiss, then grimaces as she examines the bruising on my neck.

I reckon she's going to ask about what happened, but instead she says, "It was lovely to meet Sam."

"Mum doesn't want you to be lonely," says Poppy.

"Yes. Well, that's not exactly what I ... but it's nice to know... I mean, you never bring friends home from school anymore, so we weren't sure..." Mum trails off as she dishes pasta bake into waiting bowls. "Anyway, Sam seems nice. Why don't you ask him for tea sometime?"

I mumble something vague about asking him soon and manage to avoid being quizzed about him, or what happened at school, by claiming I need an early night.

Everything in my room is as I left it. Curtains half-drawn, revision spread over my desk beside a pile of Ollie's books, folded clothes on my dresser. Dante snuffles at my hands. I scratch behind his ears.

Knowing Harrow can't just walk through the wall anytime he pleases should make me feel safe again.

It doesn't.

The Ragged Children have never come near me before. Maybe the girl saw me talking to Heather on The Shambles and has come to ask for a favour. Or she's a Hungry One and is here to tear my skin off. But I don't think so.

Either way, I can't hide in my room for the rest of my life and I can't keep relying on Heather and Audrey for everything. I'm not a kid. I know in my guts what I've got to do, and I swear it's got absolutely nothing to do with Sam-bloody-Harrow. Or the quiet pairing of hope and dread I feel at the thought of seeing him again, which is likely if we're both digging up answers.

I've got to uncover why the Hanged Man's deathloop shifted in case it happens again. And I've got to sort things out with that Ragged girl. I can't have strange ghosts turning up on my doorstep. Audrey owes me answers. As soon as I can, I'm going to tell her about the missing ghosts and ask her what the hell is going on with Harrow.

Time to recruit an eager accomplice.

"Ollie," I say as I unclip my prostheses, "I've got a mystery for you."

It's well past midnight when Dante starts to whine. I sit up and he presses a wet nose into my neck. I wince as my bruises protest. What's gotten him so rattled?

My room isn't pitch black because there's always a bit of light coming through my curtains from the porch, but it's shadowed enough that I can't make out much. I think about waking Ollie up, but don't move. The atmosphere is thick and tight, like something nearby is holding a breath.

Is there someone else here?

All kinds of fears flurry through my thoughts: violent ghosts I've faced, terrifying deaths I've been pulled into, obsessive spirits who've stalked me. I've always been shite at keeping the nightmares away. When I wake shaking in the night – and it happens all the time – it's best to roll over, snuggle Dante close and sleep it off.

Except now I can't, no matter that I'm bone tired. My head is pounding, probably from the ache in my neck. Maybe I should get up and take another painkiller. Instead I lie back down, but I can't get my mind off the Hanged Man and the Ragged on my porch. It's better to worry about literally *anything* else, so I let myself think about Sam Harrow for a while.

His fingers were ink-stained and he smelt of some kind of spicy citrus soap and musky wood.

"We should have stayed dead, but we came back and we came back changed."

"There has to be a reason, right?"

"Gifts are meant to be used."

Ugh, he sounded just like Audrey. Or Ollie. After telling Ollie about the missing ghosts he wanted to go striding off into the night to check Mad Alice's alley there and then.

My mouth is really dry and the glass by my bed is empty. Maybe this is a dehydration headache.

Transferring into my wheelchair, I make for the hall, leaving Dante to curl up atop my blankets. I never thought about how creepy everyday things look in the dark. It makes the smells and sounds of home distant and strange.

A shape flits across the kitchen doorway.

I stop, hands sweating where I'm gripping the handrim, ready to jerk my chair away if something lurches out of the shadows. Shallow breaths. It can't be one of my sisters out of bed, nothing living moves like that: like gravity doesn't quite have a hold on them. Again, I get the strange sensation that I'm being watched.

I wish I'd woken Ollie, but if I call for him now, or whistle for Dante, I'll wake Mum and I don't want her asking why I'm up at this hour.

But there is an uninvited spirit in my house.

Shite. Shite. Shite.

Edging forward I flick on the light switch by the door. Cool light spills over the table, counters and sink. The fridge hums softly. Our kitchen smells the way it always does at night, of lemon spray mixed with the fading scents of cooking.

There's no one here.

Filling a glass with tap water, I take a long drink. Then fill it again to take back to bed. I spin my chair around, but stop short. The glass slips from my grip, striking the lino with a crack. Water spills across the floor.

Slender red-nailed fingers. Half a brown face, vanishing quickly behind the door frame. Silver eyes. The overhead light flickers and pops, plunging the kitchen into semi-darkness as the hand whips back into the hallway. Gone.

Fuck.

"Charlie?" Ollie is in the doorway.

"Someone's here," I whisper. The light switch isn't working. All the bulbs in the hallway and kitchen are out. A blown fuse? Or did the silver-eyed ghost do something? No, of course not, because that's impossible. Ghosts making lights flicker, moving objects about and all that, it's made up Hollywood nonsense.

"You all right?" asks Ollie.

"Yeah, just that Ragged kid being creepy." I pick up shards of the broken glass.

It wasn't her.

A hand too big to be a child's, red nails, bright silver eyes.

No, don't even think it. It was the Ragged girl. I didn't get a good look at her is all, and it's just because of the low light that her hand looked larger and her eyes were … strange.

"We'll go see them and sort this out," says Ollie. "They know better than to come here."

As I cross into the hall, I can't help brushing the spot where her red tipped fingers touched the door frame. No, not touched, *sunk through*, because ghosts can't touch wooden door frames, or turn off lights. There's no such thing as a poltergeist.

7

THE RAGGED CHILDREN

Round the back of Goodramsgate, where a short ginnel leads to some garages and brick apartments, the ghosts of the Ragged School play in the late afternoon sunshine. It's the nicest day we've had in weeks. Fluffy clouds pillow above the pitched roofs of the old town. The air smells of dusty stone and something vaguely metallic. Ollie and I hover beneath Bedern Arch, watching the mass of grubby-faced kids running barefoot around the street.

"Who knows how many old George killed?" says Ollie, peering around me. "Dozens at least."

No one else is back here, living or dead, but I'm on edge. There's a deathloop somewhere down the side of the garages and we still don't know if the Hanged Man's shift was a one off, or if all the loops in York are changing. I need to be careful.

"You might have to wait a while." Ollie says, "The

Raggeds don't trust people much."

They trust Audrey, but there's been no sign of her since she warned me away from Sam.

Heather is good with kids too. We should have brought her with us, but she's more likely to have stopped us coming than to have agreed to help. It was hard to give her the slip. For the first time in years she came with me to school, both today and yesterday. She wasn't too chuffed about me going back with the bruises still fresh on my neck, but I can't miss any more revision, and I had to face the rumour mill sooner or later.

It was shite.

No one bothered to keep their voices down when they talked about me, and the staring – bloody hell. Also, I reckon Leonie and Mitch are tailing me. I'm not daft. They even showed up at the public library when I was going through old news articles trying to find something on the Hanged Man.

No luck yet. Access to old police reports would be handy, but I've no idea if they're even available to the public. Ollie offered to ghost into the records office at the station, but what's the point? Unless someone's got the right files out and are already leafing through them, he'd just be aimlessly haunting the place.

I've changed into the grey trackies, hoody and cap I brought with me. I don't want anyone recognizing my uniform and calling my school to complain that one of their students is behaving oddly. Especially since I'm supposed to be at an after-school revision club right now.

When I risk stepping out into the sunlight the Ragged kids

take one look at me and scatter into the surrounding buildings. I curse. Nothing's ever easy, is it? Ollie goes to see if he can entice any of them out.

I wander down the road a little, not sure what I'm looking for, just not wanting to be standing around. There's a smudge on the brick wall at shoulder height, like the scum ring inside a dirty tub. The line has marked the garages too, and the road down by the corner, and the edge of the lean-to beside the alley to Goodramsgate.

It's probably just old dirt. I quickly spot something more promising. Where the cobbled route of the old ginnel meets modern pavement there are splashes of what looks like blood leading to a small red puddle of the stuff. I crouch – pleased with how comfortable my new sockets are even after a full day of wear – and give the puddle an experimental prod. It's solid, hard and shiny.

"What is it?" asks Ollie, coming over.

I scratch at it with my nail. "Looks like wax."

"Maybe someone spilt a candle. Or, like, sealed up a really big letter."

"Both probably. Well done, Hastings, you're working those little grey cells."

"Sod off."

A curious face peeks round the side of the garages. The dirty child is small from malnourishment so it's almost impossible to guess his age. A second later the girl with the stained blouse and colourless pinny appears through a patch of ivy. I shudder and force a friendly smile.

"Y'all right there? I'm Charlie and this is Ollie. We just want to talk."

She pulls the boy close, studying me carefully, maybe reassuring herself that I'm not the bogeyman. I never supposed some of the dead might be afraid of me.

In the end the boy talks first. "Have you come to stop the Shadow Man?"

Ollie and I exchange a glance.

"The Shadow Man?" I ask.

"He took our friends Peter and Little Beth, and that other lady."

"What other lady?"

He points towards Goodramsgate. "The lady crushed by the cart. Ophelia saw the Shadow Man take her."

"Ophelia is our friend," says the girl.

"Is that why you came to my house?" I ask.

Head down, she bunches up fistfuls of her pinny. I've got to be careful how hard I push this kid. It won't take much for her to bolt and not come back.

"Ms Nightingale asked me to," she says.

"Audrey sent you?"

"She went to look for our friends. If she didn't come back by the quarter moon I had to find you and give you a message." The girl bites her lip. "I know we're not supposed to go to your house. I waited as long as I could."

So, this is what? A test set by Audrey to see if I'm ready to learn whatever secrets she's got to share?

I pinch the bridge of my nose to keep from snapping.

"What's the message then?"

The girl squares her shoulders, as if what she's about to say is very important. "Remember the capital of ruins."

Ollie seems a little unnerved. I just feel hacked off. It's so like Audrey to refuse to tell me anything and then send a ghost to my door with a cryptic message because it suits her.

"Do you know where she went?" I ask.

The girl shakes her head.

I try to remember if Audrey said or did anything that might give me any clues, but nothing strikes me. She might not want to be found, but I've got an uneasy feeling in my bones. "When did you last talk to her?"

"Eight nights ago."

Thursday. Right after she helped me escape from Sam, back when I thought he was a ghost.

He spies us. Audrey disappears. It can't be a coincidence, can it?

But, if she already knew ghosts were going missing then why didn't she just say so? Maybe she didn't think I'd care. The thought makes me uneasy.

A couple of strides towards the corner and the children scramble off.

"Wait!" I call, following them around the side of the garages. Both Raggeds dart through the brick into nearby shops and gardens. I swear under my breath.

The two women are standing hand in hand, just staring at me. I'm spluttering an explanation when I hear a shout. Heather dashes out of the alley at full sprint. At first, I think she's pissed off because I disappeared on her, but she looks terrified. Ollie raises his palm, motioning for me to stop.

I freeze, remembering there is a deathloop around here.

It's too late. A lad appears in front of me. One side of his head is caved in, flecks of white amongst the mangled tufts of his hair. He gasps and blood flows down his chin.

I turn away and my vision shifts, the street melting away. I'm in a badly lit room. A rat scuttles over my trainers and darts beneath a pile of rags. The stink is overpowering: unwashed bodies, stale air and dirt. I'm starving, the ache in my belly acidic and hollow. There are children pressed against the walls, most too weak to move. Some cough, others are crying.

The lad is standing in the corner, as yet unmarked, but his fear is bitter. I know things I shouldn't know, his memories and emotions bleeding into mine. Footsteps in the hall, coming closer. I try to pull back. I know what's coming because he does and my dread sets me shaking.

He knew he'd get it after he filched that bread, but Sal was starving and he'd woken that morning to find his best friend Isaac dead from a fever in the vermin-infested rags they shared for a bed. He couldn't face it if Sal, his only family, died too.

The door opens and a man flies in, spitting anger on gin-infused breath. The boy's memories give me a name: George Pimm. He fells us in a single backhand.

The crack against my jaw sends me crashing to the floorboards. Blows rain down and I raise my arms in a paltry defence. Pimm's boot meets my stomach. I tense in agony, inhale the pungent reek of alcohol and cower beneath the fury in his bloodshot eyes. He's yelling, calling me a thief. He'll teach me a lesson I won't forget in a hurry. Spittle dashes my cheek. I'm dragged across the boards, thrashing to get away.

"Charlie!" A distant voice calls, but I can't answer.

The dead lad watches me.

I am not this kid.

His death is not my death, but I can't break free.

"Charlie!"

Heather. I reach for her and she pulls me up. Ollie is there to steady me. My head reels from the quick shift from Victorian Ragged School to twenty-first century back alley. That and the kick to my belly make it likely I'm going to chuck up. I stagger to the garage wall and lean against it, breathing slowly until the world stops spinning and I'm not going to splatter the cobbles.

"How bad?" I ask, tasting blood on my tongue.

Heather inspects me quickly and efficiently. I wince when her hands touch my jaw. I feel raw all over, but it's probably from the shock.

"Not too bad considering," she says. "You've a cut lip, a small laceration inside your hairline and you'll come up with bruises. Your jaw and arms took the worst of it, but nothing's broken. We need to watch out for concussion, though."

How much longer until George Pimm would have caved in my skull?

Local legend tells how he took in orphans and used them as labour whilst pocketing the money for their care. When starvation or sickness took them off he'd stash the bodies to keep the income. He was caught and hung himself in prison.

A hanging, I realize, but dismiss it straight away. Wrong man, wrong place, wrong time. My Hanged Man's death was more recent and there was no fury in him, only sorrow.

"Thanks for getting me out." I pick up my cap. "Any witnesses?"

Heather grimaces. "Those two lasses tried to help you, but ran off after you were dragged along by something they couldn't see."

Ollie is watching me like I might suddenly topple over. "We'd best move. They might come back with pitchforks, or a priest."

I can't help a snort of pained laughter. "More likely they'll come back with a livestream and a ghost tour."

"What were you thinking, coming out here?" Heather puts her arm around me. "We should get you home."

"Not yet."

"It's not safe to—"

"I *know*," I say, determined.

She's right. It's not safe, but something in me aches at having left that lad behind. George Pimm murdered him, and in that pocket of memory he's still doing it. For a moment of utter insanity, I consider going back in to try and help him, but I can still sense his fear as if it were my own. It is mine, just like the Hanged Man's sorrow was mine. Inside the loops I become linked to the dead soul, I lose myself to their memories and I'm helpless to save myself, let alone anyone else.

I wish there was a way to break the cycle and free their souls.

I remember what Harrow said: "*If it was one of your ghost friends...*"

"Audrey's gone," I tell Heather, quickly explaining what the Raggeds said about Audrey investigating missing ghosts, the talk of a Shadow Man, and the strange message she left for me. Then I admit Sam told me about the ghosts and asked me to help.

With each revelation the fine lines around her mouth become more defined. I've hurt her feelings by lying, but I can't deal with that right now.

"Well, I have questions for this Sam Harrow if I meet him. But, yeah, something's going on isn't it? Audrey wouldn't have left a message like that if it wasn't important." Heather's got her thinking face on. "Though why she had to make it so sodding cryptic is beyond me."

"I want to talk to Ophelia, the friend the Raggeds mentioned," I say. "Find out what we can about this shadow bloke."

"Sounds like they saw him take Millie. She was hit by a brewer's cart outside the Snickleway Inn back when the pub was called The Anglers," says Ollie. "We passed it on our way here."

"Harrow did say one of the missing was called Millie," I say.

Heather looks worried. "You really think this Shadow Man got Audrey too?"

Wiping at the bloodstain on the inside brim of my cap, I pull it back on. "Only one way to find out. I don't know about you two, but I could do with a drink."

8

SHADOWS AND SNICKLEWAYS

The bloke behind the bar at The Snickleway Inn raps his fingers on the counter in irritation. "No ID, no pint, mate."

No point in stewing, it was always a long shot.

"Coke then," I say, trying not to look at the ghost in a fine blue doublet and ruff hovering beside the barman.

"Ice?"

"Nah."

"You want a straw?" he asks. "It's paper, environmentally friendly."

I shrug and lick the fresh cut on my lip, wincing as it stings. He adds the straw and takes my change. I look for a place to settle.

A few patrons sit glugging pints. The Snickleway Inn is one of York's famous haunted taverns and boasts seven permanent ghosts; though now I'm here I reckon at least half the customers are dead and buried. The Elizabethan gent trailing the barman and the old woman by the front window are definitely ghosts. I suspect the middle-aged Korean man propped up at the bar is also a goner. He doesn't have a drink, and the barman hasn't acknowledged him once since we arrived.

I head past the alcove tables to the empty panelled room behind the stairs. It's small, made smaller by dark red curtains and walls cluttered with old sepia photos.

My left prosthesis squeaks as I sit on a bench. The foot has loosened from the pylon, but there isn't enough space here to get out my screwdriver and fiddle with it, besides, I'm aching all over from Pimm's beating. The little wood burner in the old brick fireplace is roaring and I gladly soak up the heat. When the first sip of Coke hits my stomach, I think I really will chuck up, but the nausea passes.

Heather sits beside me. I try to avoid looking at her, not wanting to face the disappointment in her eyes. When I give in, there's only concern.

"You really want to do this?" she asks.

I swallow and look down. "Yeah."

She dips her chin. "OK then."

"Really?"

"It's your choice. What do you make of Audrey's message?"

"Haven't the foggiest, to be honest." I type "capital of ruins" into my phone, but the wifi here is shite and it's taking forever to load.

A pink cheeked woman wearing long skirts and a frown steps through the wall. I almost knock over my drink. She nearly jumps out of her skin herself, then a knowing smile broadens her face. "Well, at least you look like you've eaten a decent meal in your life. That other seer is far too skinny."

"A lad my age, curly hair?" I ask.

"That's him. Comes in with that notebook of his, always bothering Roderick about what happened to Millie. If you see him you tell him he left a mark on my nice clean tabletop."

I quickly slide a coaster under my glass. "So, what happened to Millie then?"

The woman rolls her eyes. "Nothing. Broke her tether and took off. It happens sometimes. Marmaduke Buckle was stuck next door for two centuries, and now he's out and about. Millie will be off seeing the world I s'pect."

Heather looks thoughtful. "Have you been here long Mrs—?"

"Tulliver. I've been landlady going on three hundred winters now. This place takes a firm hand." She nods at the front bar and the bloke who served me. "At least he's not filling it with gunpowder like the last lot."

Two sleek black cats sprint through the back door with a yowl. Seconds later a large ginger tom follows at full speed.

"Tsk! Seamus, leave them creatures alone," Mrs Tulliver hollers after them. "I wish the pair of them would stay down at the Starre. They give my Seamus no peace, it's enough t' want them back in that wall."

"Mrs Tulliver," I say, "are you sure Millie wasn't … taken?"

"Taken?" She throws up her arms. "That girl! Hasn't left that blasted room in eighty odd years and she's still causing trouble. Ophelia's got it into her head that Millie was nabbed, says she saw the whole thing, but she's a fanciful girl."

I'm already standing. "Could we speak to her?"

Mrs Tulliver frowns. "She's wary of strangers and talks all kinds of nonsense. Chances are you won't make head nor tail of her chatter, but I can't stop you. She's upstairs."

Muttering my thanks, I grab my drink and take the rickety staircase to the next floor. Heather and Ollie follow. The room is poky with windows made up of small diamond panes, and the same dark panelling and upholstery as the downstairs bar. Away from the heat of the stove I'm starting to ache with cold again.

Curled on the bench beneath the window is a slight woman in a woollen gown. She's not wearing a linen cap or coif, unusual for a ghost of her era, and her hair is loose down her back.

"He promised to come back," she whispers. There are tears on her cheeks.

Two steps into the room I notice we're not the only ones here. A group in their early twenties have spread out over one of the tables. I hover, uncertain. I can't talk to Ophelia with them here, but if she's as skittish as Mrs Tulliver says then I might only have one chance at this.

The ghost starts wailing, a long mournful sound that

breaks into sobbing. What am I supposed to do? She isn't in a loop, she knows she's dead all right, but some kind of spiritual superglue keeps her tied to this room.

I sit, casually as I can, putting a decent distance between us so as not to scare her, but close enough that I don't have to raise my voice.

Heather's smile is forced. She doesn't reckon I'll have much luck and she's anxious, ready to spring between us if Ophelia turns nasty. Continuing her vigil at the window, Ophelia's not paying us any attention.

We need answers or we've got nothing but the mention of a Shadow Man from a bunch of skittish kids, a tidemark on the wall where waters don't reach, a mysterious puddle of wax and a cryptic message.

If the group in the corner noticed me come in they've not given me much thought since. I've earbuds in my pocket. They don't have a microphone, but from this distance no one would know the difference. I plug myself in, pretending to make a call, and settle my nerves with a deep breath.

"Ophelia, I'm … I'm Charlie," I say.

Her lips part in surprise. She's missing teeth. There's a riddle of pox scars across her temples and cheeks.

I try again. "I suppose you see all the world's turnings from up here, yeah?"

Her expression darkens. "He promised not to leave me alone, promises made, promises broken." Reaching out, she slides a finger along the swelling in my jaw.

I flinch and Heather tenses, then holds a hand up to

stop Ollie launching himself between us. Ophelia's touch is gentle. She tips my head and hisses in sympathy at the bruising on my neck. "Shouldn't let them hurt you like that, no good at all. You have to help them remember so that they can't."

"Can't what?"

"Take you with them." She levels her gaze at me. "Is that why you left me?"

"I didn't leave you."

She blinks. "Of course. Not you. Do you know where my Simon is?"

"No. Sorry." I clear my throat, "I, er, came to ask about Millie. Mrs Tulliver said you saw someone take her." I gesture to my friends. "We want to help."

Earbuds or not, the group in the corner have clocked I'm nattering to nothing and nobody. I try to ignore the hot prickle of humiliation at their tense whispers and side glances. Not much time before they'll call down to the landlord and I'll get turned out on my end.

"Ophelia, what happened to Millie?" I whisper urgently.

She rises and points to the street below. "Taken where she died. Just there, where the ash fell."

I mimic her, swinging so I'm on my knees, elbows to the windowsill. I don't see any ash, just a few leaves and an old plastic bag dancing in the breeze. Some kid has dropped an ice cream and is screaming hell and fury.

"When was this?"

"Weeks, weeks now and nobody listens. I sung it to the

children, I sing to keep them safe, see, but then the ash came for them too." She leans into the sill. "Ashes and shadows and dust to dust."

"Did you see who did it?"

"A man made of shadow."

"You didn't see his face then?"

Ophelia shakes her head. "Millie liked to test how far she could go before her tether drew her back. She called up to me, one step further than ever before, and said I should come down and try too, because surely I have to find Simon myself. He'll never make it back if they got him, and he'd been so worried, what with his daughter called away and that man coming to ask questions. Millie was to go with me, if I would only come down. She swore it. I put my head out the window to watch her, then the Shadow Man was there, and ash rose from the earth. When it cleared … she was gone."

I look back at Heather and Ollie. The people at the other table are full-on staring at me now, nudging each other.

Time to go.

I thank Ophelia and say we'll let her know if we learn anything new. Despite my rule not to, I find myself wanting to ask if there is anything I can do for her. I never ask that, never. Because I can't solve three-hundred-year-old mysteries or deliver final messages or sort out whatever unfinished business it is that keeps ghosts like her tethered. I open my mouth to say something reassuring, but she shakes her head.

"Don't make promises you can't keep." She turns back to the window.

Abandoning my drink, I take the uneven stairs faster than is sensible. There's no sign of Mrs Tulliver in the bar so I head out front, catching sight of my reflection in the glass by the entrance. My cheekbone has puffed up, my jaw is raw and my bottom lip is smeared with dried blood. Mum's going to think I got into another fight.

The paint on the outside wall is too dark to show up any scum lines, but I look for one anyway.

Ollie joins me. "What are you peering at?"

"There was dirt on the wall down by Bedern. Could be left behind by the ash Ophelia talked about."

"Or it's just dirt," says Heather.

I go to argue, then think better of it. I hate this. I just want to be able to have a chat without worrying, but we can't talk freely here. Tourists might think it's for their benefit – a performance put on by the pub to attract drinkers – but out here on the street I'd just be some gibbering lout with a face that looks like someone took exception to his strangeness.

"Millie, Ragged Peter and Little Beth didn't vanish in a puff of smoke," says Ollie. "How do you even make clouds darker than the night?"

I scan the street for a trace of red wax. Nothing. It's been a wet spring. It sounds like Millie went missing a while ago, any evidence is likely washed away by now, or has been trampled by the trainers of a thousand tourists and blokes on stag weekends.

Is the wax even connected?

Heather looks like she's puzzling something out, but she doesn't say anything. I check the time. It's coming up to five. Not late, but the study club I'm supposed to be at finishes soon and Mum will expect me home.

I remember Google is still open on my phone. The search for "capital of ruins" has loaded. The top entry is a radio programme written by Samuel Beckett in 1946. I can't listen to the recording, but there's a black and white photo. I click the link and a ruined townscape fills the screen: piles of rubble, pools of standing water, churned mud and the skeletal remains of burnt out houses.

Saint-Lô, Normandy.

My knees feel weak. Fear wraps around my heart and for a half-second I'm back in the square, a line of my classmates walking in front of me. Mitch and Leonie are teasing each other about something. It was always the three of us back then. I'm laughing, and then the buildings are gone, replaced by bombed-out ruins. The air smells of dust and burnt stone. Something, or someone, pulls me into a dark room.

"Charlie?" Heather's hand is on my arm.

I swipe the app closed. "I'm fine, just tired is all."

"We should get back."

Yeah, we should. I want to get home, curl up with Dante and forget this whole business. But going home now feels too much like retreat. How can missing ghosts in York have anything to do with the dangerous deathloop I fell into in Normandy?

"We should cut through Mad Alice Lane on our way," I say. "See if there are any marks on the walls."

To my surprise, Heather doesn't argue.

9

✝HE SCEN✝ OF SORCERY

Lund Court, formerly known as Mad Alice's Lane, is a brick ginnel linking Low Petergate and Swinegate. It's a tourist trap, and there is a ghost tour in progress when we try to pass through it. I vaguely recognize the guide, a lanky middle-aged white bloke with a tall top hat. He's gathered his flock where the thoroughfare widens into a cramped yard, using it like a little stage to tell the legend of Mad Alice, who murdered her and who she herself had murdered before that.

A woman in an expensive coat gives me a long, drawn-out glare, as if to remind me she's paid to hear entertaining tales of terrible suffering and gruesome death, and I've not, so I really should be on my way.

As if I haven't heard Alice's story before.

She's one of the most famous ghosts in York. She has a whole blasted ginnel named after her. Alice Smith lived on the alley sometime in the 1860s. An unhappy wife to a violent husband, she took a knife to him and was executed in York Castle for the unfortunate crime of being mad.

Yeah, a right feel-good tale of frolics and giggles.

I look around for an ashy stain and spot a faint line below the windows on the left side of the alley, but I can't get close, not with this crowd. The guide is going on some, milking the tale for all it's worth.

"He just looked right at me," Ollie hisses.

Heather snorts. "No he didn't."

"He did, I swear down. Charlie, you saw that, right?"

"Nope," I say.

"He's dressed all in black, could be our Shadow Man."

Really? How would we know? Still, I watch Top Hat carefully. He looks like a parody of a Victorian undertaker: a long coat, black waistcoat, that daft top hat and silver framed half-moon glasses folded up on a chain around his neck. He's squinting at the crowd, voice lowering. Everyone in the alley leans in, expectant.

A shout. He lurches forward, miming Mad Alice slashing up her husband. There are screams, and a few nervous giggles. He finishes up the tale and gathers his tour to move on.

As he passes the sooty line on the wall, he pauses. Ollie flaps his hand at me, excited. I shush him as the guide rubs a thumb along the mark and frowns. A punter asks him a question. His head snaps up and he's off, chattering as he abandons Lund Court for some other gruesome story of untimely death.

Was that something? Is he the Shadow Man?

As the alley clears, I realize there is one other living soul left behind. Someone I reckon is a better suspect than some old tour guide. Sam Harrow is leaning against a downpipe, his leather notebook sticking out of the front pocket of his waxed jacket.

I clench my fists. "Oi, what did you do to Audrey?"

He blinks. "Who?"

"Audrey Nightingale, she helped me give you the slip on The Shambles, warned me to stay away from you. Now she's missing."

"A ghost?"

"Yeah, a ghost. You were gawking at her."

"I was looking at *you*."

Heat rises under the bruising in my neck. I don't know what to say to that so I just scowl at him.

Harrow looks me dead in the eye. "I didn't take your friend. But I'll help you find her."

I shake my head. "This isn't your city and they're not your mates, so why do you give a shite about any missing ghosts?"

Sam's smile evaporates. "Because someone has to."

It feels like a dig and I'm about to tell him to piss off, when he looks up and I see something in his face that I recognize well enough: sorrow.

Audrey didn't want us to meet. Now that she's missing, sticking with Harrow might be the only way to make sense of all this. Maybe he'll let something slip and confess, or maybe he's got something helpful in that notebook of his.

Grudgingly, I make the introductions. Ollie merely nods a greeting, pretending not to care for my sake, but I can sense his interest. Heather is polite, but distant, the way doctors are when they're assessing someone and they're unsure of the answers.

"So," Sam stuffs his hands in his pockets. "Any theories?"

"Ollie reckons it was that tour guide," I say. "On the basis that he wears black and he noticed that strange mark on the wall."

"Which mark?"

I point out the dirty line streaking the brick. "There's a line like that over at Bedern and we went to The Snickleway Inn and had a word with Ophelia—"

"She spoke to you?"

"Yeah." Mostly in riddles but I'm not going to tell him that. Instead, I share what the Raggeds and Ophelia said about the Shadow Man.

Harrow pulls out his phone and flicks through some photos of famous locations around York to an image of a wall with a similar scum mark.

"The end of Walmgate," he says. "James Reid's remains were strung up there after he was hung, drawn and quartered. I think he was the first to go missing. And look…" He points to a puddle of red wax at the bottom of the photo where the wall meets the pavement. "Whoever, or whatever, is taking the ghosts leaves behind visible traces, which means it's a physical phenomenon. They're not crossing over, and I don't think another ghost did this."

Heather nods. "This is the work of the living."

Something about her agreeing with him annoys me. "You know a lot for someone who's only been seeing the dead a few months."

But Sam's not even listening to me. He's got his face upturned, nostrils flaring. "There's that smell again too."

"What smell?"

"Not smell exactly, a tingly feeling in your head, it's … itchy."

"I don't get that."

"No?"

"There's no such thing as sixth sense."

"There is, you're just being stubborn." He bends down to examine the line on the brick. "Salt. And charcoal." He sniffs again, dusting his hand on his jacket as he straightens. "You really don't smell it?"

He's starting to piss me off.

"Look, close your eyes and breathe in," he says. "Come on, eyes closed. Focus. Open your mind."

Ollie shrugs to say "can't hurt". Heather is silent, watching Sam.

This is well daft, but I close my eyes anyway and breathe deep. Right, open my mind, or whatever.

The pungent funk of stale urine registers first. It's so acrid it burns away the other smells, and there are others, layered like sedimentary rock. Cooking from a nearby café, wet stone, some kind of musky wood scent. Not what I'm looking for, all that is here, it's real and now.

I take another deep breath. I bet I look like a complete tosspot. Harrow is probably having a proper chuckle at my expense. I'm about to give up and tell him where to stick it when I get a sudden whiff of charcoal and something fresher.

My eyes flare open in surprise.

"Got it?" His grin is bright. "Good, what else?"

I bristle, then realize he's talking to himself. He turns away, wondering out loud how long it would take for fresh wax to be tracked away by footfall.

What is it about him that has me so on edge? He seems to be well meaning, I can't fault him on that, but it's in the swagger, just like Mitch … no, Sam strides, not swaggers.

Getting out his notebook, he flips through its densely packed pages. "What do you know about spells?"

"Spells?" Now he really is taking the piss.

"Yes, spells. Magic."

I snort and turn to Ollie, expecting him to be cracking a grin at something so daft. He isn't. Heather looks perplexed, but she doesn't tell Harrow he's chatting bollocks.

"I mean … come on," I say. "*Magic*?"

Harrow gives me a level look. "You can see, talk to and touch the dead and you don't believe in magic?"

Well, when he says it like that I feel like a prize idiot. "No, I don't know anything about any bloody magic spells. What about them?"

"Well, the smell for one." He rifles through more pages in his book. "Charcoal and salt are used for concealment."

I scratch the back of my neck. "Whoever did this didn't

want to be seen then?"

"Obviously." He starts to wander in circles, like some great detective orating to the poor prick that hasn't a clue what's going on.

Namely, me.

"The kidnapper did their best to hide how the victims were taken," says Sam. "Firstly, that means there's someone in York they're concealing their activities from. It could be the ghosts themselves, or it could be you, Charlie."

I snort. Yeah, right, I'm not much of a threat. Or maybe there's someone else in York besides me and Sam who knows about ghosts.

Could it be Top Hat the tour guide? He rubbed at the mark on the brick, like he was trying to erase it. Maybe he was. Maybe he didn't realize he'd left evidence.

Or, he's the one the Shadow Man is afraid of.

Or, he's just a plain old tour guide who happened to notice something different about his regular spot, and that's all there is to him.

"And, secondly," Sam goes on, "it means whoever did this is probably planning on striking again."

"Alice was targeted?" asks Ollie.

Sam nods. "But how was she contained? Unless she was destroyed."

Destroyed? Something cramps in my chest. I don't know if it's possible for the dead to die again, but the idea makes my skin crawl. Ghosts are souls: they have personalities and memories and ideas. They're people.

Sam taps his chin, pacing towards the mark then pivoting on his heel. "We need a spell, well, not even a spell really just something to cleanse the space. Is there a good teashop near here?"

Ollie gestures to the street. "Plenty."

"Show me." It's an order, and it's like Sam has no idea he's even given it. There's fire in his eyes and his excitement is catching. Ollie hesitates, as if waiting for my permission, which I'm not going to give because he can do what he wants.

"Charlie and I will guard the site," says Heather.

Sam and Ollie are off and, even with Heather staying too, I feel like the unpopular one getting left behind.

"He's very different to you," Heather says when they're out of sight. "How long has he been a seer?"

"Six months."

"Hmmm, and he knows about magic."

"Wait, do *you*?"

"I can sense some things that are … outside of the physical world, all souls can, but spells and all that? No, that's new to me."

"You think he's full of shite then?"

"Let's wait and see." She looks over at the sooty mark on the wall. "I wish we understood Audrey's message."

"We can't trust him."

"Sam?" She's quiet for a long while. "I don't think he hurt Audrey and he seems sincere when he says he wants to help." An hour ago, she was set on getting me home as quickly as possible. Now, it seems Sam Harrow's irksome charm has won her over. "I think when Audrey warned you off she was trying to keep you out of all this. But something must have happened and so she left you that message and, well, you've gone and got mixed up in it all anyway."

"You think we should keep working with Sam, then?" I ask.

Heather nods. "It wouldn't hurt to find out what he knows, and you've always needed … you know…" She clears her throat but doesn't finish speaking. I leave the silence open.

A couple of minutes later Harrow and Ollie hurry back down the ginnel, Harrow carrying several boxes of loose tea and a white teacup, while reading something out of his notebook. Instead of sticking it back in his pocket, he hands it to me. I'm so surprised he has to practically shove it into my hands. The cover is warm from his fingers. I want to open it up, but it feels intrusive. Not that that stopped him poking through my life, so I'd have every right to read his stupid journal.

I don't though.

Crouching, he opens the packets of tea, throwing up the pungent freshness of peppermint and something citrusy. Blending the herbs together in the cup, he pulls out an old-style flip lighter. The dried leaves take like flash paper. Smoke billows and he wafts it around the alleyway.

Any minute now I swear he's going to start chanting.

I must look well confused, but he just smiles at me.

"Most of the really good herbs for this are toxic and the shops don't sell them, but peppermint, nettle and lemon are all decent for purification and cleansing." He waves his arms through the smoke. "It's the best I can do, I just hope it's enough."

My grip on his notebook tightens. "How do you know all this?"

"Google. There's a lot out there, but most of it is misleading. Modern pagan practices, namely magic as religion, don't always match up to the practical elements of what actually works. The old superstitions and sympathetic rituals, if you can find authentic ones, are most trustworthy for real world application. Wait, what's that?"

He points, but all I see are the same grey slabs riddled with weeds. Then, a patch of air becomes a shimmery blur, like heat over hot tarmac, and a rusty mark appears plain as day on the flagstones.

Sam crouches for a closer look. Part of the design seems to have cracked away, but it's mostly intact: a broken circle, like a rounded horseshoe with a vertical line through it and a shorter line crossing it dead centre. Something about it reminds me of a Viking rune, but it's the wrong style. Whatever the symbol is, it feels … familiar. I've seen something like it before, but where?

"Definite similarities to Elder Futhark, but also cuneiform, which is a much older writing system," says Sam. "Interesting."

I've no idea what he's on about, but I'm not letting on that I'm baffled.

"What is it?"

"A ghost trap." He holds his palm over it. "A spirit crosses this, they get stuck. Easy prey."

"Did you Google that too?"

Ignoring me, he takes back his notebook and starts sketching and scribbling notes into the margins.

Ollie's staring straight at the mark. I touch his arm and he flinches.

"I know who took Alice," he whispers. "I know who took them all. There is a soul catcher in York."

10

CABINE† OF SOULS

We detour back to Bedern Arch so Sam can waft smoke around in the hope of revealing a second ghost trap. It simmers into view on the road within seconds. I don't want to linger, so Sam takes us somewhere to talk.

The place he picks is well up itself. There's distressed wood, neon lighting spelling COFFEE in bright swirly letters above the counter, and seventeen different kinds of herbal tea. It's busy, filled up with tourists and students and dickheads on laptops pretending to write novels.

The waitress is probably wondering what we're doing here together. We don't look like the kind of lads who'd be mates, or boyfriends even. Sam asks for a booth. He gestures for Heather and Ollie to slide in before he lollops beside Heather and orders a flat white. I'm not really into hot drinks, but I ask for a black coffee and hope I can choke it down.

Sam turns to Ollie and Heather. "Would either of you like anything?"

What's he playing at? It's not like they can eat or drink. I probably look as baffled as the waitress.

"A ... hot chocolate?" Ollie ventures.

Sam looks to Heather, who shakes her head.

He orders the hot chocolate. When the waitress hesitates, he flashes her a grin. "Humour me."

She's wearing the stretched nervous smile of someone faced with the strange and unpredictable. "Would you like cream and marshmallows?"

"Ollie – yes? Yes, please, that would be lovely." Either Sam doesn't realize he's making the waitress uncomfortable, or he doesn't care. After another brief hesitation, she notes it down and sods off to tell her colleagues about the weirdo table.

Ollie's not meeting my eyes in case I'm pissed off with him. I am pissed off, but with Sam. I lean over, keeping my voice low. "People are staring at us."

"Really?" He looks around. "Oh yes, so they are. People do that, a lot. It's hard to stop them."

"You could try not being so obvious about it."

"So, I've got to be something I'm not just to make strangers feel more comfortable? No thank you. They'll just stare anyway."

I clench and unclench my fists under the table, trying to breathe through my anxiety. If any Hungry Ones see the four of us sitting together – two living people and two ghosts –

96

then we'll be in trouble.

Opening his notebook, Sam pulls out a metal fountain pen that probably costs more than my mum earns in a month and asks, "What's a soul catcher then?"

"A ghost hunter," says Ollie.

It's Sam's turn to look confused. "Do you mean those pseudo psychics on TV?"

I know the shows he's on about. They have daft names like *The UK's Most Haunted Kebab Shops* and are presented by "experts" who couldn't spot a real ghost if they walked right through one. Not that I can tell from the shows if those places are really haunted. The dead appear on film about as often as they do in photographs or mirrors.

"Nah, the real deal," says Ollie. "They can't see or touch us, not like you and Charlie can, but they have their own ways to hunt us. My first week undead, Earl Percy told me catchers can extinguish our souls, one stab with a magic dagger and we're nothing, like we never even existed. But he's a prick, right, so I reckon that's as much bollocks as his stories about ghosts possessing people. Everyone knows possession is a load of rubbish, can't be done. Nah, I heard catchers trap us somehow, keep us on storage shelves like trophies."

Sam frowns. "Like a cabinet of curiosity?"

"A what?" I ask.

"Wealthy white people used to purchase, or often just steal, curiosities from around the world and put them on display in their homes to show their friends how sophisticated and learned they were."

"Right," says Ollie. "But instead of stuffed endangered species, fossils and shrunken heads, catchers have *cabinets of souls*. Imagine shelves and shelves filled with trapped ghosts."

It sounds like a make-believe story to frighten ghost children into being well behaved, but Ollie's sincere. All the missing ghosts are famous, part of tours and featured in guidebooks. Surely the more famous the ghost, the bigger the score for any collector building a ghostly trophy cabinet. Unless it's just because they're easy pickings.

The waitress is back, placing the hot chocolate in front of the empty spot beside me with an awkward smile. My coffee is bitter and strong. I have to stir four artisan sugar cubes into it to make it bearable. Sam watches me with amusement in his eyes.

At the sight of his hot chocolate Ollie's face lights up. He makes a show of dipping his nose into the steam for a deep sniff.

And then I get it, and I hate myself.

It's not about the hot chocolate, it's about being a part of the living world. I'm pissed at Sam for noticing what Ollie needed, when I didn't. And I hate that I don't have the guts to order for an invisible person, or the brass to just buy something no one's going to drink.

"There used to be a handful of catchers about," Ollie goes on, "but then that nun from down near The York Arms, the one who got bricked up in the wall for getting knocked up – Sister Agnes I think her name was – ate the last seer in York. A catcher went after her in the end, got her good; least, no one's seen her for decades so I reckon she's on a shelf somewhere. A symbol just like the ones at Mad Alice's Lane and Bedern was burnt into the cobbles where she vanished. I saw it myself."

"Hold on. Sister Agnes *ate* the seer?" asks Sam.

"Some ghosts reckon our flesh and blood will bring them back to life if they eat and drink it," I explain.

"Will it?"

"Nope. But that doesn't do you much good if they decide to give it a try."

"Heard of Jack the Ripper?" asks Ollie. "They say them lasses were all seers who got caught by a nasty soul who couldn't let go of the old ways."

"It's one of the reasons I keep to myself, and you should do the same." I pretend to drink more of my sweetened coffee.

"Good to know," says Sam. He looks rattled.

"I'm not kidding about keeping your head down, Harrow. It's not only the Hungry Ones you have to watch out for. Some ghosts are just pissed off and we're something solid they can take it out on. And then there are the Mouldy Oldies—"

"Mouldy Oldies?"

"The Old Souls," says Heather, breaking her silence. "Powerful old ghosts who form a kind of ghost council and keep the peace amongst the dead here in York. There are seven of them," she counts them off on her fingers. "Lady Alice Peckitt, Sir Gosselin Danville, Earl Henry Percy, Saint Margaret Clitherow, Inga of Jorvik, King Aelle and Emperor Septimus Severus, their leader. He haunts the Minster. It's built over the administrative hub of the Roman fort and, luckily, he rarely leaves it. But I can't say the same for the others, so you need to be careful."

I can tell Sam is puzzled.

"There's some ancient ghost custom that says seers only exist to serve the dead as links to the living world," I say.

"Or so the Old Souls claim," says Heather. "They tried to make Charlie their servant once, but … I stepped in."

She lays it out for Sam, warning him which spots to avoid. I can tell from the flush in his face he's already been all over town for his survey of the dead. If he got himself noticed by Mrs Tulliver, there will be others who know he's in York. It's a miracle the Mouldy Oldies haven't tried to execute or enslave him yet.

Ollie is staring into the cream on his hot chocolate, the marshmallows having sunk into the foam. "Thank God not many people come back from the dead with the power to see us," he says.

"But we did." Sam's gaze meets mine. I duck my head into my coffee cup and take a great big gulp, wincing at the bitterness. When I glance back up, his expression seems to ask, *"Don't you want to know why?"*

No Sam, I don't. Shite just happens.

He steeples his fingers and leans in. "What about poltergeists? Aren't they dangerous to everyone, seers or not?"

"If they were real, yeah," says Ollie.

I shake my head. "I've never met a ghost who can affect physical stuff other than … well … seers like us."

The kitchen lights flickering ... fingernails on the door frame ... strange silver eyes.

Am I wrong? Nah, a fuse blew is all. Bollocks, I forgot to check that Ragged girl's nails for red polish, though now I think about it, nail polish was way after her time. The hand was too big, the fingers too long, nails too sharp. So, who was in my kitchen and why were they there? Did I imagine them?

"Then unless the Shadow Man is a seer like us, ghosts won't be able to touch him, let alone fight him off," says Sam.

He's right, and it makes me sick. To be trapped and taken by someone you can't touch, unable to defend yourself and then ... nothing? True death? Stuck forever? I feel a stab of anger, then sadness for all of the missing, even Mad Alice.

Heather looks troubled. "We're too predictable. Mad Alice rarely left her ginnel, James Reid the piper was on a schedule like clockwork. We souls like routine; we haunt the same places or people."

"Easy to target if you know what to look for," I say.

"The question is: does the Shadow Man have what he wants, or will he target more ghosts?" Sam asks, looking in Ollie's direction with concern.

Heather's wearing the serious expression she uses when she's about to give an order. "I'm going to speak to the Emperor, see if I can get him to call a soulmoot."

"A what?" asks Sam at the same time I say, "The bollocks you are!"

"A soulmoot is a meeting for all the free ghosts of York," Ollie explains to Sam. "Heather, remember what Septimus said last time—"

"I can handle him," says Heather. "I agree that the Mouldy Oldies are dickheads of the highest order, but they need to know about this and we need to warn everyone to be on the alert."

"Yeah, against tour guides with top hats," says Ollie.

"You really think it's him?" asks Sam.

"He's a possible lead we should follow up at least," I say, wanting to have Ollie's back. "I'll do some research."

I get out my phone, meaning to look up Top Hat's website, and curse. I've got two missed calls and a message from Dad. He went by the school to pick me up after my study session only to be told I'd never signed in.

"I've got to get home."

I've no idea how much a coffee costs here, probably more than I can afford. Fishing a fiver out of my pocket, I toss it on the table and stand to leave.

Sam looks at the money. "I'll get these."

I want to take my cash back, it's not like I'm flush, but I'm too proud. He's staring at me again, expecting what?

"Right, well, I'll see you around," I say and just walk off. I hear him call my name. When I steal a glance over my shoulder he's turned to say something to Heather. It makes it easier to keep walking. That and the panic of knowing I've got to face my parents.

When I message Dad letting him know I'm fine he tells me to meet him at the station. Ollie and Heather catch me up, deep in conversation about soul catchers and how best to approach the Emperor without getting torn into incorporeal confetti.

Dad pulls into the taxi bay. I clamber in. He takes one look at the state of me and starts shouting.

II

GLASS WALLS

M um almost cries when she sees my cut lip and swollen cheek. "What happened to you?"

Dad parrots the lie I told him in the car. "Says he fell."

Our bungalow smells of baked potato and laundry detergent. There are dishes in the sink, clutter on the counter and Lego bricks scattered over the lino. I itch to clear the floor so I can swap my prostheses for my chair, but Mum gives me a long look – the kind that tells me to stay put while she roots through the medicine cabinet for disinfectant. I dutifully sit at the kitchen table, tight lipped, as she dabs my stinging cuts with TCP.

Heather and Ollie are walking home. Dad was in a hurry, and pissed off, and after he saw the state of me I couldn't find an excuse to open the car door for them to get in. Dad should be starting his shift, but he shows no sign of heading out right away. He puts the kettle on and drops a teabag in my favourite mug. The blue, white and red of the London 2012 Paralympics logo is badly faded from too many goes through the dishwasher.

Mum inspects my jaw like she's trying to X-ray me for secrets. "Did you get in a fight?"

"Course not, I tripped over a cobble." I shift my left leg and the prosthesis gives an obliging squeak.

"We thought you were going to the study group."

I shrug and look away. "Changed my mind, went into town with Sam last minute."

Whatever she's going to say next she swallows it and glances at Dad.

"What?" I say. "You want me to have mates."

Dad sets the brew down beside me. "But you lied about where you were."

I'm lying about a lot more than that.

"So I forgot to call! I'm not a kid."

"No, but you're..." Dad trails off.

I'm what, Dad? Disabled? Different?

"Still our lad," he says after the silence stretches too long. "Look, if someone's giving you trouble again we'll sort it, but we need you to tell us what's going on. Is it someone from school?"

"I handled that."

Another lie.

Last year Josh Girshaw started heckling me, only stopping

short of thrashing me so bad that I'd get the school involved. And then it stopped. Overnight. He wouldn't even look at me and hasn't since. Maybe he just got bored.

"Or is it one of the lads round here?" says Dad.

"No one's bothering me." No one alive, anyway.

I can tell they don't believe me by the way Dad shifts on his chair, and the puckering in Mum's chin that appears whenever she's upset. There's a pressure in my chest, like one of them alien things is about to burst through my ribcage. All I do is lie to them. I'm sick of it. It's a good thing my seeing ghosts is a fluke, because if someone made me like this—

I don't think I could ever forgive them.

My eyes sting. I bite the inside of my cheek until I taste iron.

"It came out!" Poppy and Lorna charge into the kitchen in their matching unicorn and astronaut pyjamas, Lorna holding a small, bloodied incisor up in triumph. She grins to show the new gap in her bottom teeth.

"She was brushing it and it went all dangly and there was blood!" Poppy squeals.

Mum pivots, her frustration with me sliding beneath an instant smile. "You'd better wrap it in some tissue then." She tears off a sheet of kitchen roll.

"Will the tooth fairy come?" asks Lorna, bouncing about.

"I expect so. Put it at the edge of your pillow."

Wrapping her tooth in tissue like it's a precious jewel, Lorna hurries back to their room, Poppy following.

There's a long silence. Dad takes a breath and I brace

myself, knowing whatever he asks I'll probably have to lie again.

A mobile rings. Mum snatches it up and greets the caller with, "What's wrong?" then looks at the clock over the fridge. "I'll be right over." She turns to Dad. "Chrissie needs us to take the kids for the night."

Dad heaves himself up with a tired grunt. Bags shadow his eyes. He's wearing a full day's worth of stubble and he's about to go back out to work some extra hours. Money's always been tight, but right now they're under a lot of pressure. I heard them talking about it when I was up late letting Dante out for a pretend-piss. Mum has been taking more and more time off work to help Chrissie. Dad's picking up the slack, but they're still not making ends meet, especially when a chunk of what he makes goes to keeping Chrissie afloat as well.

"The girls?" asks Mum.

"I'll do bedtime," I offer.

"Fine," she says, grabbing her coat and keys. "But no letting them stay up and set traps for the tooth fairy like last time."

I almost smile at that. When they stop bickering and work together the twins are capable of dangerous things. Dad still has the scar on his finger to prove it.

"And this talk isn't over," she warns as she swaps her pompom slippers for her knock-off Uggs. "I've got my phone if you need me."

Dad goes to follow her out, then hesitates at the door. I keep my gaze fixed on my cooling tea.

"Lad, whatever it is, you can tell us." He shifts his weight from one foot to the other. The dodgy bit of lino creaks. "We love you no matter what, no matter who you…" He clears his throat. "You can always talk to me, about anything, or anyone."

"Anyone?" The way he said it. *"Any-one."* And the look they gave each other when I mentioned Sam. *"No matter who you…"* Who I what? My head goes light and my throat tightens.

He knows. He knows. He knows.

"Dad… I…" My mind is a vacuum. I've practised this moment in my head a thousand times over and now it's here all I feel is the nausea of blind acceleration, my thoughts spinning.

When I came out to Heather she reckoned I should trust my parents on this when I was ready. Am I ready? I don't know, but the need to reach across this chasm between Dad and me is overwhelming. The pressure in my chest ruptures and my words spill out in a rush, "I'mgayandiknowitmightnotbewhatyou—"

He's beside me in two big strides, his heavy hand on my shoulder. "Slow down, Charlie. It's all right."

"Does Mum know?"

"She's got a fair idea, aye. And she loves you. We both love you." His voice catches and he swipes at his eyes. "Look, no homophobic arsehole is gonna give my lad a hard time, so we'll sort it, all right? You and me."

For a second, I feel lighter than I have in a while.

"We'll sort it."

But then the vice in my chest clamps tight again. They think I'm getting the shite kicked out of me for being gay. If I say nothing they'll stop asking questions. But it's another lie, and another thing for them to worry about.

"It's not like that," I say.

Dad's expression is open, waiting for me to make some kind of sense. If he's all right about me liking lads, maybe he'll understand the ghost thing. Later Ollie can ruffle my hair or lift me up, or *something*, and Dad will see it's not all in my head—

"Paul!" Mum hollers from out front.

The truth sticks somewhere in my throat. I can't risk it. So, I swallow and nod, looking at the ticking clock, the box of Yorkshire brew by the kettle, anywhere but him because if I do I'll cry and neither of us can deal with that right now.

"Thanks for having my back," I say.

He taps the steaming mug. "Milk, two sugars. Don't let it go cold." A heartbeat, then he sniffs and heads to the car.

Hands shaking, I take a long sip of the brew. I remember what he'd said the day he gave me this mug: "You can do anything you set yourself to do."

"Except tap dancing," I'd joked from my hospital bed, still sore from another surgery.

"Don't count it out, lad," he'd said.

After a quick tidy up, I transfer to my chair. Although my trainers are pretty battered where they dragged on the cobbles, the damage to my left prosthesis is minor, a loose screw is all. I can fix it when I've got the girls to bed.

Poppy insists she needs to brush her teeth again, just in case she can coax one of her wobbly teeth to fall out too. I reassure her she'll get her gold soon enough and herd her to their bedroom where she helps Lorna set up the trundle in the gap between their beds for when our cousins arrive.

"You can read for ten minutes," I say, knowing it'll be way longer than that.

My phone buzzes. Unknown sender. I wait until I'm alone in the kitchen to open the message.

Let me know when you have something on that tour guide. We need to find out more about soul catchers too. Hope you got home safely. S

Sam. I didn't give him my number, but it doesn't surprise me he got hold of it. I feel a familiar flicker of irritation, mellowed by something else.

"We need to."

We. Like we're a team now.

My fingers hover over the keys. Should I tell him about Audrey's message?

The shadowy ruins of Saint-Lô loom over me. My breath catches in my throat. Harsh voices. Footsteps. Metal on skin. Blood. My forearms throb: I gulp for air.

I don't want to remember.

Dante whines and puts his chin on my knee. His familiar doggie smell brings me back to reality.

I am alive. I can breathe.

In the end I don't text Sam.

After helping myself to leftovers, I dig out a screwdriver and fix my prosthesis, trying to think things through. Soul catcher spells, red wax and a stupid message from Audrey, who might also be missing. A suspicious ghost tour guide who might be involved, or not. What about the dislocated deathloop? That seems to be a different mystery entirely, and I don't see how what happened in Saint-Lô is important either. I sit a minute, senses off kilter, like I've been spinning on the spot.

I just came out to my dad. Holy fuck. What about Mum? What will she say? What if Dad's wrong about her knowing and she isn't all right with it?

Deep breaths. Stay in control. I decide to do press-ups and crunches to keep my mind off things. Dad will go straight to work after dropping Mum and my cousins home, and Heather and Ollie will be back soon too.

In the end Ollie comes home alone, which sucks because I wanted to tell Heather she was right about my parents being chill with me being gay.

"She's gone to petition the Emperor for a moot," says Ollie when I let him in. "I tried to talk her out of it."

We're both tense, waiting for Heather to check in. Ollie wants to go over the clues again and get excited over the fact that Sam can do magic. Maybe there's some kind of spell in

Sam's notebook that could help protect us from them.

"Why didn't you tell me about magic?" I ask.

"Well, it's not *magic* magic, is it?" Ollie shrugs. The hunched way he's sitting makes me think of a wise old man trapped in a boy's gangly body. "Sam isn't about to hop on a flying skateboard and make friends with an owl. It's more superstition and stuff, and hardly anyone believes in it anymore, not even the dead."

"But it is … real?"

"I reckon there's as much magic in the world as you let in." He grins. "That didn't sound half bad, eh?"

I think of Sam wafting the smoking teacup around Mad Alice's Lane, brow creased in concentration, eyes hopeful.

Yeah, not half bad.

Mum gets back with the terrible trio. I know from the way she hugs me that she and Dad had a chat in the car, and that she really is all right with having a gay son. Actually, she's known for a while.

After the carnage of the bedtime story, I slip away. By the time Mum pokes her head round my door I'm tucked up pretending to sleep, but I can't settle. If I sleep I'll dream, and I don't want to dream.

Instead, I scroll aimlessly through TikTok: my favourite wheelchair basketball team, fitness accounts, hot lads in "Love Wins" hoodies lying with cute boyfriends in cornfields, or curled up on the couch together, their lives way better than mine. One lad kind of looks a bit like Mitch. I unfollow him.

I can't help looking at Sam Harrow's profile pic again. I should message him back. He might be my only hope of finding Audrey.

Thinking about Audrey reminds me that I need to research Top Hat. It doesn't take long to find his website. His name is Peter Rawley and he's been at this ghost-tour business a long while. Apparently, he was one of the first to start doing them in York. But if he's a soul catcher then why start taking ghosts now, and not a decade ago? What's changed?

The skin on the back of my neck prickles. I turn my head. There's a figure at my window.

I lurch upright.

Mr Broomwood waves.

I curse, ignoring Dante's barking and Ollie's exaggerated groan from the hammock, and slip out of bed. My stumps are weight bearing. I can walk on them for short distances, though it aches. My dead neighbour waits impatiently as I make my way over, unlatch the window and slide it open. Cold air stirs against my hot skin.

"If this is about your bloody roses—"

"What's Heather up to trying t' call a moot?"

I look at my phone. It's four in the morning. She has been busy for word to get around so fast. I count down from five to calm myself. I could tell Mr Broomwood to piss off, but he'll just rant at me. Instead I tell him what I can. It's nothing he'll not hear at the moot in any case.

"Well I can't go anyhow," he says. "What if some louts come by and vandalize the close like what happened down York Cemetery way?" He shakes his head. "Good-for-nothing kids and their voodoo hocus-pocus. Young'uns today have no respect for the dead." He wraps his dressing gown tighter. "I watched it on the news with David's renters. At least they watch local news, not like the last—"

"Yeah, well Heather can fill you in after the moot." Stifling a yawn, I reach for the latch, ready to draw the window closed, but Mr Broomwood isn't done.

"There ain't going t' be a moot, lad. The Emperor tried to strike a bargain and Heather wouldn't sell, least, that's the way I heard it."

My elbow whacks the window frame. "Is she all right, did he—?"

"No, no, but he gave her a good talking to for getting above her station. The Old Souls won't ever let her call a moot herself y' know, not even dead a decade. I'd speak up for her, but I can't go all the way t' the Minster with my old bones."

I'm polite enough to not point out that he doesn't have bones anymore and, as he's only been dead for a few months, the Mouldy Oldies are unlikely to listen to him either.

"Though, if those ancient busybodies get their act together they'll want me there," he says. "What with my neighbourhood-watch experience."

"I'll be sure to mention it."

He snorts and bumbles off, grumbling.

It's only when I'm back in bed that something about his

mention of vandalism at the cemetery clicks. There was a report on the news when I was at the hospital. Something I saw on the screen … what was it?

There's a short article online in the local paper. I scroll through, no suspects, shock and outrage, blah blah blah. My thumb freezes over the phrase "possible occult connection". There's a photo of a broken grave, police tape across one part of it and the cemetery chapel in the background. On the edge of a gravestone is the deep red of hardened wax. But that's not what's got me hissing at Ollie to wake up. Nearby, something has killed off the grass in a shape that looks very familiar.

The Shadow Man has claimed another victim.

12

THE KING'S FAVOURITE

"Gates locked in a half hour," says the man over the top of his newspaper as we approach York Cemetery. I recognize him from the news. When he spots the roll of paper under my arm his bushy brows migrate up his forehead.

Wandering around a cemetery isn't what most lads do on the first day of their Easter holidays, especially when they have exams coming up, so I nicked some art supplies from my sisters. If anyone asks I'm doing a grave rubbing of – oh, sod it, I can't remember, a famous geologist buried here – for coursework I actually submitted weeks ago.

The gatekeeper must think I don't much look the type to be into grave rubbings, and for a moment I worry he won't let me in, but he waves me through with a warning.

"Stay away from the chapel. And careful not to damage

anythin' when you're making them rubbings." He flicks the corner of his paper. "And don't you make me come looking for you. A half hour only."

Of course, like a complete pillock, I didn't check what time this place closes. Apparently, corpses don't like visitors after four fifteen. Must be because their social calendar is already heaving.

"He's still watching," says Heather.

Ignoring the road up to the chapel, we take a round about way on to one of the tree-lined avenues between the plots, Ollie hurrying ahead of us. Snowdrops and spring crocuses poke up between the graves. Traffic is a distant rumble. I smell grass clippings and things growing.

"Remind me why you haven't called Sam," says Heather.

I make a non-committal noise. "I just don't want to bring him all the way out here if it's nothing."

Heather opens her mouth, closes it and smiles. What the hell does she find so funny?

"What did the Emperor want?" I ask, changing the subject.

Heather stops. "Want?"

"Yeah, in exchange for hosting the moot? Broomwood said the Emperor wanted to make a deal, but you turned him down."

"There was no deal. I don't have anything he wants." She walks off and I have to hurry to keep up.

Standing watch over an area of gravelly tarmac, the columned chapel seems more like a Greek temple than a place of God. It was probably white once, but the weather has beaten

117

it grey at the base. The front looks normal enough so we head around the back, keeping our distance. The graves go right up to the wall where there is a little door in the foundations.

The ghost trap is burnt into the grass beside the vandalized grave. It looks identical to the other traps. I snap a pic with my phone.

"Who d'you think was taken?" says Ollie, keeping his distance from the mark.

"A tethered soul, maybe?" says Heather. "I'll ask around. Someone might have an idea whose patch this was."

Like most cemeteries there are very few ghosts here. Spirits don't actually like graveyards. I mean, why would they?

I wander up to the back of the chapel, noting all the names on the gravestones in the hope something will stand out. Most of the inscriptions are too weathered to read. The lock on the back door looks like it might have been jimmied open at some point. I turn to ask Heather what she thinks, but she and Ollie are still beside the ghost trap, pressing at the air like they've joined the circus as mimes.

A cold hand crushes my heart. If they get caught I've no idea how to get them out.

I hurry back. "You stuck?"

Ollie shoulders the air and bounces off. "Nope. Blocked."

"More magic?"

"Nah, invisible force fields I can't cross always appear around stuff. It's dead annoying."

They're not stuck, they just can't move closer to the chapel. We walk the line, Heather and Ollie testing it at every step.

No matter if there's gravel, gravestone or grass beneath our feet, Ollie and Heather can't get closer to the chapel than ten or so metres.

When we've gone full circle Heather asks, "What now?"

Something pulls me cruelly backwards. Cold steel bites my neck as a thin blade presses against my skin.

A ghost? I'm thinking yes because no one living walks around with a real sword, they'd get themselves nicked.

Ollie and I lock gazes. When he moves so do I, slamming my elbow into my captor's torso as Ollie rushes us with wild bravery but not a whole load of accuracy. Whoever has hold of me twists, avoiding the worst of my elbow and – still keeping the rapier against my jugular – shifts us both to the side. A well-timed kick to Ollie's arse as he stumbles past sends him flying.

"Let Charlie go," says Heather, calm but firm.

"Charlie, is it?" says a male voice in my ear. "It seems your companions want you back unharmed, seer. I am not unjust. I propose an exchange. The woman for your life."

Heather folds her arms. "In your dreams, creep—"

"You mistake my meaning. A figure cloaked in darkness apprehended Mistress Nightingale from that spot thither, nine days ago."

"You saw Audrey?" I ask.

"Well it wasn't Charlie, so get your hands off him," snaps Ollie.

"You swear to this?" asks my captor, tightening his arm.

I try to nod and the blade bites into my throat. "We're

looking for the missing ghosts, not taking them."

He releases me. My instinct is to jerk away, but on the slippery grass I risk falling, so I turn slowly to face a well-built gentleman in a black doublet with gold trimmings, chestnut hair curling on to his broad white collar.

"Souls taken, you say?" Sliding his rapier back into its scabbard, he strokes his neat triangular beard. "Yes, something is indeed amiss."

"Can't get anything past you," scowls Ollie, rubbing his arse.

My neck is bleeding, but it's just a nick. "Who are you?"

The man gathers himself up, nose in the air, one hand to his chest, the other on the hilt of his rapier. "I am George Villiers, First Duke of Buckinghamshire, former Lord Admiral of the king's fleet, Knight of the Royal Garter and the favourite of *three* kings."

That sort of rings a bell from my Jacobean history module.

"I've heard of you…" says Ollie, unsurprisingly. "You were knifed in a pub in Portsmouth."

Now I remember. George Villiers had a bit of a bad run of things and someone did him in.

The murdered man nods gravely. "Cruelly assassinated by that villain Felton and cursed to wander the earth. I came to York to discover my errant son. Alas, no luck, but this city doth appeal far more than my old haunting ground. As such, I have settled to make it my home. Mistress Nightingale, whom I did meet through James Reid, an excellent fellow, implored me to take up station here and warn her if any persons of villainous character should approach the chapel."

"Did she say why?" asks Heather.

"Nay, only 'tis of vital importance." He places a palm back over his heart. "I am one who hates to be idle. I seek redemption, to remedy my wrongdoings and thus end my perpetual wanderings—"

"Right, so you watched the chapel for Audrey," I say. "Then what?"

"After a week at my post, well, mostly at my post, there was time spent with dearest James…" He clears his throat. "A villain picked the lock on the chapel door, lingered inside for some time and upon departing, locked the door anew."

"Did they take anything?" I ask.

"I saw nothing, but a smaller item may hath been concealed about his person. Mistress Nightingale was most concerned. When James missed our arranged foray along the River Foss, I feared something untoward had occurred and came seeking counsel. I saw Mistress Nightingale thither" – he points towards the ghost trap – "facing the villain. Living shadows obscured his face, writhing like the very demons of hell. I started towards them in haste, but he scattered about a darkness so foul it did clog up mine eyes. When I was able to situate myself, Mistress Nightingale was gone."

"The Shadow Man." Ollie's voice is a taut breath. "A soul catcher took her all right, just like Reid and the others."

"James was taken?" Villiers' hand shoots to his rapier.

"Aye, I mean, yeah. But we're going to get him back," I say with more confidence than I feel.

121

Villiers nods. "Tis a noble endeavour. I shall join you."

Heather snorts. "Oh, will you?"

"Madam, I was a courtier, a statesman and an admiral. I commanded His Majesty's forces and undertook negotiations on his behalf. I was the favourite of *three* kings. I can be of use to you. And James is … very dear to me."

Heather stares at him, giving nothing away. "Did you see the Shadow Man's face?"

Villiers nods with enthusiasm.

"And you'd recognize him if you saw him again?"

"His foul countenance is burnt into my every waking moment."

After considering Villiers for a long while, she offers him her hand. "Heather Noble, junior doctor."

"A pleasure, Mistress Noble." Scooping up her hand, he bows to kiss it.

Ollie waves. "Ollie Shuttleworth, sickly waif."

"And this is Charlie Frith, seer." Heather gives "seer" a certain gravity I don't deserve.

I give him an awkward nod. "This villain you saw, did he have a top hat?"

Villiers face lights up. "Aye, he wore a bonnet of unusual height."

"I knew it!" says Ollie. "It *is* him."

I've got to agree. It's looking more and more likely that Peter Rawley is the Shadow Man. I want to go find him in town on one of his tours right now. But what good will that do? I don't know how to fight him, don't know how the magic works, or how he's even holding the ghosts, let alone how to free them. We need more information before we confront him.

"Do you know how to pick locks?" I ask Villiers.

He sniffs. "Such a skill is beneath a man of my standing, but I have been known to … well, there were letters incriminating … I had to…"

"So, yes?"

"If 'tis a pin and tumbler system."

Leaving the three ghosts on the boundary, I take a quick photo of the crypt lock and show it to Villiers.

"Aye, I can pick it, at least I could if I were still flesh and bone. Alas, I hath no mortal form."

"Could you teach me?" I gesture towards the chapel. "If Rawley broke in then we should take a look inside before we go after him. Either he was after something in there or it's where he's stashing the ghosts he's taken. I need to get in."

"But we can't go in with you," warns Heather.

Villiers snaps his fingers. "We require a magus to end the magic barring spirits from the chapel."

Ollie gives me a pointed look.

I think about Sam sat in the café, the tip of his pen jammed between his teeth, loose curls sticking up where he's run his fingers through them. He makes me feel like I'm not in control, like anything could happen when he's around. That scares me worse than falling into a deathloop with no one to drag me out again.

I clench my jaw, but I know Ollie's right. I'd go in alone, but that would be daft. I'm about as magical as a teaspoon.

"All right, *fine*."

I drop Sam a message. I don't want anything to do with him. I don't. He complicates everything and he's confident and pushy and … infuriating. This is for the sake of the missing ghosts, not because I want to hang out with him or anything.

He replies within seconds: an address and a time.

I've only got five minutes before the cemetery closes. Picking a grave that looks suitably swanky, I make a quick rubbing as Heather and Ollie fill Villiers in on our investigation.

The grumpy bloke is waiting for me, tapping his rolled newspaper against his arm as if he's assessing the likelihood of me breaking in later to perform an unholy ritual atop a gravesite.

I'd say there's a one hundred per cent chance, although I'm not sure about the specifics yet.

He makes a big show of checking his watch. "Cuttin' it a bit fine, lad."

"Sorry. I'm slow on my feet." I lift up my trackies to expose my prostheses.

The old man softens. "Got what you need?"

"Yeah, I think so. Thanks for waiting."

He even wishes me a good day as he locks the gates.

I dump the grave rubbing in the first wheelie bin we pass.

13

SEEKING SAM

"This can't be it." Ollie squints up at the five storey townhouse on one of the nicest terraces in York.

"Why not?" I ask, opening the gate. "He acts like he owns the world, maybe he actually does."

The front garden of the address Sam sent me is pristine, and the glossy front door stands at the top of curved marble steps. This street is arsehole central – brass doorknockers, huge sod-off four-by-fours, and pretention. The people who live here probably have monogrammed stationery and, like, go on holiday to second houses, and call going to London "going-down-to-town".

I hesitate before raising the big brass knocker and letting it fall. The door is opened by a tall, well-dressed white man in his late fifties. He's sharply featured, all upright angles, neat-cropped hair and tailored suits.

"I… Does Sam live here?" And then, because he's not saying anything, I add, "I'm a mate from school."

"School?" He frowns. I've messed up. The boys from St Matthews probably don't wear battered trackies and baseball caps, or use the word "mate". "Sam's not home."

"Oh, right." I try not to fidget. "Do you know when he'll be back?"

There is a strange sheen to the man's eyes. They seem a little too bright, a little too wet. He's staring past me, like he's looking through Ollie to where Heather and Villiers are deep in discussion on his front lawn. His gaze snaps back to me. "He won't be long. Why don't you come in and wait?"

The invitation catches me off guard. I want to bolt, but the bloke is striding into the house, expecting me to follow. It would be rude to take off.

Ollie trails me over the threshold. "Do you think they have an Xbox?"

Inside, the place is sodding magnificent. I'm serious. Everything gleams: the floor, the window drapes, the paintings. Above the doors there are carved panels of men riding chariots and lasses pouring water from big jars. A marble staircase winds down from the upper levels. There is a huge dresser at its base, cluttered with family photos. In the centre is a shot of a glamorous woman with skin the same golden tan as Sam's. Her hand rests on the chest of a younger version of the bloke who opened the door. Mr and Mrs Harrow. Sam's got her nose and his chin, dimple and all.

An older photo sits at the front of the dresser. In it, two

blokes – one with Sam's curls – lean against the nose of a small military plane. The bright angled sun sharpens their jaws and shadows their eye sockets so that their faces look like skulls.

I flip the frame over and read:

August with Henry S before deployment, 1943.

"What's your name?"

I jump, not realizing Mr Harrow has come up behind me.

"Charlie," then I add, "Frith," because he seems to be waiting for something more.

"Related to the Friths of Upperwhelmingcotte?"

I swear he just made that place up.

"Uh … I don't think so." My voice sounds incredibly loud in the echoing hall.

"Shame." Taking the photo from me, he taps the image of the man with curly hair. "My grandfather, August. He was a scientist and engineer, advance tech, worked in weapons development during the war. Clever man. The firm he and his college friend Henry" – he points at the second man – "started after the war is still going strong, and still in our family. What do your parents do?"

"Mum's a senior hairstylist. Dad drives a taxi, but his dad was a farmer until he retired and sold the land."

"I'm sorry he had to sell." Mr Harrow stares at the photo. "I've had generous offers, but I could never part with my grandfather's legacy. It's my responsibility to keep it healthy. It's a shame your father didn't continue your family profession."

Not really. Dad never wanted to be a farmer, used to hate getting up early as a lad to traipse about in all kinds of weather after sheep too stupid to stay alive. And as much as Gramps used to talk about the Dales with fondness, he never begrudged Dad for wanting something different.

I don't want to disagree with Mr Harrow, so a muttered "I suppose" and a half-shrug is all I manage.

He puts the photo back. The way he's looking at me makes me feel measured and categorized. "What happened to your legs?"

Seriously? I get that people are curious, but it's really none of their fucking business—

Wait. Did he just glance over to the door to where Ollie is peering into an unusually ugly urn?

Nah, Rawley's got me on edge, thinking everyone who just happens to look in Ollie's direction can actually see him. Sam would have mentioned if his old man was a seer too.

To my relief Sam arrives home, an expensive looking rucksack slung over one shoulder. "Sorry I'm late."

Unlike most men his age, Mr Harrow hasn't dyed his hair. It's salt and pepper grey, and neatly groomed. Now I see Sam's wild curls and rumpled shirts for what they are: defiance. He might look like a floppy-haired posh git to me, but next to his dad he's slumming it.

A phone rings somewhere on the floor below.

"I must get that," says Mr Harrow. "A pleasure, Charlie. You are certainly unexpected."

I mutter something meaninglessly polite as he

heads downstairs.

"Nice place, mate," says Ollie into the gaping quiet.

"Thank you." Sam looks about as comfortable in this house as I am. He drops his bag at the foot of the dresser. We look at each other, the awkwardness growing.

"So…?" he prompts.

Remembering why I came over in the first place, I show him the photo of the ghost trap in York cemetery and tell him about George Villiers, Audrey's disappearance, the circle around the chapel, and Peter Rawley the tour guide likely being the Shadow Man. "And yeah, that's about it. Rawley's stashed something in that chapel, or wants something in there, but I don't even know where to start with the whole magic-ghost-line thing."

Sam's lips curl into a wry smile. "Ah, you're here because you need me."

"No. I can go in alone. I just … you're better at magic and at sensing stuff, and … I thought you wanted to work together—"

"You walked off and left me in that café, Frith. You've ignored my messages since then, and now I'm just supposed to trust that you want to work as a team? I've been completely honest with you from the start."

"Honest?" A hot prickle runs up my neck. "Not likely, you … you didn't even tell me that you're trans." I don't know why I say it. As soon as I do I regret it, because it doesn't matter, but it's out there now and I can't take it back.

"Really?" He smirks. "It's literally the least interesting

129

thing about me, but sure, why not. Sorry, let me reintroduce myself." He mimes shaking my hand, big, exaggerated movements, laying it on thick. "Nice to meet you. I'm Sam Harrow, trans-man, I just thought you needed to know that so you can make a shit-tonne of unnecessary judgements."

His expression is intense, focused, and I feel peeled and shredded and wrong. "I just wish you'd have told me, is all."

"You don't have an inherent right to know," he says flatly.

There's a feeling hanging between us, broken and awful. All that bolshie confidence irritated the hell out of me, but now his lips are trembling and I feel like I've taken something from him without even meaning too. I want to give it back, but I don't know how.

Ollie is staring at us with a funny look on his face. "I'm just going to check on Heather and Villiers."

Sod this.

"Forget it." I flick my hood up and head for door. Ollie's in such a hurry he starts to walk right through the wood. I look away, catching sight of Sam's monochrome great-grandfather. It strikes me how similar they look. Sam's a bit narrower in his frame, but there's that family dimple, and the same eyes, same brow, same curly hair.

"Charlie, wait" – he catches my arm – "I didn't say that I wouldn't help you. Finding the missing ghosts is what matters."

We're standing close. I could reach out and grasp his forearm in return and we'd look like two lads from opposing gangs making a pact.

130

Ollie pokes his head through the front door. I flinch. Sam lets go of me.

"I know, I know, rule number one," says Ollie. "But they've gone off to the Minster."

"What?" I'm outside in less than three seconds.

The street is already empty. What the hell is Heather thinking?

"Fuck sake! We don't need a moot, ask Broomwood to keep it all a secret and the old gossip will have it spread around York by sunrise."

"Some folks won't believe it," says Ollie. "Heather thought it was worth another try. Villiers *is* an eyewitness, and he's been dead for at least three hundred years. Longer than some of the Mouldies."

"That doesn't mean they won't hurt her."

"What's going on?" Sam is hurrying down his front steps.

"Heather's gone off to see the Mouldy Oldies."

"The scary ones? I thought she'd already spoken to them."

"Yeah, she has, so going back is proper daft." I don't know what they do to her, but last time they decided to punish her she came back semi-translucent and unable to talk for days. "Let's go, Ollie."

Pulling open the gate I start up the street, Ollie a step behind me.

"Didn't Heather tell us to stay away from them?" Sam calls.

"I'm not letting them hurt her again," I shout back.

"I'm coming with you."

"No way."

"Fuck sake, Charlie." He catches us up. "Either you want my help, or you don't."

14

THE GRAND OLD SOULS OF YORK

They've had the power washers in to scour the Minster walls to gleaming many times over, but as we enter the vast belly of the building I still feel the years. This place is really bloody *old*.

"Perpetuity in every arch and line," says Ollie.

The stained-glass windows bring the pale walls to life with soft washes of colour, but the space still feels like the inside of one of the leviathans from Ollie's graphic novels, the columns like ribs.

While he hurries off to look for Heather and Villiers, Sam and me have to queue. It's paid entry and I don't have enough to get in. The young woman on the desk asks if I'm a resident of York and when I say "yeah" she tells me I can get in for free if I fill in some forms. I hesitate, wondering if we can break in round the back instead because paperwork is a drag and the

Mouldy Oldies could be hurting Heather *right now*.

Sam pays for me. I don't have much choice but to let him. It pisses me off. I don't need him flashing cash just because he's got it.

Whispered voices bounce around the arches as we head deeper into the Minster. This is the kind of place that makes you walk reverently, like something is watching your every step.

Something *is* watching. The Minster is packed with ghosts. An officer strides up the aisle narrating to a bundle of floating monks. Down the nave, a group of gents in big ruffs huddle together, gossiping. Not far from the crossing tower a man in a powdered wig is lying on the floor with his arms and legs spread out, just staring at the ceiling.

I mean, why the hell not? If you can't do weird stuff when you're dead, when can you?

We wander on. Hammering starts up. There's some grand restoration project going on. The organ is covered in scaffolding; most of the giant pipes are laid out in racks. There are memorials all around the Minster walls, actual statues of the dead kneeling in prayer or lying on their coffins. Beneath our feet are mouldering bones, shelter for worms and dust. There really shouldn't be so many ghosts here, this place is essentially one big graveyard. Maybe they stick around because the Mouldy Oldies like to play court.

"Where are they then?" Somehow Sam's whisper sounds louder than normal talking. I spin him so that we're facing the ornate tomb of some devout bloke with an impressive nose.

"Whatever you do, don't make eye contact with any ghosts," I hiss. "This isn't a game, OK? If we're caught…" I let the sentence hang in the air like an axe about to fall.

Realizing I'm still holding his arm, I drop it. This is stupid and dangerous. I'm going to get us both gutted if I'm not careful. And if the Mouldy Oldies don't kill us for coming, Heather will.

Sam leans in, pretending to read the plaque on the tomb. "What did the Mouldies do to you?"

"Nothing." I don't look at him. It's all I can do not to start shaking. "But trust me, you don't want them to know you exist."

They cornered me not long after Nan died. Mum was going through a bit of a religious phase, seeking comfort in the church after losing her parents one after the other. I was in my old chair, the one on loan that I hated because it had push handles. The service was over and the girls were wailing, distracting Mum and Dad. Me and Heather headed towards the far end because the stained glass was mildly spectacular. I'm not a big art buff but back then doing anything without my folks was a big deal.

Seconds later I was surrounded by the ancient dead. I remember agony in my chest, trying to get away, but they had hold of my arms and I couldn't reach the wheel rims to get myself out of there. The Emperor and Earl Percy were the greediest, leaving painful scratches on my chest and shoulders as they wrestled, each trying to grab me until Heather came flying to my defence. The Emperor challenged her, but she stood up to him, giving me enough time to haul myself back to my family, blubbering and terrified.

I never found out how Heather got the Mouldy Oldies to leave me alone and agree an accord, but she did. I don't enter the Minster and they don't claim me as their servant.

We *really* shouldn't be here. I wipe my sweating palms on the inside of my pockets and bite down on my fear until it's a glowing, painful thing beneath my diaphragm. I should get us out of here, but I can't, not without Heather.

Ever since she stood up for me, the Emperor is always looking for another excuse to punish her. The dead can't wound most living people, but other ghosts are fair game. They might not leave permanent physical marks, but Heather assures me it still hurts like a bitch. I'm not letting them do that to her again. Not ever.

Ollie wanders close and as he passes us he whispers, "Undercroft," naming the vaulted space beneath the choir.

We can't go down there. It's too cramped with all the visitors milling about. Although there are pillars we might be able to hide behind, our escape would be limited to only two ways out, both up wonky stone steps.

Sam offers to go down to the Undercroft while I wait up here. "They don't know that I can see them."

I tell him to shut up and drag him across the aisle to where there is a gap in the stonework. A decorative grille covers the broad hole. It's low down so we have to crouch, but it offers a partial view into the Undercroft. The vaulted room is full of tourists breathing pious air and taking selfies in front of the hell-stone carving. They shuffle away to look at the dead king's tomb in the next chamber and I spot Heather and Villiers.

We're too late.

They're side on to our hiding place, facing Emperor Septimus Severus, a broad and bearded man draped in crisp white and purple cloth. St Margaret Clitherow is on the edge of the group, her face like thunder. I shift closer to Sam for a better view. He smells good – kind of woody. Now I can see the edge of Inge of Jorvik's fine fur-trimmed cloak and the glint of armour and velvet that means Earl Henry Percy is beside her. Gentleman highwayman Sir Danville is there too, red haired and swaggering alongside Lady Peckitt and King Aelle of Northumberland.

A full house then, all seven Old Souls.

I close my eyes to steady myself. Sam is sat close enough to bring goosebumps up on my arms, or it's the cold – it's cold in here – or the fact my blood is two parts anxiety to one part panicked exhilaration. We're not in direct view, but that could change if they move.

"Imperial Majesty, I pray listen to Earl Percy's warning," says Lady Peckitt, a neat woman of middling years dressed in a pastel gown with lace at her elbows. "No tethered soul can speak freely for they are bound by the chains they forged in life. To put faith in Ophelia's testimony is to place trust where it is not deserved."

"With all due respect, Lady Peckitt," says Heather, in a tone that suggests zero respect at all, "my tether to the city does not affect my ability to think rationally. To dismiss Ophelia's experience because of mental illness is callous, antiquated and harmful."

I forget she always has to talk like this in front of them, all "thee" and "thou" and "m'ladies". Older ghosts can speak like modern people do. I mean, it's not like the dead aren't listening in to everything all day. The Mouldy Oldies are snobbish, preferring to stick to old style speech, though they've dropped the Latin and Old Norse out of sheer necessity.

King Aelle of Northumberland steps forward and Sam and I shrink back from the grille.

Don't look left, don't look up and left or we are dead.

The Anglo-Saxon king is a jowly man with bulging eyes. "I put it to you that Ophelia hath had not mere discourse with our enemy but" – he pauses for effect – "*relations*."

Saint Margaret wrinkles her nose. "Sins of the flesh."

"Again, *not* relevant to the discussion," says Heather.

The Mouldy Oldies are all princes, kings and lords, all except Saint Margaret Clitherow who remembers herself in a simple shift, her hair tucked under a cap. She's proud of her sainthood, raised up after death to be something more. Right now, she's glowering at Heather like she's something nasty she shat out earlier.

"Ophelia witnessed Millie get taken," says Heather, pressing on. "And we have evidence of a magical mark where—"

Earl Percy holds up his hand. "Verily, Ophelia's beloved was a foul taker of souls and n'er her loyalties rested with us."

With his blue velvet cloak-coat, white hair and beard he looks a bit like a wise old wizard. Or he would, if Gandalf had been a mean old bastard with a hooked nose and a devil's smile.

Villiers steps forwards with a flourish. "Thou mayst put faith in mine own loyalties, Your Excellency. I am George Villiers, First Duke of Buckinghamshire…" He launches into his long-winded introduction, adding titles and accomplishments like my sisters add chocolate sprinkles to cereal.

Is he … flirting? Yeah, like a boss, throwing in smooth compliments as he postures. The Mouldies are lapping it up. Sam and I glance at one another. I can't help a little eye roll. Sam's lips twitch and he huffs an amused smirk. For a second, I'm glad he insisted on coming along.

"Thou art most welcome in York," says Sir Danville, clearly flattered by Villiers' peacocking.

"Indeed, such a charming and affable soul is a great addition to our glorious city," adds Lady Peckitt.

Villiers bows to each of them in turn. Maybe he's a better statesman than history gives him credit. "The very stones of this city doth whisper of thy wisdom, and I, thy humble servant, have come to seek thy counsel. My dear friend, James Reid, is amongst those poor ensnared souls…" He goes on and on, describing what he saw in the cemetery and the Shadow Man, his account smattered with more compliments. It's all going well until he mentions "Mistress Nightingale".

"Audrey Nightingale?" asks Inge. A low rumble of disapproval runs through the assembly. At once the atmosphere turns sour.

"Will you please listen to him!" says Heather. "Peter Rawley, a soul catcher, is trapping souls, innocent souls. You vowed to protect us from—"

"Be silent." The Emperor's voice is thick with anger. Heather shuts up fast.

I'm gripping the stone lip above the grill with enough force that my fingers are turning white. This is it. This is where they hurt her. We need a distraction. Where the hell is Ollie?

"Mine heart doth pain for thy loss," the Emperor tells Villiers, "I shall appoint one to gather sufficient argument in the matter."

"Imperial Majesty," says Earl Percy. "I volunteer for such an enterprise, and shalt speak to all who endure in the matter of the missing, and while it lasteth make provision to keep secure our great city."

"But we already have witnesses and a suspect," says Heather. "Everyone needs to be warned *now*."

"I hath set my terms for a moot, Mistress Noble," says the Emperor.

She bristles. "Never going to happen."

"Does thou then think I wouldst distress our people without good cause?" The Emperor's lip curls. "Leave Earl Percy to settle this matter. Give me not cause to descend upon you, and those who aid you, with un-tempered wrath."

Walk away, I urge Heather silently. *C'mon, don't be daft.*

"Oi, lads, you can't sit here." My attention snaps to the man standing over us. Security. No, he's actual police, badge and all.

"Sorry, officer," says Sam, jumping to his feet. "We were just…"

I stay where I am and slip an Allen-key out of my pocket. Stretching out I lift my trackies and pretend to adjust my prosthesis. "Almost done. This one's giving me some trouble today."

"Oh, well there are plenty of seats in the choir or some stone benches down the far end," says the officer. "You'll be more comfortable. It's a trip hazard if you sit right here." He offers me a hand up.

"Thanks, and sorry to be a bother."

"No bother at all. Have a great visit."

The conference below us is breaking up, ghosts vanishing straight into the bones of the building. Heather, used to obeying physics because of me, is walking up the steps. We scramble inside the toilet block to hide, ignoring the fuss of mothers and prams. Ollie meets us there. We give it a few minutes then head out. I make sure my cap brim is pulled low as we pass under the crossing tower and make our way out through the gift shop.

Outside, rain is brewing, clouds amassing over the city and the streets are clearing as people duck into shops and restaurants to avoid a soaking. As the first drops fall, Sam pulls me under the awning of an antiquarian bookshop and peers back towards the Minster. He lets out a nervous laugh. I'm rattled, but he catches my eye. There's mischief dancing there, and it sort of stops my breath a moment.

"Tell me you didn't go in there?"

We lurch and spin. Heather and Villiers are standing in the rain, untouched by the weather. Her expression is desperate and afraid.

"Charlie wanted to be here when you got out," Sam says quickly.

Relief in Heather's face. She believes him. Another reason I'm glad he came along. I'm a terrible liar.

"The pups have pluck," Villiers chuckles. "This must be our scholar of the occult arts. Delighted, Master Harrow." He extends his hand and they shake. "I am George Villiers, First Duke of Buckinghamshire, Lord Admiral of the king's fleet, Knight of the Royal Garter and the favourite of *three* kings—"

Heather isn't done with me. "Charlie, you must never enter the Minster."

"You're one to talk."

"I had it under control."

"Will they help us?" asks Sam.

Heather's expression sours. "Earl Percy is going to" – she makes air brackets – "*look into it.*"

"You don't think he will?"

Ollie snorts. "Earl Percy? Not likely. I doubt the Mouldy Oldies care if soul catchers take their pick of us, but I bet they'll sing a different tune if Rawley goes for one of them."

"I agree," says Heather. "There is no way Percy is going to give this much thought, but I can't work out why they're not taking the threat seriously. We have to sort this ourselves."

"Should we tail Rawley, catch him in the act?" asks Ollie.

I shake my head. "And risk him getting you? No way."

"Let me do some research tonight," says Sam. "See if I can work out a way to break the barrier around the chapel."

"Thanks," I say. "I can come with you tomorrow."

"Best not. It might look suspicious if you go back. Rawley could be watching the place."

"OK … right."

"I'll call later."

"Yeah, thanks then." I already thanked him. He must think I'm a blathering idiot.

With a small smile, Sam shoves his hands into his pockets and dashes into the rain.

Heather watches him go. "If the Mouldy Oldies find out we're still nosing about, it could get nasty."

"I'm not giving up now," I say, hoping to sound braver than I feel.

"Charlie, they could *kill* you."

"Yeah, them and every other soul in York."

The man spits in my face. "What is the solution to the theorem?"

I turn away, dragging rank air into rattling lungs. I spit too. Blood. The next punch sets my cheek on fire.

"Good men are dying."

Angry laughter bubbles up over bloody lips. "And you'll send them out to die again." The voice is female, but it's mine.

I'm speaking.

"We know you solved it." A second person steps into a broken sunbeam, the slanted light catching on dark curls and a dimpled chin. "How did you stabilize the coterminous bonds?"

It's Sam Harrow.

"Tell us, or he'll cut it out of you," threatens the taller man.

Someone shakes me awake. I blink, expecting Ollie, but it's Lorna.

"You were screaming again," she says.

Sitting up, I wipe the sweat off my face with my sheets. No Ollie. No ghosts at all, just Lorna, and Poppy is peering around the door.

"Sorry." My jaw is still swollen, and the dull pain brings my nightmare back in sharp flashes. "I didn't mean to scare you."

"I wasn't scared," Lorna says, striding away.

Poppy lingers as I get myself up. I want to scream, so I bite down on my sore lip until tears spring to my eyes.

"Are you remembering when you died?" Poppy's voice is soft.

I look up, surprised.

"I'd be frightened too." She smiles then, sweet as anything, and before I can gather my wits she adds, "Mum says don't sleep all day because you've got to revise."

And then she's gone.

Blood pumps through my aching temples, knotting my thoughts. The men in my nightmare are from the deathloop in

Saint-Lô. I dream about the taller of them leaning over dead bodies on the battlefield – I can't ever see what he's doing, only that it feels wrong – and I dream about the other one in the dark room with the blades and the blood. I know it's not really a nightmare. It's a memory belonging to the ghost in the deathloop I fell into.

Remember the Capital of Ruins.

OK sure, Audrey, but remember what exactly? Her? Those blokes and what they did to her? I dream of them, but I've never seen either of their faces clearly before, and I didn't even see the killer's real face, I saw Sam's.

Shite. I want Sam Harrow out of my head. I want to get rid of this nasty, hot weight when I think of him. I was a prick to him, that's why I'm dreaming him into my nightmares.

Ollie is at the door. "All right?"

"Fucking fabulous, mate."

"Thought so. The kettle's on."

I check my phone. No messages from Sam.

Breakfast. Revision. Press-ups. More revision. I check my phone again. Nothing.

Sam doesn't call until lunchtime the next day.

"What?" I shout, cupping my mobile as Lorna charges after our cousins with her hands full of something sticky.

"I said I've been down to the cemetery to have a look," says Sam.

145

"You find anything?"

The line crackles. "Whatever spell or curse is keeping the ghosts out of the chapel, it's too strong for me to break."

I don't know what his room looks like, but I picture something grand. Him, sitting on the edge of a giant canopied bed, his curls flopping over his forehead, that lightning shock of hair caught in a beam of light peeking past silky curtains.

Not that I'm imagining him in bed or anything, just … there, in his room.

"Charlie?"

"I'm here. Look, I thought you knew loads about magic."

"I'm more of an observer of the occult arts than an accomplished practitioner."

"You don't know anyone else then?" I ask. "I mean, what about your friend?"

"Who?"

"That magic lass you got to find me."

"Miri is a hacker, not a witch."

"Oh."

Another long silence. I should say sorry for being a dick the other day. I mean, I don't care what he thinks of me. We don't have to like each other to work together, but I was out of line.

No, it's best to leave it alone right now. Anyway, I should apologize in person.

When it comes to the chapel, we can't wait. Ollie and I prepared a plan B. I was hoping we wouldn't need it because it's dangerous, especially if the Mouldy Oldies are going to take offense to our snooping.

"All right," I say. "We'll have to go in, you and me."

"Break in?" I hear Sam's surprise.

"Round the back of the cemetery there's a second gate. It's at the end of Belle Vue Terrace. Meet me there Wednesday. Midnight. Wear dark clothes."

"How are we getting into the chapel?" he asks.

I look at the assorted padlocks I dug out of the garden shed this morning. "The first Duke of Buckingham is teaching me how to pick locks."

"Right." Sam clears his throat. "It's a date, then."

15

A MODERATE AMOUNT OF PERIL

The gate at the end of Belle Vue Terrace is as tall as me and made of thick bars tipped with spikes. Houses overlook this spot on both sides. I need to be careful. There aren't many reasons anyone carrying a torch, crowbar and homemade lockpicks would hang around outside a cemetery.

"Do you think Sam's actually coming?" asks Ollie.

"He bloody better." I told my folks I'm staying over at his. If he doesn't show then I'm stuck out here all night with no place to kip.

The clouds are low, the air so moist it feels like it's drizzling. Ollie strides into the street, waiting for Sam. Sat on a low wall, Heather presses pleats into her grey slacks then releases them. Little things like that let me know she's quietly freaking out.

"Audrey was right," she says. "I just thought I'd have more time."

I'm about to ask her what she's on about when Villiers emerges through the front wall of the house opposite and glides towards us. I shudder and look away.

"Really, Master Frith, for a seer thou art most squeamish about the incorporeal nature of souls. The older we become, the less inclined we art to pander to the limitations of the material plane. Incidentally, hath thou seen a show called *The Witcher*? They're binge watching it in number twenty."

"Stop perving on people in their own homes, it's intrusive," says Heather.

Villiers exaggerates a sigh. "Alas, I am forever a student of the human condition."

"And just because the Mouldy Oldies think you're charming doesn't mean you get to hover like one of them. If you're going to stick around, you play by Charlie's rules and walk."

Seriously, where the fuck are you?

It's my third message to Sam in the past half-hour. Nothing back. I don't want to worry that something has happened to him, so I call him every kind of pillock under my breath instead.

"He's here," shouts Ollie.

Ghost eyesight is better in the dark than living eyes. Still, I almost tell Ollie he's got it wrong. The lad walking towards us looks nothing like Sam Harrow. He's got the brim of a baseball cap pulled low over his face, a navy puffer zipped up against the cold and hands stuffed into the pockets of trackies that have seen better days. But, yeah, it's Sam all right. He's still got his notebook. Even looking like a lad from round my way he's got a gentlemanly nature about him. I reckon they'd still let him in the golf club or wherever.

"You look well daft," I say when he reaches me.

"Obviously. I'm dressed like you." His grin is wicked. "What's the crowbar for? In case you can't pick the lock?"

My cheeks go warm. "Nah, I just … you know … thought it might come in handy."

"I assure you I am a tutor of great skill and Master Frith is a fine student," says Villiers. "Now, the night is no longer young. Let us meet adventure, and not a moderate amount of peril."

We head for the gate. A stark light floods the road from the driveway of a nearby semi. We duck and scramble, flattening ourselves against the ivy dripped wall encircling the cemetery, muttering prayers and curses and God knows what else into the night.

A tuxedo cat darts from the porch. After a few more seconds the light switches off.

Sam whispers the poshest *"fuck me"* I've ever heard.

The gate has those iron spikes to contend with, so we go over the wall instead. Sam's up and over in a jiffy. He's smaller in the arms and shoulders than me but stronger than he looks, and nimble. Getting me over takes a lot more grunting and swearing. Villiers lets me climb on his back and hefts

150

me up. Dangling off the wall by my fingertips, I drop down. My knees jar painfully, my sockets and prostheses don't have much give, but I stay upright, secretly chuffed the press-ups have paid off.

This place is really bloody creepy in the dark.

We enter one of the tree-lined avenues leading to the chapel and I stumble to a halt. I can't see a blasted thing, but I've walked this way before. To get to the chapel we need to follow it and turn left. Arms outstretched, crowbar pointed like a sword, I inch forward and immediately catch an uneven paving slab. Someone grabs me before I fall.

"Steady going, young Frith." Villiers pats my back.

Somewhere behind me Sam swears. "We'll have to use a torch."

"Link up and we'll guide you," says Heather.

Hooking the crowbar into my waistband, I grope about until a hand falls into mine. I think it's Ollie, but the hand is far warmer with longer fingers.

Sam.

There's sweat on his palm too and I swear I can feel his heartbeat through his skin. I want to pull away, but that's childish, so I panic and accidentally end up squeezing instead. *Let go of him, just let go.* No, then he *will* think there's something in it.

I hold on.

Hand in hand we stumble through the dark with the dead. The trees open up and I get a sense of the looming presence of the chapel. When I finally let go of Sam it feels like he slips away into the darkness, but really he's still close enough that I can hear his breathing and smell his expensive soap.

We stop at the ghost line.

Villiers clears his throat. "Be cautious and, above all, be vigilant."

"Yeah, don't die," says Ollie.

Heather hugs me tight. Her silent anxiety is giving me the jitters.

Me and Sam head for the crypt door. Crouching against the turf, I take out the lockpicks I made from two of Mum's hairpins. Sam switches on his phone torch. The brightness is jarring, but it illuminates the lock. I get to work.

It's harder to pick a lock out here than in the safety of my bedroom. More than once I have to take out the picks, wipe my brow and start again. Sam stays quiet, even as the minutes stretch. I listen to the pins, pressing each in turn while twisting with the lever pick, feeling the resistance and waiting for the soft tell-tale click of the notches lining up. I count four and slide the pick against the last. It catches. I twist both picks together and the door creaks open.

"Not bad, Frith, not bad." Sam claps me on the shoulder and heads inside without checking if Rawley is lurking in the shadows to kill us.

Reckless git.

The crypt smells like it needs a good airing out. A green emergency light reveals a main switch just inside the door. I flick it. Nothing happens. I take out my torch, the beam joining the glow from Sam's phone. The lights dance down the short corridor to a wall of granite tombs stacked three high and mottled with age.

"Why would anyone want to be sealed up in this airless place?" asks Sam.

I wince. Seriously, he has a loud whisper. "I guess they think they'll be better preserved or something."

"What's the point? No one opens up a grave and says, 'gosh, doesn't grandfather look good for a corpse?'" He kicks a pebble and it rattles across the flagstone. "I want to be buried under a tree. Worm food."

"If it goes wrong tonight, I'll let your dad know."

"Don't bother. He doesn't care." There's bitterness in Sam's words. I don't know what to say, so I keep quiet. Eventually, he says, "So where's this lair then?"

"I never said it was a *lair*, just that Rawley broke in. According to Villiers he stayed in here a long while." Where the corridor splits, I shine the light left and right. Down one end is a metal box, probably something to do with the electrics. At the other is a window which is half bricked up.

"Right, you look over there." Sam motions towards the box. "I'll go that way." He points at the window.

I've seen enough horror movies to know splitting up is the worst move to make. I'm about to tell him, but he's already wandered off.

Taking the crowbar from my waistband, I focus my torch on the floor and lower walls, looking for anything that seems like it might be interesting to a soul catcher or could house a trapped ghost, but there's basically nothing here. One alcove is full of stacked chairs; another is full of maintenance equipment.

"Anything?" Sam calls. Apparently, we've given up on the whispering.

"Nah."

We meet in the middle again.

"I could cleanse the space; it might reveal a trap or some other kind of magic mark," says Sam.

"You got some with you?"

He flashes a grin. "I'm always carrying."

Pulling out a folded paper bag, he tips the herbal blend on to the floor and sparks up a lighter. I stand back to avoid a face full of pungent smoke. If there are fire alarms down here, we're buggered.

We search the walls and floor for any newly-revealed catcher marks.

"Nothing my end," I say, trying not to cough.

"Hang on," says Sam. "There's something behind these tombs."

Most of the stone slabs carry a name, date and epitaph, but the central column of three are bare stone. Unmarked. The smoke curls into the cracks either side of the central stack, as if a hoover is sucking it into an empty space on the other side.

"This is it." Sam begins pushing with his fists, first on the centre of each slab, then the corners.

"Wouldn't it be handy if someone brought a crowbar." I wave it at him.

He pulls a face as I wedge the end of the bar in the groove

between the stacks. Sam puts his hands beside mine and pulls as I push. Stone grates and the bar slips. I fall into him. He braces me until I find my balance. I blush. We try again.

After another slip he shakes his head. "It's not going to budge."

Maybe he's right. Maybe we're just trying to break into some poor sod's resting place, but Rawley must have had a reason to come in here. We don't have any other leads. I lean against the granite. Despite the chilly air, my forehead is beaded with sweat.

A name.

I've no idea where it comes from or why I just thought it, but I let it trip off my tongue, too quiet for Sam to hear.

"Rachel."

A grinding reverberates through the crypt, a rolling and a thump, like the sound of a door unlocking. The three panels swing inwards as one, revealing a narrow stairway heading down into the earth.

16

DOWN IN THE DARK

"Do you think it's safe?" Sam shines his phone light down the steps.

I inhale the stale air. "Shite no."

"Right. I'll go first."

I follow his lead, abandoning the crowbar so I can keep a palm against the wall. Why are there always stairs? I hate stairs, especially old uneven stairs. If we ever meet whoever built this place, I'm telling them they should consider putting a lift in their next creepy underground lair, or whatever this is.

God. It's best to not think about what might be waiting for us down in the dark. I focus on each step instead. If I slip I'll send Sam flying, and if I snap his neck he'll probably haunt me.

The stairwell turns at a right angle, then again, wrapping back on itself.

Sam gasps. "God, that is seriously rank."

I smell it too: mould, damp and a lingering putrescence that makes me gag. We reach the bottom and my torch beam catches a brief glimpse of a wide room before a rush of freezing air blasts us. The torch flickers and dies. Sam's phone light goes out.

All I can hear is my own tight breathing. Then something crunches underfoot. Gravel? A light sparks up. A grotesque mask appears beside me. With a yell I lurch away.

"Charlie, it's just me."

Sam. He's got his lighter out, the warm flame catching in the hollows beneath his eyes.

I put my hands on my knees and lean down, sucking air through my teeth. "Bloody hell, Harrow."

"You should have seen your face." He's grinning that wicked grin of his.

"You're a prick."

There's broken glass on the floor. Down the centre of the room is a long table, but I can't see much by the lighter's small flame. That stale ammonia reek catches in the back of my throat.

I try my torch, but it's buggered. "Check for candles or lamps or something."

Sam's already on it, moving deeper into the room. I follow, because somehow the little puddle of light around him feels like safety.

"Aha!" He lights two old-fashioned storm lanterns, then hands me one and we start to explore.

On the tiled counter to the left, a load of empty tins with vintage packaging teeter next to a half-full ration book dated August 1944. The large table is covered in old lab equipment and brittle rubber tubing that breaks apart under my fingers. I pick up a pair of half-moon spectacles with thin frames. When I turn them this way and that the glass has a slight bluish sheen.

I've seen these before.

The smell, the tiles…

Sam is rooting through a stash of booze. He pulls the stopper from a dusty bottle and takes a deep swig. "Ugh. That's got a kick."

He offers it to me. I grab the bottle and take a greedy gulp, choking on the fiery liquid, and point into the darkness at the opposite side of the chamber.

"I've been here before."

Sam edges forward, the light from his lantern reaching the end of the table and the corpse hanging above it by a thick noose.

"Shit!" He leaps back.

The body is shrunken inside the remains of the clothing, which has rotted around the skeletal limbs. Leathery skin, blackened and hardened with age, still clings to the skull like shiny plastic. The chair the man climbed lies on the floor.

I look away. "That deathloop you pulled me from, it's him."

"You sure?"

"One way to check: he burnt letters and a photo before he did it…" Giving the corpse a wide berth, I head to the far end of the underground room. There's the sink, just as I remember, and in it the ashy remains of a fire. Nothing survived except a featureless curl of yellowed paper. "Yeah, it's him."

"Do you think he was a soul catcher too?" asks Sam.

"There is a magic line outside keeping the dead out, so yeah, I reckon so. And these—" I hold up the half-moon glasses. "Rawley has a pair just like them."

I slide on the lenses and the walls shimmer into focus, riddled with softly glowing catcher marks like the ones I saw in the Hanged Man's loop. They circle around the room, no gaps, but they look faded and weak. When I peer over the top of the lenses, the marks vanish.

"Shit, Sam, look through these."

I hand them over. Sam slides them on and whistles low and long. "These reveal hidden spells. Very useful. You say Rawley has a pair?"

He passes the glasses back to me and I slide them into my pocket. "On a chain around his neck."

"So, he breaks into the lair of a long dead soul catcher to what … compare magic glasses?" Sam takes a moment to think. "Is anything different from what you remember in the loop? Is something missing? Or did he leave something behind?" Sam starts opening drawers and rifling through the items on the table, then under it.

I scan the room as best I can in the dim light. "Maybe. No … I dunno. To be honest, I was kind of focused on not dying—"

"Charlie. We've got to go." Sam is standing, frozen. In his

hand is a glass bottle the size of a clenched fist. I remember it from the deathloop. It was sitting in a mount – that bit of metal on the floor under the table – and must have been knocked over when the man kicked the chair away.

Sam holds the bottle up, the light from his lantern shining through it. The stem is sealed with thick red wax, and inside it a fleshy mass writhes and twists, offering flashes of a bloodshot eye, a toothy mouth and clawing hand.

We got this so wrong. The magic barrier isn't supposed to keep ghosts out. It's there to keep the dead in.

17

TOOTH AND NAIL

S hit. I'd take on the Old Souls right now. Hell, I'd take on the school bullies while dressed up in a sodding knob costume. Anything other than what's in that bottle.

"Put it down. Carefully." I struggle to keep my voice steady.

We know soul catchers trap ghosts. Now we know how they contain them. If the bottles are sealed with red wax, that explains the puddles of the stuff where the ghostnappings took place. Whoever is trapped in that bottle has been there a long while, and they look pretty pissed about it. If it breaks…

Sam's breath puffs in the chilly air.

Static raises goosebumps on my arms.

Something crunches beneath my trainers – shards of broken glass, *curved* glass, covered with flecks of wax.

Two bottles. There were two bottles on the metal stand, not

one. One unbroken globe is in Sam's hands, and there's no sign of a second bottle. Which means...

The sound of sobbing echoes from the walls. Fear carves out a chasm in my chest as I step in front of Sam and lift my lantern like it's a weapon. But no ghost was ever scared by a light.

A nun in a grey habit appears from behind the stairs, as if exhuming herself from the walls. She's unusually tall – way over six foot – and slender, her milky eyes watchful as she glides towards us. I smell brick dust and sweat and stale beer. At the end of her life someone slashed off her hair and made a fair mess of it. Bloody patches on her scalp glisten wetly in the lamplight.

Her gaze locks with mine. It's like being plunged into an icy river. I try to move but my muscles won't obey. My brain is screaming blind panic. There's a buzzing in my bones.

She's chanting something, a singsong hymn I recognize as part of the Lord's Prayer, "Deliver us from evil." She reaches for us. "Help me. Please."

Sam takes a hurried step backwards. "The walls."

Rust seeps through cracks in the tiles, merging into dark patterns like the ones I saw through the glasses. Dust and debris shift, like an earthquake is rattling the bones of this place. For a second, I think it's Sam and his magic, but his eyes are wide and I can tell he's as shit-a-brick-scared as I am.

"Bricked up alive for being with child." The nun presses the drapes of her habit around the small mound of her belly. "I need you."

"Um, what exactly does she need us for?" asks Sam.

I don't know, but I'd bet on my afterlife it isn't two-for-one cinema tickets or long walks on the sodding beach. Ollie told us about a pregnant nun – Sister Agnes – who got bottled by a catcher for murdering a seer. She's a Hungry One, and to get out we've got to go past her.

"Stay away, or we'll put you back in the bottle." It's a desperate, empty threat.

Sister Agnes's laughter is cruel and hungry. She knows it.

She strikes. Lips stretch over pale gums and yellowed teeth. A clawed hand shoves me aside. I twist, dropping my lamp and breaking my fall, rolling in time to see Agnes push Sam on to the table, smacking the second bottle from his grip.

I swear time slows as it falls. The bottle hits the stone floor and shatters. Air is sucked in and released.

A figure with a strong stubbled jaw materializes between us, his bowler hat low over a broad forehead. His tattered coat and long fingers are stained with crusted blood. When he catches sight of me he grins, flashing sharpened teeth.

"One each," says the nun. "Enough to breach the ward."

"Agnes, love, you spoil me." Sharp-teeth raises his hands. Shards of glass lift into the air. Wood screams as huge splinters tear from the table. He twists his fingers. Warped metal, enamel plates and broken bottles begin circling him like a storm.

"He can't … do … how?" I stammer. The dead can't touch the physical world, *so what the hell is that?*

Fumbling for my footing, I duck beneath the maelstrom.

Shoving Agnes off him, Sam dives around Sharp-teeth, who seems to be more interested in playing with his food than landing a killing blow. He lets Sam slip past.

They probably want us alive when they eat us.

Flames burst to life on the table, licking down a trail of oil from the spilt lamp. Catching on the rubber tubing, the fire spreads, pumping out dark smoke.

"Run!" Sam shoves me up the stairs and I grapple in the dull light, feeling my way forward. My muscles throb as I push my prostheses to their limits, but I have to keep going. Acrid smoke billows up the stairwell behind us, chased by Agnes's cruel laughter.

I trip, my senses off-kilter. My chin hits the step and I bite my tongue. Sam's atop me, scrabbling over, arm under my chest to haul me up. His lungs sound as ragged as mine. I struggle to find my balance. He's pulling me on and up.

The granite around us trembles and cracks. Sharp-teeth lunges up the stairwell, grasping for me. I kick out in panic and my prosthesis sinks through him until my stump connects with his belly, sending him reeling backwards into Agnes. Sam's got me fast in his arms, keeping me from tumbling after the ghosts. I spit blood and keep going.

We stumble into the crypt together. Flaming wooden splinters and chunks of granite sail after us. Sam rushes to close the door.

"Leave it!" I gasp.

Sharp-teeth rises up the stairwell. Agnes's waxy face is only seconds behind him. Fresh panic charges through me, but the adrenaline keeps me upright. Our only hope is to cross the ghost line.

We make a break for the main door and stagger into the graves. Compared to the funk inside the crypt the night air is freshness and freedom.

Something smacks into my back, sending me flying. As I land, my left leg twists painfully. The grass is damp and cold. I curse the agony and roll over. Sam, desperate and panicking, is pulling the heavy oak door closed. It clatters on its hinges and swings shut.

Waste of time, he's not thinking clearly, but I don't have the breath to tell him.

Arms burst through the door either side of him, pulling him hard against the wood. Sharp-teeth's head emerges through the solid door and he sinks his choppers into Sam's neck. Sam bellows in pain. Blood, dark and glistening, leaks between Sharp-teeth's lips.

NO!

I haul myself up, but there's something wrong with my left prosthesis again. The foot flaps about, useless. Doesn't matter. Get to Sam.

Throwing myself towards the door I go for Sharp-teeth's eyes, sticking my thumbs into the soft fleshy parts of his sockets, grimacing at the wet squelch of his eyeballs against my fingers. He pulls back, howling, and I tear Sam away.

One hand pressed to Sam's neck, his arm around my waist, we half-stumble half-hop side by side through the graves. He's got me as much as I've got him, keeping me balanced.

He makes a terrible gasping noise. I grip him tighter, willing him to hold on; it's not far, not far now.

Where's that magic-circle ghost barrier thing?

For a horrifying moment I think it's gone, somehow evaporated whilst we were inside.

Then I hear Heather, Villiers and Ollie screaming at us. An angry screech echoes through the gravestones. *Don't turn around.* Only metres to go. My muscles burn. I can't do it. I can't take another step. But I do.

We're over the line.

Sam slides away, though I try to hold on to him. Heather has me. We put more distance between us and the chapel. I'm starting to feel the pinch of my injuries and every step takes more than I think I have to give. Villiers has a hand over Sam's wound.

God. It's bad. It's really bad.

"He got bit," I tell Heather. It's all I can manage right now.

A few more metres and she helps me to sit. I go down against a gravestone, sinking into the ache of my legs.

Sister Agnes and Sharp-teeth rush us, stone and flaming wood bursting into the night around them. The fragments reach the ghost line and sail across it, arching down. A chunk of flame-licked wood flies through Villiers, striking the gravestone above my head. Ollie swears. Sam tries to shield me.

The Hungry Ones tear at the barrier. If the magic doesn't hold, they'll be on us in seconds. I can't fight – can hardly move.

Heather's expression is one I've only seen on her once

before. Standing slowly, she walks back towards the chapel. Sister Agnes sneers in her face. Sharp-teeth bares a manic grin.

Silently Villiers draws his rapier and goes to stand beside Heather. Ollie is only a second behind, fists clenched, facing down the enemy. The night air tingles with something electric.

"You'd better hope that line holds," Heather's voice is serious, steady. "For your sake. Do you think we're the only souls who'll step up to defend these boys? There is a city counting on them and the spirit who kills them will find their afterlife cut very short."

Bluffing, of course, but I still feel a hopeful stirring beneath my heart.

Agnes steps back first. Sharp-teeth hacks phlegm, spits, then turns, like retreat was his idea all along. Debris from the underground room is still churning around the chapel, but they're no longer throwing it at us.

Heather and Villiers hurry back. Ollie gives Agnes and Sharp-teeth the middle finger before following.

Sam slumps against me, holding his neck, face taught with pain. I'm injured too, but it doesn't matter. It will be all right as long as Sam keeps breathing.

"Light," says Heather.

I get out my torch, but it's still not working. Sam hands me his lighter with shaky fingers. It's smeared with his blood.

At Heather's order he takes his hand away. Several deep scratches on his collarbone seep sluggishly into his polo shirt, but it's the bite that looks bad, two nasty gashes where ghostly teeth ripped into his flesh.

"We need to stop the bleeding," says Heather.

Sacrificing the light, I pull off my puffer and hoody. The hoody is old and full of holes. It doesn't take much to tear a bit off to use as a compress. She tells me to keep the pressure against Sam's neck. He leans in to me and my breath catches.

Ollie sits close. "Sam, mate, exactly what part of 'don't die' confused you?"

The barest flicker of a smile. "I'm not actually dead yet."

"We need to get you to A&E," Heather tells him.

He shifts himself up a bit. "And tell them what exactly? That a ghost bit me?"

"I don't care what you tell them." She's doing her doctor voice. She'll not suffer nonsense when there's a hurt in need of healing. "It needs cleaning out and stitching up—"

"No hospitals."

"Company incoming," says Villiers.

A wash of artificial light moves through the graves to our right. Shite! We probably set off an alarm some place. Or the Shadow Man has come back to finish us off.

18

STITCHES

Sam staggers to his feet, the night breeze plucking at his curls. I left my crowbar inside the chapel, and with a broken prosthesis I'm stuck where I am. The torch shines in our faces. I squint and put up my hand.

"Charlie?" The light wobbles, then lowers.

Leonie. She's wearing an oversized coat with her pyjamas stuffed into boots, hair tucked under a silk bonnet.

"Shit me, Olympics." Mitch is behind her, carrying a shovel. He looks one loud noise away from swinging it. "Did you set the chapel on fire?"

Leonie's torch beam catches on Sharp-teeth's grimace and Agnes's clawed fingers. Sam and I flinch. Although Leonie and Mitch can't see them, they can't miss the debris sailing around.

"Is that a fucking wind tunnel?" asks Mitch.

"Hungry ghosts, actually," says Sam, before I can stop him.

Ollie throws his hands up and makes a *tusk*ing sound. Villiers looks almost amused.

Mitch snorts in disbelief. "So, you broke into a cemetery at night to hunt hungry weather ghosts and commit arson?"

"Never mind us." I nod at his shovel. "You out for a bit of late-night grave robbery? An unusual idea for a date, but top marks for originality."

"It was the best weapon we could find in Leonie's garage." He sounds a touch defensive.

Leonie steps between us. "I live on Belle Vue. We saw someone sneaking over the gate."

"Since when did you move this side of town?" I ask.

"Mum's buried here."

Guilt twists my stomach. I should have remembered about her mum. Still, I don't buy their story. "You followed me here."

"We didn't!"

"I'm not stupid. You've been tailing me these past couple of weeks."

Leonie folds her arms. "You were acting weird."

"I'm always acting weird."

"Well, weirder than usual, and after what we saw on the playing field—"

"You weren't there." I cut her off.

"We were … er, in the pavilion," says Mitch. He can't meet my eyes.

They must have headed straight out there while I was

catching my breath behind the science block.

"We know you two weren't fighting," says Leonie. "And that there was something else there." She glances back at the chapel and the flaming debris. "Something we can't see."

"Let's not do this here," says Heather. "The fire service could be on their way and the police station is only down the road."

"Agreed," says Sam.

Villiers offers me a hand. I grasp it, and he hauls me upright in a single, smooth movement.

"How the hell—?" Mitch splutters. "Are you a wizard or something?"

I can't help a startled laugh. It comes out wild and broken. To them it must look like I lifted an arm and just commanded my body to rise up, like a vampire out of a coffin.

"Or something," I say.

With my torch and Sam's phone fried, we ask Leonie to light our way. Villiers and Heather support me on either side so I can limp after the others. We hurry along the grassy avenue towards Belle Vue. Leonie keeps glancing back at me, wide-eyed disbelief mellowing her usual calculating look. After what they've seen there's no point trying to hide the fact that something otherworldly is going on.

Sirens wail in the distance.

"Hurry!" Leonie hisses, scrambling over the wall, followed by Sam. Mitch gives me a boost. Ollie warns me to look away and the ghosts slip through the brick. I dangle off the wall until I feel hands on my arse and back. Villiers has me. I let go and drop the rest of the way into waiting arms.

It's not Villiers but Sam, breathing heavily and smelling of smoke and blood and night air.

"I've got you," he says.

"Get that compress back on," Heather snaps before I can stammer a reply.

Villiers pulls my arm around his shoulder and Leonie leads us into the driveway of the red-brick semi with the porch light. The motion sensor clicks and a second later we're bathed in the same harsh beam.

"Your dad?" I ask.

"In China with Al. We were all supposed to go next year, but Al's birth dad is sick so it was very last minute, and flights to Zhengzhou are well expensive, plus, you know, I've got exams. Joe's in Leeds. Terry's at a house party."

She unlocks the door. We pile inside.

The living room is like I remember it: white walls and natural wood, houseplants everywhere, Mrs Agyemang's artwork on the walls, handsewn cushions scattered on the understated couch. Except this is a different house. I never played here as a kid, never ate ice cream and peanut brittle on the lawn out back. Leonie's mum never lived here and Leonie and me aren't mates anymore. This is a stranger's home. It smells the way other people's houses do, of different bodies living unfamiliar lives.

Sam looks done in. How much blood has he lost? Heather pesters him to peel back the scrap of hoody and show her the damage in better light.

Leonie sucks in a breath at the sight of it. "Oh my God, are vampires real?"

"If you won't go to hospital we need to treat this here," says Heather. "Tell the girl to stop gawping. We need to wash this out. Does she have any iodine?"

I relay the question to Leonie who makes a face. "I-I don't think so."

"Soap and water will have to do. Right, we'll take whatever first aid supplies she has."

Leonie sends Mitch to check the first aid tin in the kitchen as she shows us upstairs to the bathroom. My broken prosthesis is getting in my way so I take them both off and dump them in the hallway with my liners, knotting the ends of my trackies.

The bathroom is plenty big, wider than the hall downstairs, with a tub and sink to the left of the door, a separate shower and toilet to the right.

Mitch brings the first aid tin. Leaning on the bath, I root through it, listening to Heather instruct Sam on how to properly wash the bite out.

"We need nylon thread, a curved needle, tweezers and scissors," she tells me. The scissors and tweezers are no problem, but there's nothing in here I can use to stitch the wound.

Leonie appears at the door with an opaque plastic box. "Joe ordered this off eBay for his gap year, never took it with him."

It's a suture kit with needles in sterile casings, forceps, even a pair of latex free gloves. Scrubbing my hands, wrists and forearms in the sink, I lay out everything we'll need.

"Have you ever done this before?" asks Leonie.

"Heather has," I say. "She'll guide my hands."

"Who's Heather?"

The doorbell sounds through the house.

We freeze where we are. Blood drips to the tiles.

"Police! Open up please."

"You called the rozzers on us?" I hiss.

Leonie makes an apologetic noise. "I told you, we thought you were those vandals come back."

"What do we do?" asks Mitch.

Leonie kicks off her boots and shrugs off her coat so she's just wearing her pyjamas. "I'll go talk to them."

"And say what?" I ask.

"I don't know yet, whatever it takes to get them out of here."

Mitch removes a stray leaf caught on her bonnet. Leonie squeezes his hand and he gives her a reassuring smile.

"Try not to make any noise," she says and disappears downstairs.

"Shouldn't you go too?" Sam whispers to Mitch.

Mitch rubs the back of his neck. "Her dad doesn't know I'm over this late."

There's the sound of the front door opening.

"We received a call from this address about a break in at the cemetery," says the low and even voice of authority.

Leonie's reply is muffled. Has she stepped outside?

Trespassing is the least of our worries – we're also looking at property damage, arson, and if they find that body, murder.

No, they can't pin that on us. There's no crime in finding a body.

The front door clatters shut and Ollie gives me a double thumbs up, but I'm not so sure it's over. Heavy footsteps sound below us, followed by a man's voice. I close my eyes and strain to hear.

They're in the house.

A soft click.

My eyes flare open.

Mitch presses a finger to his lips. He's carefully closed the bathroom door. Sam hisses in pain and I focus on him. He needs fixing up. We've got to stay quiet and trust Leonie to get rid of the police.

"Are you sure you don't want to go to the hospital?" I whisper.

Sam tries to shake his head and winces. Usually his whisper is loud, but now I have to lean in to hear him clearly. "Too many questions we can't answer plus, I'm supposed to be over at yours, remember? My father will want to talk to your parents and then they'll know you lied—"

"He'll notice a bloody great hole in your neck."

Sam blinks. "I look really good in scarves."

"As a man who has lost many a comrade and friend to the rot, may I advise you against this," says Villiers. "As deft as I am sure Charlie's handiwork will be, antiseptics of the enlightened age should not be overlooked."

Sam winces. "Thanks, Villiers, I'll bear that in mind."

"Who are you talking to?" Mitch's gaze darts around

the bathroom.

"Just get out of the way," I tell him. To my surprise, he moves over without argument.

I pull on the latex-free gloves. Sam settles on the floor beside the bath and I kneel in front of him.

"Line up the skin. If it's uneven the scar will be twisted," says Heather. "We're going to do individual stitches bisecting the wound, all right? That means across, as few as possible. When we start, don't pull on the needle, guide it through gently from the back with the tweezers."

The grazes on my palms sting inside the gloves, but I have to steady my hands. I give Sam an apologetic grimace. "This is going to hurt."

"I should have brought that whisky up with us," he says.

"Last chance to change your mind."

"Just do it."

Heather settles her hands over mine. I take a deep breath and start to stitch.

19

LOST

Leonie arrives back just as I'm finishing up and looks horrified at the sight of my blood-slicked gloves. Sam is breathing in shallow gasps, his skin sweaty and grey. Having watched the whole thing, Mitch is a similar colour.

"It's done," I say, stripping off the gloves. Heather pats my shoulder. She's proud. I'm just relieved it's over.

Sam inspects my handiwork in the mirror over the sink. "Not bad, Frith, not bad."

Fishing a tube of Savlon out of the first aid tin, Leonie offers it to Sam. "Whatever bit you might have rabies."

"The last death in England from indigenous rabies was in 1902," says Ollie, because stuff like that just rattles about in his head. I repeat it to Leonie, who rolls her eyes.

"Well, aren't you just full of fun facts, Charlie." She waggles the tube at Sam. "You've a nice face, wouldn't it be

177

a shame if it rotted off?"

Heather gives her an approving look. "She always had a sensible head on her."

Yeah, except in Normandy. Not then.

Sam tries to open the screw cap and fumbles. I take the tube. He tilts his head to the side and I realize he means for me to apply it for him. Something flips over inside me. I'm light-headed – must be from the shock of sewing someone up. The cream smells of that oddly blank medical odour. I smooth it on his stitches.

"Done."

"Thanks." He pulls away. Something between us stretches and snaps.

"The police gone?" Mitch asks Leonie, catching her waist.

"Yeah. Seriously, I deserve an Oscar." She drapes an arm over him. The sight of her hands curling through his hair freezes me up.

"You think they'll come back?" I ask.

"Not tonight. They've got to assist the fire service and stuff."

"But they'll see the freaky shite going on out there, right?" says Mitch.

I curse under my breath. Sister Agnes and Sharp-teeth won't be able to hurt the living, but there's no way even the dimmest police lackeys are going to miss floating masonry.

"Yeah," I say, feeling uneasy. "And I left my hoody out there and our caps."

"So?" says Mitch. "They'll think those belonged to the

vandals we said broke in."

"They'll be covered in my fingerprints—"

"Ever been arrested?"

"N-no."

"Ever been fingerprinted for some other inexplicable reason?"

"No."

He shakes his head. "Then good luck to them."

Sam sits on the edge of the tub. "He's right. They can only go through their databases and look for a match, which they won't find. Plus, that body is decades old, not exactly a fresh missing person."

"Body?" asks Leonie. "What body?"

Sam and I exchange a glance.

"Under the cemetery chapel." How much can I tell them? I decide to stick to the simplest answer. "Dead for decades, we just found him." Which gets me a raised brow from Leonie and a frown from Mitch.

He leans forward. "All right, you're not wizards and you're not vampire hunters, so what the hell are you?"

The ghosts and Sam are silent, all watching to see how this will go down. I open my mouth, then hesitate. Mitch and Leonie were with me in Saint-Lô; they saw what happened and they made everything worse. What if they go telling people about tonight, saying I lost it again, saying – I don't know – *stuff*. Bollocks.

"Don't you push us out again, Charlie," says Leonie. "Not now."

Push them out? That's rich.

"It's dangerous," I say. "There are … things!"

"Things?"

"Dangerous things," I stress. "You could get hurt. You shouldn't be involved."

"But we are!" Leonie stabs her finger at me. "You break the laws of gravity, and he" – she points accusingly at Sam – "just bled all over my bathroom, so we're involved now, whether you like it or not."

"They could have turned you in to the police," says Heather softly. "But they haven't."

Yet.

"Better to forge an ally than risk them seeking answers with our adversary," advises Villiers.

"Unless we erase their memories," Ollie suggests. "But I don't have a Men-In-Black flashy thingy. Sam, you got some magic spell in your notebook-of-wonders to make them forget what they saw?"

Sam shakes his head, sways a little, and then clambers into the bathtub. "I … need to lie down for a sec."

"You can lie down so long as one of you answers our questions," says Mitch. "Or we get the police back here and you can tell them what's going on."

"Mitch," says Leonie.

But his mind is set. I know that look. His charm is fraying, the real Mitch breaking out, the lad I see laughing at me from behind his fake smile, the one who is mates with Josh Girshaw even though he beat me up. There's no smile now, just tight anger and fear. Mitch is afraid. And scared people do stupid, dangerous things.

So, I tell them the truth.

"When people die, sometimes they sort of stick around as ghosts – souls, really. Me and Sam, well, we can see them." I hardly recognize the sound of my voice, but I'm speaking all right, spilling secrets. "There are loads in York, old ones from hundreds of years ago as well as the newly dead. I don't know what makes them stay, difficult deaths or unfinished business maybe, but yeah, there are ghosts all over the place. Lately, someone has been taking them. We reckon it's a tour guide called Peter Rawley. The ghosts call him the Shadow Man."

I tell them about soul catchers and the truth of what we found in the chapel and the deathloop on the playing field. The more I talk the easier it becomes to keep going. When I finish, the living are sat in a cramped circle on the bathroom floor, all except Sam, who is curled up in the tub like a chick inside an egg. Heather is by the door, close to me. Ollie and Villiers have crammed themselves into the shower to save space.

"So, you can see dead people?" Leonie asks, as if waiting for me to admit I'm cracked, or that this is just some prank.

"Yeah." I watch Mitch. I've never seen his face look so blank.

"And so can Sam?"

An arm raises out of the top of the tub. "Guilty as charged."

She looks around, pausing on the mirror as if she might see spirits dancing in the glass. "Are … there any ghosts in here now?"

I make the introductions. Villiers bows with a flourish of his hand. Heather smiles. Ollie doesn't do anything. They can't see him anyway.

"Anyone else?" asks Leonie.

"Three spirits are plenty for any suburban bathroom."

She shakes her head. "I'd call bullshit, but I saw what happened at school. It was like on the trip to Saint-Lô, you know, like that all over again."

I don't want to talk about Normandy.

"And in the cemetery" – she has her hands clasped in front of her, like she needs to hold on to something – "the way you moved was impossible without someone else there ... so, yeah, I trust the evidence. Have you always seen them?"

I'm sweating. "No, only since the meningitis."

Mitch stands up, fists clenched and shaking. "Why didn't you tell me? We were best mates."

Best mates? We were almost more than that.

I didn't tell him because it was something else that made me different from him and everyone else. Because I was already dealing with losing my legs. Because seeing and hearing invisible people is odd and unnatural, and I didn't want him to think I was weird.

If he doesn't get that then I'm not going to explain it to him. When I don't answer, he shakes his head and walks out.

"That went well," says Ollie.

The world feels crushed, a tiny pinpoint in a vast darkness. After everything he did to me, how can Mitch storm out like he's been wronged?

Leonie dashes after him, catching him halfway down the stairs. I can't hear what she says because she speaks quietly. Mitch nods, then he's gone and she's coming back upstairs.

"He just wants to help you," she says to me. "That's all we've ever tried to do."

"Help?" I snort. "You abandoned me."

"You're the one who suddenly stopped being our friend. We tried—"

"Because you told everyone I was crazy." I stare her down.

"We didn't…" She takes a deep breath. "Shite, Charlie, we were kids and we were scared. One moment you were beside us, the next you were dragged back into that pharmacy and … you were, like, sitting in mid-air for a second. I mean, it was impossible. There was blood all over you, your arms. We didn't understand what we saw – how could we? You wouldn't talk to us!"

"So, it's my fault then, is that it?"

Heather puts her hand on my arm and the touch takes the edge off the pounding in my brain.

Leonie closes her eyes for a long moment. "Let's just get some sleep, yeah? Take Al's bed. Sam can have Joe's."

I look at her, surprised. She sucks her teeth at me. "I'm not gonna kick you out in the middle of the night, no matter how much of a pillock you're being."

"All right. Harrow?"

Sam doesn't answer.

"Oi, Sam?" Panic pinches my voice. I lean over him. He's

breathing deep and even breaths. I touch his shoulder and his lashes flutter, but he doesn't wake up. "I don't think we're getting him out of the tub."

"Get some sleep," says Heather. "I'll sit with him."

"No, I'll stay." I haven't seen Leonie's brothers in more than five years. I don't want to sleep in either of their beds.

"You want to crash in here?" asks Leonie.

When I nod, she shrugs and disappears into the hall. A minute later she's back, holding bedding. There's just about enough space to stretch out beside the bath. When the floor is clean, she pads it with a few woollen blankets and brings in two quilts. "Do, uh, your ghosts need anything?"

"What a delightful young lady," beams Villiers, then proceeds to recite a long list of demands including a black-work linen nightcap and something called a posset.

"Nah, they're good," I say quickly.

"OK, well. Night then."

"Leonie?"

She stops at the door.

I clear my throat. "Um, thanks for … you know."

"Yeah." She nods and is gone.

I tuck Sam in, propping a pillow under his head, being careful not to strain his stitches, and then I lean against the bath on top of my nest of blankets. Heather joins me. Ollie curls up on her other side.

Villiers sits against the wall below the window. "You must sleep. I shall keep watch."

My adrenaline is draining away, leaving me withered and

aching. I should get up and wash my liners. I could do with a scrub myself, but Sam is in the bath and the shower would be a right faff. I'll deal with it in the morning.

Pressed close to Heather, I let exhaustion suck me down. I want to reach up through the dark and take hold of Sam's hand, just to reassure myself he's still real. He saved my life again tonight, but I reckon I saved his too. We were an all right team.

I think on what Heather said about us being important to the ghosts of York. It's almost sad that it's not true. Maybe I want it to be. When she was alive she dedicated her life to healing people, the Hippocratic oath – do no harm. Then in death she's cared for me like a big sister, so her threatening them like that, saying she'd cut short their afterlives … I don't know if it scares me, or makes me love her more.

"Heather?" I nudge her with my elbow. "I thought souls were immortal. Can ghosts really die again, like, die *for real*?"

Taking my hand, she squeezes tight. "Nothing is forever, Charlie."

20

†HE RUINS

Stumbling into the crumbling house on the square, I sink into shadows and wait for the men to pass. They're looking for me. No, for her. She's standing in the ruins of Saint-Lô, rust dripping from her fingertips, making the ground bloody.

She doesn't run. She must not show fear. They almost caught up with her at Caen, but she bluffed her way out before they found her. She used glamours to change identities, made it this far. She can do it again, be someone else, new name, new person.

I peer around the crumbling doorjamb and breathe in dust and the stink of mud and smoke. I know what comes next.

A truck pulls up. Door opens. Two cold-eyed Englishmen. It's too late to run. The taller man leans over a torn-up body in the rubble. Whatever he whispers chills my spine and I feel my disgust quicken.

The man with thick curls and Sam's face calls me by her name. I spit at him, cursing. Rough fabric scrapes my skin. I'm pulled down, hitting muddy water that squelches through my fingers. I gasp against a stench that makes me heave: rotting flesh, ammonia, charcoal, hot metal and burnt earth. I'm lost, I'm lost in her memories and I can't get out.

Rope bites my wrists. My skin burns.

Someone shouting. "Cut again, dig deeper. Carve it out of her if you have to."

The woman watches me from the corner. Her eyes are dark pools, the life long gone. The blood dripping from her fingertips becomes a trickle, then a stream.

"Charlie." My name. Spoken again, closer this time. I'm in bed, no, I'm on the floor. Sam is kneeling beside me. The bathroom is dark, but I can still make out his messy hair and his profile. The sight of him brings me back to a world without ruptured flesh and the stink of blood.

"You OK?" he asks.

I grunt "fine", running fingers through sweaty hair, then look at the backs of my hands – chunky with chewed nails – because I can't quite believe I'm awake.

The bathroom is stuffy with dry heat. At some point I've pulled off my clothes and kicked away the blankets. I'm suddenly self-conscious with just my boxers on, which is daft, because Sam's seen me in shorts at the hospital. But he wasn't this close to me then, we hadn't just escaped an underground lair together, and I hadn't stitched up a hole in his neck.

I tug the covers over my stumps. "Where is everyone?"

He leans back against the bath. "Heather and Ollie went to keep an eye on things in the cemetery. Villiers is on watch outside."

It's not like them to leave without waking me. My first instinct is that Sam's lying and something terrible has happened to them, but I know the anxiety is lingering from the dream. I force myself to take several more breaths.

"Nightmare?" he asks.

"Yeah, old memories. Not mine."

"Deathloop?"

I nod.

"You don't see the loops, do you?" he asks.

"Not until I'm close enough to get pulled in. What, you can?"

"Yes, and I feel them before I see them. There's a sense of danger, a shiver up the spine. I've … er, well … never actually gone into one." He sounds like he feels guilty, as if he's skipped a rite of passage.

I rub my knuckles into tired eyes. "You don't want to, trust me. It's like the ghost's memories become yours. You know what they knew. What happened to them happens to you and it's … brutal. If I'd died in the Hanged Man's loop my spirit would have joined his, trapped forever, or that's what Ollie says."

"You weren't dreaming about the Hanged Man just now."

I frown.

"You were speaking French," he says.

"I dunno any."

"Well I do, and that was French." He leans in slightly. "Is there something else you're not telling me?"

I duck my head.

"Talk to me, Charlie." He waits, eyes in shadow, his own secrets glinting there. Maybe he already knows about Audrey's message and he's playing with me.

"I hardly know you."

He tilts his face and a curl flops over his forehead. He looks at me from under it. "Do you want to?"

Audrey doesn't trust him.

But Heather does or she wouldn't have left me alone with him. And I want to, so yeah, I'd like to get to know him better. Sitting with him now, the way he's settled close enough we could touch, I've never felt surer of anything. The world ends right here with him and me, something dark and hollow in the shadows, waiting, but if we just stick together maybe we'll make it through.

"Ask me anything," he says.

"Anything?"

"Anything except my dead name."

I wince. "What I said at your house, you're right, I don't have any right to know about any of it, not unless you want to tell me. I was a prick."

Sam grimaces. "You were."

"And I'm sorry."

"Apology accepted."

"All right," I hesitate. *Ask me anything.* "So, how did it happen? Dying, I mean. You know, coming back and all that?"

He blinks, surprised, and I regret the question straight off.

"You don't have to say if—"

"I drowned in our lake."

"You have a *lake*?"

He actually chuckles, but it's fragile. "At the villa. My mother is Italian; it's her old family home. We go out there a lot, or … we used to." His smile fades and he tucks his legs tighter against him, hooking his arms over his knees. "I was walking with a friend. I slipped on the bank and hit my head, went under. I remember almost everything I see, I've no idea why, I just have a good visual memory. I remember how green the water was. It had little bits of algae floating in it and tiny, perfect creatures." He blinks. "Luci – my friend – jumped in after me. She lifted me up towards the surface and then I was in the ambulance coughing out lake water and my father was there. He saw it happen from the house, ran down, pulled me out." He pauses. "They didn't find Luci's body until the next day."

"I'm sorry."

He swipes at his cheek. "Mother thinks drowning shocked my system into revealing a latent extrasensory talent I've always possessed, no matter that I never experienced any ghostly phenomenon before the lake."

I blink. "You told your parents?"

"Yes."

"And they believe you?"

"My mother once spent an entire winter holding séances in a castle in Hungry. Not only does she believe me, she's thrilled. And my father, well, you'd never think it, tech and engineering businessman that he is, but he humours her, funds all the cognitive parties and aura-building retreats she spends her time organizing. He's used to putting up with grandiose claims of psychic ability in our family, so he just lets me get on with it."

My gaze finds his in the dark and we sit there for a moment. If I reach out will he let me take his hand?

Nah, that'd be weird. Wouldn't it?

I should tell him about the deathloop in Normandy. How Audrey pulled me out and, because I was so terrified, came home with me to York. And the woman in the loop … the woman…

Remember.

I can't. The nightmare is still too close to talk about, so instead I ask, "Would you change it if you could? I mean, of course you'd want to save Luci, but like, the seer thing?"

"Mostly no." He shakes his head. "But I want to understand what I'm supposed to do with it. My mother might pump out an above average amount of pseudo-spiritual drivel, but she's right when she says this is an opportunity to help souls who can't help themselves. I don't know if someone chose me for this, but I accept it regardless."

"I don't," I say quickly, trying not to let my envy show. Seeing the dead is right for him – it fires him up, it beats me down.

"I'll go back to the lake one day," says Sam. "I'll find Luci's ghost, if she's still there, but I need to understand everything I can about spirits first. I don't want to show up without answers and fail her all over again." He gives me a sad half-smile. "How did you die?"

I shrug. "You read that newspaper article; you know what happened."

"Not from you."

"There's not a lot to tell. I don't remember much of being sick. I definitely don't remember dying or coming back, except that Heather was there. But it took me a few days to realize no one else could see her. She was stabbed in the parking lot, bled out. Her soul went right back to work because she's selfless, and healing people is what she cares about most. She came to check on me and that was it, we've been mates ever since."

"You're lucky to have her," says Sam. And I hate myself, because he's right and here I am wishing I was normal, which is like wishing Heather and Ollie away.

"I didn't lose any close friends when I came out as trans," he goes on, "but the lake changed things. My mother told everyone about my gift and people were either scared of me, or they thought I'd had some kind of mental break. Imogen and Suze stuck around, but they're all the way down in Surrey. I've met some amazing people like Miri, and my friends Hunter and Jake through the online trans community. We WhatsApp and video call all the time, but we don't get to meet in person."

"I'm sorry you had to move."

"I'm not, not really. Some cis girls in my year said I was making up ghosts to get attention, like I wasn't already getting enough of that as the only boy in an all-girls boarding school. But they were the idiots who said I couldn't possibly be trans because I'm into guys, so fuck them." He sighs. "Honestly, I was ready for a fresh start. York's all right, except for soul catchers and missing ghosts."

He likes lads.

My hand, close to his, pulls back. I thought he might – he did pretend to be my boyfriend – but wondering and knowing are two different things. Suddenly I don't know what to do with the parts of me that are closest to him.

"Charlie, say something."

I look at that curl over his forehead, at the dimple in his chin, at his lips. I know he's waiting for me to say we're friends because we're hunting the Shadow Man together, and yeah, maybe we are mates now. Heather was right. Sam's not a scary lad; he's generous and brave and selfless. I've been so set on not trusting him that I missed that. I've been telling myself that I'm working with him just to keep an eye on him. And I was wrong.

I don't just want him as a mate. I want something more.

Mitch kissed me and it felt right. I look at Sam and I get that same hopeful rush. But Mitch betrayed me, and the saddest thing about it is that he didn't even mean to. It's easy to give too much, fail, and lose everything. That's what would happen with Sam because I'm a selfish, cowardly mess, and it won't take him long to see it.

My pledge of friendship slides back down my throat and instead I say, "I don't understand why you can see deathloops and I can't." And then I feel like an utter pillock.

Sam leans back. "Maybe you just need to open up."

"I *am* open."

"Are you? Because it seems to me that you spend a lot of time pushing everyone away."

He clambers back into the tub.

21

OVER EASY

66 I know you said there's no such thing as poltergeists—"
Leonie digs a screwdriver out of the toolbox at the end
of the table and passes it to me.

"Thanks," I say, turning over my broken prosthesis.

"But then how was all that stuff flying around the cemetery
like that?"

The pylon and most of the hardware look fine, though the
screw needs tightening. Twisting the screwdriver, I pry away
the foot shell so I can have a look at the damage underneath. I
really hope it won't need to go in for repair. I used to bust my
prostheses a lot as a kid, but now I'm expected to know better.

"Charlie!" prompts Leonie. "Poltergeists, the cemetery…"

"What? Oh, I dunno. I've never seen anything like
that before."

I blink – *silver eyes … lights flickering … red nails against the door frame* – and turn back to my task. That was just my nightmare-befuddled brain playing tricks. Besides, neither of the ghosts under the chapel had silver eyes.

I examine the foot shell. There's a big tear through the top. "Ah shite, this has gone right through." I've messed up the bushings and the split toe is at the wrong alignment, a much harder repair, but I can at least get the foot facing the right direction again.

"Leonie has a point," says Sam from his spot at the far end of the table. "Either there's a fourth type of ghost out there that we didn't know about, or something is changing them."

Sharp-teeth's bite is an angry blotch on his neck, but my stitches look to have held. Maybe it's because he's still dressed in trackies and not his usual chinos and jumper, but he doesn't seem like himself. This thing between him and me is in the air like static. If I look at him for too long I'm sure I'll be stung, so I go back to working on the busted foot, wondering if I can get away with duct-taping the shell for now.

A bead of moisture from my hair, still wet from the shower, drips into my collar. I shiver, though it's plenty warm in here.

I like Leonie's kitchen. It smells of breakfast. That's got everything to do with Mitch, who is skulking over by the hob, poaching eggs. Next to him, Villiers natters on about the culinary preferences of long dead kings. Mitch can't hear him, but that's not curbing Villiers' enthusiasm for the subject.

Leonie turns back to her laptop, fingers dancing over the keys as she types. "What if a ghost's essence isn't fixed, but malleable, and being trapped inside a ghost bottle somehow changes that essence?"

"How?" asks Sam, and I'm glad he asked because I got lost at "malleable".

"I don't know yet, not without examining a bottle for myself. One data point isn't really enough to prove containment turns a regular ghost into a poltergeist—"

"If that's what they are," I say.

"Polter-geist, from the German meaning angry ghost," says Ollie from the door. "Seems spot on to me."

Relaxing a little now that he and Heather are finally back from the cemetery, I relay what Ollie said for Leonie and Mitch.

"Let's summarize the facts," Leonie ticks them off on her fingers. "Fact one: most ghosts can't touch or interact with the physical world, except with you two." She points to Sam and me.

"Fact two," says Sam, raising a finger. "Ghosts that have been trapped in a bottle and then freed can interact with physical matter."

"That's more of a hypothesis at this point but fine, yeah, probably true."

I look up from rummaging through the toolbox for some duct tape. "Does that mean that when a soul catcher bottles a spirit they're actually making them stronger?"

"Only once released," says Heather. "And it's temporary. That bowler hat bloke can't lift so much as a pebble now."

"They were lobbing masonry about," says Ollie. "That's got to eat up a lot of energy."

"Does that mean they're granted a finite amount of additional energy from being in the ghost bottle?" asks Sam. "And when it runs out they're back to being regular spirits?"

"Slow down for those of us who don't speak ghost," says Leonie.

I relay the full conversation, and then, when Ollie and Heather update us on what's going on in the cemetery, I translate that too. Apparently, the fire crew put the flames out, but the place is almost gutted. The police found what was left of the Hanged Man and opened an enquiry. News crews are already shadowing the cemetery gates.

"Clear the table," Mitch calls, waving a spatula.

There's a scramble to get my prosthesis and the toolbox off the table, Leonie's laptop away and cutlery out of the drawer. Sam gets up to collect the plates, leaving his notebook open. Its pages splay like a fan and I spot a familiar face. Mine.

Everyone is distracted, so I take a quick peek.

Maybe Sam really does have a photographic memory, or near enough, because the sketch of me is perfect, right down to the little mole beneath my right eye. He's even done proper shading and stuff. I turn the page to another sketch of me, and another. Some look almost finished, others are just parts of me – an eye or an ear, or the side of my face.

"Charlie, one egg or two?" Mitch asks, as if our argument last night never happened. I snatch my hand back and the notebook pages fan again, hiding the sketches.

Mitch smiles, but it's a tempered kind of friendly. Leonie probably had a chat with him about playing nice.

"Er ... two, thanks."

I hop down to help, taking a handful of cutlery from Leonie. She opens her mouth, but seems to change her mind and closes it again.

"Ask," I say.

"Oh, um ... does walking on your residual limbs not, like, hurt?"

I shrug and head back to the table to lay out the cutlery. "Only on really hard floors, or gravel. Balancing takes practice, and I can't do it for too long."

Sam passes me a mug of coffee and then sets the sugar bowl next to me. "For sweetening."

Heat in my cheeks and neck, but I force myself to shrug, keeping it casual. I can't tell if it's a dig, or if he's flirting.

We settle round, making space for the ghosts at the table as well. Sam has made them each a mug of coffee, which makes me smile.

Heather breathes in the steam. "God, I miss caffeine."

The eggs are better than good. Mitch can really cook. Sam tells him so through a mouthful of breakfast. Mitch flushes at the praise, explaining step by step how he made the sauce. Turns out he's got a placement in some fancy restaurant in town to train as a chef after his exams.

When we're done eating, Sam holds his notebook open to a sketch of the chapel room. "We really need to work out what Rawley took from the soul catcher's lair."

"Then we need to know who the Hanged Man is," I say. "If we have a name we might also be able to work out how

199

Audrey knew him."

"I can haunt the investigation," says Ollie. "The police will be trying to identify the body, maybe they'll come up with a name."

"What about Rawley?" asks Sam. "He should be our focus. He's the threat."

"Yeah, I wonder if we can see his ghost traps with these," I say, taking out the half-moon specs.

"An old pair of glasses?" asks Leonie.

"We found them under the chapel; they're magic or something."

"They let the wearer see hidden spells," Sam explains.

"Can I try?" asks Leonie.

Sam hands the glasses over. "I don't think there's magic in your kitchen—"

"Holy shit." Leonie slides the glasses on, then flicks them up and down to look at the room with and without them, the lenses glinting a soft blue. She laughs in amazement. "I can see them."

"What?" I ask.

"Them, the ghosts." Leonie points. "Heather, right? And Villiers and … Ollie."

Ollie rocks the finger guns. "Be honest, you weren't prepared for me to be this handsome, were you?"

"You look kind of scary actually. Like, distorted, an echo of a person, but I *can* see you and I … I can hear you – how is that possible? Maybe there's a separate spell for auditory reception in the frame or something?" She lets out another blustery laugh. "Science has got some serious re-evaluating to do."

"Can I?" Mitch asks. The glasses suit his face far better than they do Leonie or me, or even Sam, whose personal style is already halfway to hot librarian.

Mitch blinks a couple of times, looking from Villiers to Heather, baffled. Ollie starts doing a jerky, robotic dance across the kitchen.

"That's ... w-wow." Mitch reaches out as Ollie passes him. For a second, I think they'll be able to touch, but then Ollie's spectral flesh washes through Mitch's hand, making me shudder.

"Probably for the best," says Heather. "If we can't touch you then we can't hurt you."

"Except with my cut-throat wit and on point banter," says Ollie, winking.

Mitch passes the glasses back to Leonie. She hesitates, then heads into the living room, calling, "I'll be right back."

"Well, I think we just found out how soul catchers see spirits," I say. "Ollie, maybe Rawley *was* looking at you that day in Mad Alice's Lane."

"Told you so," says Ollie.

Heather scoffs. "Rawley wasn't wearing his glasses in the ginnel. He didn't see us, which is good news if he's the Shadow Man."

Leonie returns, her chin quivering and her eyes watery.

"Oh, babe, I'm sorry," Mitch puts his arms around her and she buries her face in his chest.

"I just … thought she might still be here, watching over us, you know?"

Me and Sam exchange a guilty glance. Her mum. That's why she asked me if there was anyone else in the bathroom yesterday, and I just made a joke of it. I am such a dick.

"Leonie, the only ghosts here are the ones we brought with us," I say, as gentle as I know how. "If your mum stayed, she isn't here."

Leonie nods, disappointment flashing into sorrow, and maybe a hint of relief. Hooking the spirit specs on to a floral cord from the sideboard, she settles them around her neck. "So, what now?"

"We tail Rawley," I say. "Sam's right. He's the threat, but he doesn't know our faces yet so we can get close to him. Hopefully we'll find a clue as to what he's done with the stolen ghosts, and the glasses mean we can see where he's laid down a ghost trap. Maybe we'll catch him in the act."

Sam dusts his hands down on his trackies. "Well, it looks like we're going on a ghost tour."

22

DEAD SE†

According to his website, Rawley's tour starts after lunch at The Golden Fleece on Pavement, a crooked building at the base of The Shambles. No pre-booking, we've just got to go down there.

Mum cried when I got home yesterday, says I can't deny fighting when I've fresh cuts and bruises. I swore I was sorting it, and that it has absolutely nothing to do with me liking lads. I thought she'd argue when I said I was going out again – I have an exam first day back after the holidays and I haven't revised anything – but she didn't fuss. She's messaged me twice since we left, though, nonsense things that make me sure she's checking in. Normally my folks let me spend hours holed up in my room, but now every moment they can't see me it's like they're afraid they dreamed me up.

We arrive at The Fleece on time, our ghosts in tow. Good

thing my dodgy prosthesis repair job is holding because getting in here in my chair would be a nightmare. There are too many awkward ups and downs, uneven jambs and tight passages. Everything feels low and cluttered. White plaster cast death masks mounted high on the walls grimace at us as we head into the back bar where a skeleton is propped up at the counter. It smells sticky in here, the greasy tang of the Greggs next door mixing with the sweet musk of old ale and older wood.

I scan the bar, nervous that Lady Peckitt might step out the woodwork and give us what for. This is her haunting ground and she'll not be best pleased to find us investigating after Emperor Septimus's warning. Instead, a sandy-haired woman presses a startled hand to her bosom, then ups and vanishes through the sidewall. There's also a mournful bloke crouched on the upright piano at the back of the room, and a soldier in a beret watching us from the far corner.

"Geoff Monroe," whispers Sam, nodding at the uniform. "The Canadian airman who fell from an upstairs window."

Monroe's one of The Fleece's star attractions. I've heard they hold regular séances here – not that the phantom hungry tourists can actually sense him.

Mitch and Leonie are sharing the spirit specs back and forth, gawping at the dead until Heather says to cut it out or they'll blow our cover with Rawley. He might not recognize us, but he'll know what the glasses are.

"Do we meet here for the ghost tour?" Leonie asks at the bar.

The barwoman motions to a sign we managed to miss.

"Cancelled, but Bill's tour meets in Minster's Yard in a half hour if you want to catch that one."

"Actually, we were dead set on Rawley," I say. "Heard he's one of the best. Do you have his number?"

"Pete's the private type. I haven't heard from him since he called to cancel." The landlady gives us an apologetic shrug and turns to take another order.

Sam gets out his wallet. He's dressed like an absolute tosspot, a silk scarf tucked inside his shirt collar to hide the stitches on his neck. It's a cravat, apparently. Who the hell wears a cravat? To be fair, the country gent thing looks dead good on him, like, proper fit, but still … a cravat? "Let's have a drink and check the area for ghost traps, just in case."

So we stay, all of us squeezing in a little nook probably meant for a couple. It's a good spot, out of the way but with a fair view of the rest of the back bar.

With no sign of Rawley, Leonie hands me the spirit specs. Soon as I put them on Villiers, Heather, Ollie and the other spirits around us turn grey and semi-translucent. Ollie says something and I can hear it, but it's distorted, like someone's turned the volume way down. My head pulses with pain.

I tear the glasses off and pass them to Sam, who tries them on. After a moment he makes a face. "Looks like we can only use these to see hidden magic if there aren't any ghosts around."

"I'll do it," Leonie offers.

Sam shows her his sketches of ghost traps so she knows what she's looking for, and the reality of what we're doing hits me. It's noisy enough in here and we're pressed tight enough around our little out-the-way table that no one living will realize we're talking to people they can't see. But the dead notice us. No matter how this goes I've just chucked away any chance of being anonymous in York again.

There really is no going back.

A week ago, I'd be shaking, but Sam's confidence keeps me settled. He doesn't care what anyone thinks or even that being a seer is dangerous. If he can brave it, so can I.

I'm out having a drink with mates – well, almost mates – on a Friday. All right, we're checking for ghost traps because a popular local tour guide is a ghostnapper, thief, and all-round bad guy, but still, this is … good.

Mitch is sullen and distant. I've no idea what he's thinking. Leonie comes back to the table, announces there are no ghost traps nearby, then takes the glasses off, just in case. Mitch tucks her palm into his. She smiles at him and something softens in his eyes. He loves her, although he probably hasn't told her – not the kind of lad to give his cards away like that – but he does.

I expect the familiar ache of loss, but it isn't there. As Sam leans forward his knee brushes mine, probably by accident, but I feel the stab of something hopeful. I know I'm just setting myself up for disappointment, so I shift away. He inches back and even though I moved first, I feel crushed.

An unimposing young man with a patch over his left eye approaches our table. His outfit makes him stand out: a bright red double-breasted coat and a felt tri-corn, which he tips in a flourish as he bows. "I heard you were asking after Rawley."

I'm fooled by the costume and take him to be One Eyed Jack, the seventeenth century highwayman said to haunt The Fleece. Then he says, "If it's the dead you're after, I'm your man. I promise you the spookiest tour in York, frights and sights, maybe even a glimpse of a tormented spirit in one of the city's ancient Snickleways."

Which means he pays some poor lackey to dress up and jump out at his punters. One glimpse of what Sam and me see every day and this soft southern git would piss himself.

"Oi, you!" A broad-necked man with ruddy cheeks and thunder in his eyes charges our way. The highwayman pales and scarpers. "Bloody students, think they can make a few quid skimming off the real tours. Like there ain't enough competition already." He's a thickset white man, maybe in his mid thirties with a short, dark beard, crooked front teeth and small eyes. "You lot after a good ghost story then?" he barks rather than speaks.

"We want a word with Peter Rawley," I say when no one else replies. "Any idea where we can find him?"

Bull-Neck is silent but there's tension in his jaw.

Movement to my left. A man sat at the end of the bar is pretending to read the newspaper, but he's glancing our way when he doesn't think I'm looking. I can't see enough of his face to get a good sense of him, but he's white, maybe a similar age to Bull-Neck, with a blonde crew cut and his face clean-shaven. There are dark tattoos peeking from his collar, but I can't make out much detail at this distance.

"It's for a school project," Leonie says brightly to Bull-Neck. "Business and Tourism. We need a case study of a small business capitalizing on the influx of tourists interested in folklore." She gives him an innocent smile. "You know, gory history, ghost hunters and the like."

"Ghost hunters, is it? Well, Rawley would be your man for that, but he's gone to visit his sister over in Harrogate."

Something about Bull-Neck's tone has changed and I don't like it.

"Do you know when he'll be back?" I ask.

"Forget Pete Rawley. Find someone else to interview." He gives us a curt nod and strides away. Crew-Cut, the stranger at the bar, chooses that moment to turn and order a fresh pint, keeping his back to us and to Bull-Neck as he stalks off.

"Weird," says Heather.

Sam leans in. "You get the feeling we're being warned off?"

"Yeah," says Mitch darkly.

"I trust him not," agrees Villiers. "Cox-combed scullion."

But it's Crew-Cut I'm worried about. Why would he be listening in to a chat about Peter Rawley? Leonie notices me watching him and announces she's just going to pop to the ladies. When she comes back I realize she's given herself the perfect angle to take a nice long look at his face.

She slides back into her seat and hisses, "That's the policeman who came around after the chapel fire."

"You sure?" I ask.

"I only lied to the bloke for twenty minutes."

"Does he have spirit specs?"

Leonie shakes her head.

"Maybe he's just out for an off-duty pint," Mitch puts in.

One of the death masks on the wall behind the stranger blinks. A dead man with light, umber brown skin and short twists oozes out of the bricks. Can't have been dead long, a few decades maybe. His plain black polo neck and simple slacks make him look like a Steve Jobs wannabe, but he's also got a nose ring and pierced ears. His full lips are rouged with lipstick. He's not big, but he looks strong, like a dancer. Slowly, he places a red nailed hand on the bar.

On it. Not in it. *On the bar*, like he can touch it.

His long nails are red. His eyes are silver.

"Charlie?" Sam's voice is a half whisper. "Do you see…?"

I duck my head, nerves fizzing. "Yeah. He was at my house a couple of weeks back, like, *in* my kitchen, watching me."

"I've never seen eyes like that," says Ollie, unsettled.

"A devil," mutters Villiers. "Tempters and fiends sent to undo us."

The silver-eyed ghost nods at us, exaggerating the movement so there's no doubt he knows we see him. Then he ghosts right through the solid bar, fingertips sweeping the back of Crew-Cut's hand as he turns the page of his newspaper. From this angle I can't see if the ghost *touched* him, or if his hand went through his. But Crew-Cut knew the silver-eyed ghost was there. I'd bet on it.

What are the chances of this officer being another seer? Or, what if he's really the Shadow Man and we've been after the wrong bloke this whole time? But would a ghost ever help a soul catcher? The idea makes me feel sick.

Leonie and Mitch have questions. I whisper them answers as best I can, describing the silver-eyed ghost, and how he *might* be able to touch things. I can tell Leonie's itching to put the spirit specs back on, but she doesn't.

"This could mean Rawley's off the hook. What do you think, George?" Heather nudges Villiers. "Is that bloke our Shadow Man?"

"'Tis impossible to verify from such an aspect."

"Go take a closer look," I say. "Subtle like."

"You may wish to avert thy gaze, Master Frith." He slides backwards, vanishing through the wall. Moments later he appears behind the bar as he leans, trying for a gander at Crew-Cut. If Crew-Cut knows Villiers is there, he gives no sign of it.

"Well?" I ask, when Villiers rejoins our table.

He shakes his head. "'Tis possible he is our man, but…"

"But?" prompts Heather.

"It was a dark night."

"You said, and I quote, 'his foul countenance is burnt into my every waking moment.'"

"Ah, well," Villiers shifts uncomfortably. "Perhaps I was a little hot-blooded in mine desire to aid you. I assure you that he" – a nod at the bar – "is of the right height and aspect to be the fiend, but I must see this Rawley fellow to compare."

"What, you want us to do a line-up?" I hiss. There are photos of Rawley on his website, but they're only of his top-hat-wearing silhouette. No good shots of his face.

Sam leans in. "So … do we approach him?"

He means Crew-Cut. We could, but what would we say? *"Hello, officer, just wondering if you've been kidnapping ghosts for nefarious purposes. If you haven't, enjoy your pint and paper. If you have, any chance we could have our mates back? Also, just a heads up, you might be being haunted."*

Yeah, right. He'd have us down the station for antagonizing a police officer.

"Before we go pissing off the local constabulary, I reckon we track down Rawley for Villiers' line-up," I say.

"Well, I don't think he's left any ghost traps here," says Leonie. "We should go."

Everyone agrees. We leave, quick and quiet, the others heading off ahead of me. As I pass Crew-Cut I can't help glancing his way. He's spun on the bar stool, newspaper folded and is looking right at me. He's younger than I thought, late twenties with a straight, broad nose, strong jaw and serious eyes. He's handsome in an angular, chilling kind of way. I almost stumble, but catch myself in time.

"Tread carefully." His tone is kind, but he isn't smiling. He rolls his left cuff back so that I can see the tattoo at his wrist – a hand holding a flaming torch in the style of an old print or illustration. Is that design supposed to mean something to me? He frowns. "There are things you don't want to walk into the middle of, dangerous situations that are no place for children."

"I'm not a kid, mate," I say as casually as I can, then I leg it.

Outside, grey clouds curl over chimney pots like the sky is sinking towards the city. It starts to spit, then drizzle, fat droplets flecking Sam's face. His tongue reaches to taste a bead hovering on his top lip. I look away.

Ducking under the carved tiers of an imposing timber-framed house, we slip past the shopfront on the ground floor and head through the narrow opening into Lady Peckitt's Yard. The yard is actually a ginnel narrow enough to keep off the worst of the rain. The old-fashioned lanterns are already on, battling the gloomy afternoon.

Leonie slips the spirit specs back on, as if she has to check she didn't make it all up. Heather gives her a reassuring smile and Leonie returns it.

"We're on the right track," I say, as soon as we're out of the wet. "That rozzer just said so."

"What?" Heather's frown is back.

"He spoke to me on the way out, showed me this weird tattoo—"

Sam turns to head back the way we came. I catch his arm. "No, listen, he warned me off, like proper told me this shit is dangerous."

"Tell us something we don't know," says Ollie.

"Which means were close," I continue. "It's Rawley. Got to be."

"Then what's it to him?" Mitch jerks his thumb towards

the pub.

I shrug. "Maybe the police have some secret ghost-hunting division or something, but if that's true they're doing a shit job. We take care of this ourselves, hunt Rawley down. For all we know he's keeping the ghosts on his mantelpiece at home."

"You want to go to his house?" asks Leonie. "How do we even find it?"

"One minute." Sam places a call, expression brightening when whoever it is answers. "It's me. Yes, still hunting a ghostnapper. We need info on Peter Rawley and his address in York, whatever you can get us... I'm with them now ... yeah, we can wait on the line." He starts to pace. The sound of the rain hammering the roofs echoes down the alley.

A few minutes later Sam says, "OK, fine. Hold on," and holds his phone out in front of him, ushering everyone into frame as he switches to video call.

The young woman filling the screen has a round face, wide-set eyes as blue as her hair, arched brows, and a small gold hoop through her nose. She's older than us, but not by much.

"Hi, Team Spectre, I'm Miri, grey-hat hacker and waffle lover." She has a slight lilt to her words, the trace of a Scandinavian accent.

I mumble a hello.

"Miri meet Charlie, Mitch and Leonie." Sam points to each of us. "George Villiers, Ollie and Heather are also here, but they're dead so you can't see them."

"Charmed." Apparently being introduced to three ghosts doesn't bother her. "Good to know Sam's not getting into trouble on his own."

"I asked Miri to do a background check on Rawley," says Sam. "Find anything?"

"A lot of articles published in local history magazines. He has a good Tripadvisor rating. That's about it. So, I dug a little deeper, broke a few laws and I can tell you he owns his own home and has a sister living in a care home in Harrogate. But, if there is evidence of soul hunting, or whatever you call it, then it's somewhere private."

"Like his house," I say. "Which we should investigate. Could you get us his address?"

Miri arches one slender eyebrow. "Already done, sugar plum. He's local, Hull Road."

"Does he have any other property?" asks Sam.

"Not under his own name, but he could have rented a storage unit under a fake name. I need you to get his IP for me."

"Why?" asks Sam.

"Because if he has used a fake name to rent property there will likely be a digital record of it on his computer. I'm too remote to take advantage of an unsecured WiFi router. I don't care if he's into spooky shit, everyone has digital secrets. Plus, it's always useful to know who a target has been communicating with, unless ghostnappers chit-chat via carrier pigeon, in which case I can't help you."

Sam and I exchange a worried glance. What if there's more

214

than one soul catcher? It's not a comforting thought.

"IP?" I say. "That's, like, on his actual computer, right? How do we get that?"

Miri winks. "Knock on his door and pretend to be Mormons preaching the good word or something."

She ends the call. Seconds later Sam's phone flashes and a text box pops up with Rawley's address followed by a detective emoji and a link to a web page explaining how to locate a computer's IP.

Ollie grins. "I love her hair."

23

GIVE UP †HE GHOS†

The bus drops us near the garage on Hull Road. The sky is still spluttering so we move quickly, following Sam, whose eyes are trained on Google Maps, to an avenue of stocky red-brick homes with tall chimneys. The street is quiet, proper suburbia smelling of cut grass, fresh rain and privet hedge.

Rawley's rundown house is over-shadowed by a bushy evergreen, which is good because once we're up the path we're hidden from the street. Still, I pictured Rawley plotting away in some crumbly building on The Shambles or an old manor with ghosts in its timbers and magic etched into the roof tiles, not a poky semi on a bland estate like this.

But we might as well be outside a haunted house for how I feel – stretched thin and severed. I chew at the inside of my lip hard enough to taste blood. This is proper daft. If we're wrong about Rawley, this is going to be well awkward. If we're right about him then he's likely dangerous. So, naturally, we're just going to rap on his door and ask him if he's been kidnapping ghosts.

I mean, we're not. We have a plan. It's just not a very good one.

Leonie and Mitch will pretend to be collecting donations for the rebuilding of York Cemetery Chapel. We stopped off at a newsagent and print shop on the way. Now they're armed with news clippings and a fake sign-up sheet we filled out on the bus. Leonie is even wearing a phoney volunteer badge, which will hold up so long as he doesn't look closely.

While Leonie is signing him up, Mitch is going to ask to use the bathroom and unlock the back door for me and Sam. We can then check the place for ghost bottles or signs of soul catching, while Mitch finds the computer and gets the IP for Miri. He's read over the instructions Miri sent and swears down he knows what he's doing. When Villiers confirms Rawley's definitely the Shadow Man, we can come up with a plan of attack.

Basically, we're winging it.

Me and Sam stand to the side of the front door, out of sight, and Heather, Ollie and Villiers duck under the windows, just in case Rawley comes out wearing spirit specs.

"Ready?" asks Mitch.

Leonie checks over the papers on her clipboard and then nods. Mitch raps on the wooden door, paint flaking under his knuckles. We wait for a few minutes. He knocks again.

No answer.

"Charlie, close your eyes," says Heather. "I'll take a quick look."

I block her path. "Bad idea. Maybe he went out, or maybe he's lurking with ghost traps at the ready."

"C'mon, he isn't home," says Ollie. "The bottled souls could be here. Let's just break in and search the place before he gets back."

"Fine, but we stick together," I say.

I pat myself down. Shite, I didn't bring them.

"What's happening?" asks Mitch.

"Heather wants to ghost in and take a look," I say. "I reckon it's too dodgy so we need to break in, but I'm a daft sod and forgot my lockpicks."

He blinks slowly. "You have lockpicks?"

Leonie draws out one of the long bobby pins securing her printed headscarf below her curly high puff. "Will this do?"

"Perfect." I say. "You got another?"

She does. I pretty much remember how to shape them first time, inserting the pick and lever and working through the pins like a pro. When the final click sounds and the door swings inwards I lurch backwards, but the dark shape on the other side is just a coat, cape and top hat hung on a peg in the shallow entryway.

Sam goes first, as he always does. Leonie and Mitch have a playful squabble over whose turn it is to wear the spirit specs. Leonie wins – no surprise there.

The poky living room is directly left.

"Kubrick called," Leonie whispers. "Overlook Hotel wants its wallpaper back."

There is a tartan armchair beside an ugly fireplace, slippers set next to it. Newspapers on the side table, overflowing bookshelves, a coffee cup growing mould, nothing that screams "soul catcher". No ghost bottles. The curtains are partially drawn over yellowing voile, making the room dim. The air smells of must and something metallic. The underground room had the stench of old death, this is … fresher.

Something bad happened here.

At the back of the living room there's an archway where two rooms were knocked into one. It leads into what I assume was once a dining room but is now some kind of office. An old computer – on screensaver – sits on a desk beside piles of articles and papers. While Sam and Mitch hunt down the IP, I take a quick gander at the bookshelves in case there's anything useful there. It's mostly full of National Trust guides and local history books.

"Got it," Sam whispers, noting down the IP on his phone.

A strangled gasp sounds from behind a door to our left.

Sam's eyes widen, mirroring my shock. My heart starts up a charging rhythm. Is someone here? Pressing a finger to his lips, Ollie motions to the door. I get it, someone has to go look. I move towards the sound as Heather edges around the side of the living room, stepping through the archway to my side. I know my friends are just behind me, but they might as well be miles away.

At my touch, the door creaks open revealing plain counters, a kettle, a toaster and a sink filled with plates and pans. Something has splattered the cabinet with dark streaks. The floor is covered in brightly coloured fridge magnets, including a Viking with "York" emblazoned on his shield. Little notes and receipts rest in a dark tacky pool clogging up the metal strip separating the kitchen lino from the worn carpet. I taste iron in the air.

That's sure as hell not wax.

Behind me, Villiers mutters an old prayer with a lot of beseeching of heavenly fathers in it. The door thumps open against the fridge. Hesitant, I peer around the corner.

In the centre of the kitchen a man is hunched over someone lying in the dark pool.

A body. There's a body on the floor.

His back is to us. Slowly, he turns. It's Rawley, pale skin taut over the scaffolding of his bones. Whoever his victim is, I don't reckon they're ever getting up.

"Um, Charlie," says Leonie. "He's not…"

Then I look at the body on the floor. The head is slumped towards me, slack-jawed, the stare blank and lifeless. And I understand why Rawley looks so hollow and beaten.

He's dead.

"Gates is sending kids to do his collecting now." The ghost of Peter Rawley looks like a wild animal caught in a trap. "He tell you I'd come quietly like a good little ghostie, eh?"

I put my hands out so Rawley can see them. *No weapons here, mate, just a block-headed teenager trying not to chuck up on your corpse.*

"We're not here to hurt you, sir," says Sam over my shoulder.

Rawley seems to take in the fact that Heather, Ollie and Villiers are ghosts like him, then peers at me again, then Sam, the lines across his forehead deepening. "Death-touched."

I can guess what that means. I nod, nice and slow, not wanting to startle him. "Who's Gates? Is he … did he … murder you?"

"Murder?" says Rawley, as if the idea had only just occurred to him. He knows he's dead. If he didn't we'd be facing a deathloop.

"Yeah, the big dent in the side of your skull there—" Ollie points at Rawley's corpse. "That's a dead giveaway it probably wasn't natural causes."

"Ollie!" hisses Heather.

Rawley's mouth twists into a snarl. "Aye, it was murder, all because I didn't wait about idle while ghosts were poached from the streets. No one starts trapping souls in York without my say so, old friend or not."

"He doesn't sound like much of a friend," I say.

"I've known Caleb Gates since he were a lad, taught him the basics of phantasmic theory myself. He was an ambitious sod even back then, bristling over some inheritance his mam was duped out of, got interested in dangerous magics best left alone. He travelled who knows where, learning who knows what. I never expected him back, but then his mam died and he ran out of brass. A job that flush, of course Caleb was going to take the offer. I threatened to put up wards against him, so he clobbered me, the bastard." Rawley shakes his head. "I shoulda seen this coming. Caleb is a leech, takes what he needs and sods off."

"What was the job?" asks Ollie.

"Cash for the delivery of sixteen ghosts. Didn't say who the targets were, but I'm not surprised by who he's plucked so far: all famous, old and powerful."

"I'm surprised whoever hired him didn't offer you the job," says Heather coldly. She's asking if we can trust him, which we probably can't. I'm also pretty sure we don't have a choice.

"Aye, they did. Sent me an email, all very modern," says Rawley. "I could use the brass and all; my sister isn't well and there's too much competition about these days. Mine was one of the first ghost tours. Now, there's one on every corner. But I don't trap innocent souls and I don't break the old code, so I turned the offer down." He shakes his head, then mumbles. "It's odd, seeing the dead without cryptolenses."

"And you thought Gates sent us to trap you?" I ask.

"Aye, he had a bottle with him when he done me in. Newly dead souls have a lot of juice." Rawley looks down at his corpse. "Especially if the end was violent."

I want to say how sorry I am that his life ended like this, but I don't want to make things worse.

"He's probably worried I'll warn York's spirits what's coming for 'em," Rawley goes on. "He tried to nab me but I was too quick, scarpered before he could catch me."

"If he's after you then why come back here?" asks Leonie. "Isn't this the first place he'll look?"

"The place of death has a pull on the soul that died there," says Heather. "Especially in the first few days after passing over."

"And Gates knows that so you lot have to go." Rawley waves us towards the front door. We shuffle back into the dining room, but no one makes a move to leave. Unable to see or hear most of what's going on, Mitch just stands there looking totally lost.

Rawley shakes his head. "C'mon, out, the lot of you."

"Gates has our friends," I say. "We need to know who hired him."

"The email was anonymous. It's just some rich occultist too lazy to do their own collecting."

"Occultist?" asks Sam.

"Aye. Magic dabblers, conjurors and the like."

Anger charges through me. "So, he's what? Stealing ghosts for some rich, magic-obsessed prick who wants something dark and dangerous for their mantelpiece?"

"They don't collect souls for the pretty, lad." There's a cold kind of humour in Rawley's tone, like this is all some sick joke. I can already tell I'm not going to like the punchline.

A string of colourful cursing swallows the rest of Rawley's answer. Villiers is standing on the boundary between the

223

living room and the office, arms out like he might suddenly fall. For a moment I can't work out what he's playing at.

Then I see it.

Disguised amongst the ugly swirls of the patterned carpet is a gleaming ghost trap. And he's standing right at its heart.

24

PRACTICAL PHANTOMATOLOGY

I curse and call myself every kind of pillock. We knew there was a danger of ghost traps and we let Villiers walk into one anyway. Leonie is upset, saying how sorry she is she missed it because she's the one with the spirit specs. To be fair to her, the carpet's pattern hides it well. Villiers' cheeks puff with effort as he tries to pull free. The trap ripples around him, puckering the air.

"We're going to get you out," I promise, looking at Sam and hoping to see his confident smirk – *"Oh no problem, I've got some stinky herbs for that"* – but he's as flummoxed as I am.

"Caleb will've included an alarm for when the trap is sprung," says Rawley.

His words register with dull horror. I picture Crew-Cut and his silver-eyed ghost, and the seriousness of this hits me.

Gates *murdered* Rawley. What are four nosy teenagers to him except witnesses to silence?

"Right, we have to get Villiers out now." I turn to Rawley. "How do we get him out?"

"There's now't I can do."

"Bollocks there is, you're the magic man here," says Ollie.

Rawley shakes his head. "His essence has tied in, feeding the theorem. There's only one way out and that's into a bottle."

"I am exceedingly unfond of confined spaces." Villiers is doing his best not to panic, but there's fear in his eyes. If he could sweat he'd be gleaming with it. No matter, I'm sweating enough for the both of us.

"The bottle needs to be prepared special, and there's no time," says Rawley. "The ghost trap can only be broken by the catcher who put it there, or by someone just as strong. I'm dead and you lot don't look like you know one end of a fracture charm from t'other."

"There's four of us and we're fast learners," says Sam.

"Learn what?" asks Mitch.

"Magic," I say.

Mitch's eyes widen.

Rawley holds his cheeks, thinking. "Four siphons *might* do it."

"What do we do?" asks Leonie.

Rawley points to his overflowing bookcase. "Up top, the skinny volume with the purple spine."

Climbing a chair, Sam grabs the book and tosses it down to me. It's slim like a pocket guidebook, the small text dotted with graphs and diagrams showing, well, to be honest, I haven't a sodding clue. Maybe if I was better at physics or maths then I'd stand half a chance, but I'm useless at both and this is some kind of next level wizard shite.

"Page sixty-one," says Rawley.

I flip past chapter headings like "Practical Phantomatology" and "The Fundamental Principles of Mathemagics" to a drawing of a ghost trap covered in confusing lines and equations.

"Spirit Sinks, Ghost Traps and Bindings," Leonie reads over my shoulder. I let her take the book off me, trusting she'll make more sense of it than I will.

"Dissolving a ghost trap—" Her head snaps up. "We have to mark it with our blood?"

"It's all about energy in balance," says Rawley. "To take his phantasmic essence out, you've gotta put something back in. Oi, Blondie." Rawley gestures to Mitch. "My knife is in my coat by the front door."

"He's not a seer," I say when Mitch doesn't respond.

"Christ sake." Rawley rubs his hand down his face. "Tell him will you, oh, and there's a pair of cryptolenses he can have in my coat. It's not like I need them."

I'm guessing he means spirit specs.

When I relay the message, Mitch hurries off. Rawley barks orders, positioning us equal distance around the trap, warning Ollie and Heather to stand well back. He's going on about energy transference, but my panic fuzzed brain can't process it. Sam asks something intelligent about structure and stability and Rawley grins.

"You've got a feel for magic. You too," – he nods at Leonie – "both naturals, that's good."

A pathetic piece of me wants to ask "what about me?" but it's not worth wasting my breath.

Returning with the knife and specs, Mitch swallows, like he's about to put his hand into a dark hole with no promise it will come back out unscathed, then slips the glasses on and takes up his place in the circle.

We each dig the point of Rawley's blade into our thumbs.

"This is very unhygienic," says Heather.

I'm not much bothered by the bite of steel into my flesh, but as Leonie crouches and wipes her blood on to the carpet I feel a pull under my ribcage. There's not enough blood to do more than leave a few specks here and there, but the sigil she draws is clear, like she's sketched it out with a glow-in-the-dark sharpie.

Next is Sam's turn. As he drip-draws his sigil the uncomfortable feeling grows. I almost drop the book when he passes it to me. The symbol I've got to make is something like a fancy backwards J. As I draw, the pull in my ribs becomes an ache through my whole body.

Mitch goes last, and I focus on not keeling over.

"Hold it steady," says Rawley. He's standing close to the edge of the trap. "Oi, ghostie. On three you throw yourself out, hard as you can."

Villiers unbuttons his doublet, shakes out his shoulders and squats slightly. "On your count, good sir."

I spot determination and a flicker of fear in the slope of Rawley's mouth. Suddenly, I understand what he's about to do.

He counts.

Villiers leaps, grunting with the effort—

—Rawley steps into the ghost trap. The mark ripples as he touches it. Wisps of him gather and swirl. He grits his teeth.

Villiers isn't free yet. He's moving like he's underwater. I reach into the trap and grab his hands. Then Rawley is all the way inside and Villiers tumbles forward, crushing me into the armchair behind us.

Rawley is crouched in the centre of the ghost trap.

One in. One out.

A shape moves past the big evergreen outside. Ollie turns away from the yellowing net over the window. "Someone's here!"

"The Shadow Man," whispers Villiers, rolling off me and falling through the furniture. He springs up, drawing his rapier.

We're out of time.

"We can take him," says Mitch. "Four against one."

A key slides into the front door lock.

"Are you daft?" says Rawley. "He'll kill you and bottle you. The newly dead have a lot of power. There's a hole in the fence out back, takes you behind the houses. Go now."

The trap pulses and the throb in my bones worsens.

"C'mon," I say to Sam, plucking at his sleeve. "We gotta go."

"Take the book," Rawley tells Leonie. "The warding is in the last chapter; put it on every corner, every crossroads."

Leonie clutches the little volume to her chest. "We can't just leave you—"

The front door rattles as the handle turns.

Yes, we bloody can!

"Go!" gasps Rawley.

Mitch and Leonie sprint into the office, scrabbling for the back door. Heather and Ollie help Villiers, whose edges are smoking slightly. Sam's hand finds mine. We don't look back as we leg it into the overgrown garden. Behind us Rawley shouts something, maybe to keep Gates's attention on him, maybe to tell us to run faster.

The hole in the fence is only large enough for us to slip through one at a time. The ghosts don't stand on ceremony and hurry through the rotting wood. I'm too flooded with panic to care.

On the other side is a narrow path of weedy paving slabs. We plunge along at a fair pace. I raise my feet high, careful not to trip. When we round the corner, coming out in another cul-de-sac, Sam doesn't take his hand from mine for a good ten seconds.

I count them.

We keep on the move, walking now, just a bunch of teenagers out for a late afternoon stroll away from a crime scene. There's a smear of blood on the side of my right trainer. I wipe it on the grass verge.

We're lucky. The bus comes into view minutes after we arrive at the stop. Mitch flags it down. We take the back seats. Ollie keeps watch out of the rear window. Sam leans into me, just a little. I press my knee to his, wanting more but not knowing how to ask.

Sinking into the steady grumble of the engine through my back, I breathe in the ordinary scent of dirty fabric and exhaust fumes. "That was bloody close, that was."

Villiers shudders. "For a suspected villain, Rawley is an honourable man."

"We misjudged him," agrees Heather.

I can't believe how wrong I was about Rawley, and now we've lost our chief suspect. But, at least we have a new name: Caleb Gates.

"We need to go to the police," says Mitch.

"No way," I say.

Leonie shakes her head. "We broke in, and we disturbed a crime scene—"

"But we know who killed him," Mitch protests.

"And there's no evidence."

"We can't exactly say that his ghost told us who his murderer is," says Sam. "And if they take our prints they could connect us to the chapel fire."

"And Caleb Gates is a rozzer," I say. "Remember? That stranger in the pub, the one with the crew cut and the tattoos, he's the officer who came to Leonie's house after the chapel fire. He's on to us."

"That's quite a jump, Charlie," says Heather. "Are we sure he's Gates?"

"If it's not Rawley, then it's got to be him. He's the right build." I say, looking to Villiers, who nods. "Right, he shows up at Leonie's after the fire asking questions. When we go looking for Rawley – the man he murdered – there he is at the bar, listening in. Maybe he's just out for a pint, but then why that pub at that time? And then he warns me off, in a proper creepy way and all. He's involved, got to be."

"Involved, yeah, but none of that means he's the Shadow Man," says Heather.

I wish Audrey was here. She'd back me up on this.

"Well, what about that silver-eyed ghost that follows him about?" I ask. "Rawley said Gates was into dangerous magic and that's some kind of spirit we've not seen before. Can we take the chance he's not Gates? If he is and he's real police, secret ghost hunting division or not, then we need to be doubly careful. We can't stop him if we're locked up."

"Shite, OK. No police," says Mitch. He looks sullen. I get it. Leaving Rawley's body to rot doesn't sit right with me either, but we have to protect ourselves. Leonie sniffs, flicks open the little book of magic and starts reading.

Sam whips out his phone, dials and puts the call on speaker. As the sound of ringing bounces down the bus, a woman spins to give us a disapproving glare. She can get stuffed.

"That was quick. I'm impressed," says Miri when she picks up. "I'm already in and searching. There's plenty to do with ghosts, but it's mostly tour-guide stuff so far."

"Rawley got an anonymous email from someone trying to hire him to trap ghosts," says Sam.

"He just told you that, did he?"

"His ghost did," I say. "Rawley's dead."

Silence. "I'm sorry to hear it."

"Yeah, he's not our Shadow Man. That's someone called Caleb Gates."

"Email you say, hold on."

The sound of nails clattering on a keyboard. The bus turns with a whine and stops, its suspension hissing. A few people flow on and off.

"It's not here," says Miri. "No email. It could have had a timer on it, a self-destruct."

Sam groans.

"Everything leaves a trace. I'll find your sender and I'll get you what I can on Caleb Gates, but it could take a few days. I'll call when I've got something."

She hangs up.

I try not to fidget. "Sam, we don't have days. Gates might catch up with us or trap more souls."

"We need to set the warding, like Rawley asked us to." Leonie holds up the book so we can all read the title: "Wards, Guards and Boundaries". She taps a finger to the bottom left where there's a symbol that looks like two lit matches, one facing up, one down.

"For the protection of gentle spirits," reads Ollie. "It's got to be painted with hog hair on every corner and crossroads, but it'll stop anyone trying to lay down ghost traps."

"You can still get hog hair brushes in good art shops," says Sam.

"The paint's special too." Leonie frowns. "Where can we get mistletoe this time of year?"

"Online?" I venture. "You can get almost anything online."

"Gi's a look," says Mitch. Leonie passes him the book and he pours over the ingredients. "Yeah, I mean the process is hella complex, but I can cook this up. Not at mine, though. Mum will have a fit if I use one of her good pots for this, and it's gonna take three days minimum."

"That's my place out then," says Leonie. "Dad and Al get home the day after tomorrow."

"Mine too," I say. My parents will ask way too many questions, and no way I can blag this being part of our chemistry revision.

"We can use my kitchen," Sam offers. "My father's working on a big contract proposal and rarely leaves his office. He probably won't even notice we're there."

"Every corner and crossroads in York," says Leonie. "That's a lot of painting, but if we start at the centre and work outwards, we could get most of the old town covered in a week."

"You need to be careful," I say. "Ghosts might not be able to hurt you, but Gates can. He's a killer and he knows where Leonie lives. He's seen us together. He knows you're involved."

She swallows. Mitch pulls her close. I'm itching to reach

for Sam. He's sitting next to me with that stupid floppy hair of his and that dimple and his sodding eyelashes, leg pressed against mine. But what if he pulls away now we're not running for our lives?

"We're not backing out," Mitch says, jaw muscles tensing.

I stare at him and Leonie, wishing I could tell them they've done enough. Truth is, cooking is Mitch's thing. I trust him to get the recipe right. And Leonie will have that entire book tabbed and colour-coded before morning. If there's something in there that can help us understand all this, then she'll find it.

"I'm not asking you to, but we stick together," I say. "In pairs, minimum. No one is ever alone, and that goes for ghosts too. We watch out for each other."

They all nod.

Only then do I think to check my phone. Seven missed calls from Mum. I ring right back.

"Charlie." Her voice is thick with worry. "It's Aunt Chrissie. She's had a bad turn."

25

WARDINGS AND WARNINGS

It really is bad this time. Aunt Chrissie's staying on the ward for observation, so the terrible trio are with us full time. I've been helping Mum, then hiding out at Sam's, claiming he's helping me to cram Hamlet for my upcoming exams, not to cook up some foul-smelling potion and graffiti a magical symbol on to every corner and crossroad in York. I've made my folks all kinds of stupid promises about the grades I'm going to pull off this year, so they'll be pissed when I fail to pass a single subject.

True to his word, Sam's house has plenty of space and we've not seen his dad, only heard footsteps on the stairs or a door slamming in the basement below. We stick to the kitchen on the ground floor: a large cream room with gleaming counters, dangerously slippery floors and an actual crystal chandelier. Mitch is at his spot beside the stove where the magical-paint-in-progress simmers over a low flame, the steam misting up his cryptolenses. According to the recipe, when the herbal sludge thickens, we've got to blitz madder root and ochre, then mix them in.

Villiers is perched on the counter, regaling Mitch with grand tales about thwarting his enemies' attempts to oust him from the king's favour.

I'm sat at the breakfast table, hunched over Sam's laptop, countless tabs open as I search York Library's digital records for anything that could tell us who the Hanged Man is. Opposite me, Leonie and Sam trawl through Rawley's book, trying to teach themselves basic magical theory, or at least understand what magic is and why it works.

My research is slow-going. There are a lot of records – newspapers, historic photographs, ancestry information – and all we've got to go on is a possible connection to the cemetery. To double our chances, Ollie and Heather are haunting the police station down in Fulford, listening out for any leads on the identity of the Hanged Man. They're under strict instructions to run if they spot the silver-eyed ghost, or Crew-Cut, who I still reckon is Gates, but I'm on edge anyway. What if they get into trouble and I'm not there to help?

"Charlie, I can practically hear you worrying," says Sam. "They'll be fine."

Am I that obvious? I give him a weak smile, though I can't meet his eyes. It would kill me.

He's been sneaking glances at me all week. Yesterday his hand brushed mine as we chopped herbs for the paint. I swear he did it on purpose. I'd looked sideways at the line of his jaw and wanted to kiss it. I didn't. But now every time I see him I get this befuddled feeling that makes talking a hundred times harder.

"Oh my God, that's it," breathes Leonie. "I know what they're using the trapped ghosts for."

Villiers falls silent. Mitch looks over. Sam sits upright.

"You do?" I say, eager.

Leonie takes a deep breath. "How come ghosts can be caught in a bottle trap if they can't touch anything except seers? I mean, they should be able to pass right through the glass, right? So, I broke down the instructions in the book for making a ghost bottle, remember Rawley said the vessels had to be specially prepared?"

I wish she'd get to the point. Leonie is the kind of person who needs to know *why* something is the way it is, and preferably *how* while she's at it and she'll then explain it to you, even if you don't have a clue what she's going on about.

"When activated, the theorem, which as far as I can tell is just a fancy word for a complex spell, triggers an artificial ghost loop *inside* the bottle, trapping the spirit and making it stronger. If the bottle breaks, the loop dissolves and the freed ghost becomes a poltergeist, able to interact with physical matter for a limited time."

Sam runs a finger over his stitches and shivers.

"I don't get how yet," Leonie goes on. "My hypothesis is that the loop enhances a ghost's phantasmic energy, making it more concentrated. Basically, like, super-powering the ghost.

Now, this" – she taps a finger on Rawley's book – "is way too simple to cover it, but I did find references to ghosts as 'supplementary essence', which explains everything." She pauses, eyes wide, waiting for us to understand. We stare back in dumb silence. "Stored potential. Energy. Occultists are using ghosts as batteries."

Sam looks sick.

"This is so fucked up," says Mitch.

I'd like to think this is all bollocks, but Leonie's a sodding genius and, in a horrible way, it adds up. Gates and his mystery client treat ghosts as things to be used, not people with thoughts and feelings of their own.

Nothing is forever.

I feel knotted up and strange. "Do you think when a bottled soul is used to power a spell – theorem – whatever … does it, you know, kill them for good?"

"It must do," says Sam. "Why trap new ghosts if you can reuse the ones you already have?"

"A true death." Villiers' voice is tight with fear and awe rolled together. "No hell. No heaven. Just … oblivion."

The kitchen door swings open and Mr Harrow strides in. Even in casual chinos and a sweater he's as polished and put together as this house.

"Dad!" Sam pulls my untouched Shakespeare notes over Rawley's book. "What are you doing here?"

"Well, I live here, Sam, and sometimes I need to eat." Taking a loaf from the bread bin on the counter, he fishes sliced meats and wrapped cheese from the fridge. It's weird, watching him do something as ordinary as make his own sandwiches. His kitchen has paintings on the walls. It has a *chandelier*. He should have some personal chef in here whipping him up four course lunches.

"Nice to see you again, Charlie." His eyes still have the same watery sheen as the first time I met him, probably from hours spent staring at a screen.

"You too, sir. How's ... um, work?"

"Going well. In fact, I had a major breakthrough earlier today. We will be able to start tests on the prototype soon." I can hear the excitement in his voice. "Sam, are you going to introduce me to your other friends?"

Sam scrambles to do just that.

"Those are unusual glasses you're both wearing," says Mr Harrow.

Leonie smiles. "Couple goals, right?"

"Does anyone else want a sandwich, or will you stick to soup?" Leaning over the bubbling paint, Mr Harrow inhales and quickly recoils. "Are you certain this is edible?"

Mitch is flustered, protective of days and days of hard work. "No, it's ... ah ... an experiment ... for um..."

"It's dye," says Sam. "Natural dying, you know, for living history. A guy at school invited us to a medieval thing, but we need to make costumes."

"Interesting." Mr Harrow knows it's a lie. It's in the snake-like twitch of his lips and the slight scowl hovering behind his smile. "What are you using for the mordant?"

"The ... mordant?"

240

"To fix the dye to the cloth." The emphasis on "cloth" is subtle, but it's there. Obviously, we don't have any fabric ready to go into the pot. A new tension pricks through the room. Sam stares at his dad, a pulse beating in his jaw. His dad stares back.

"Piss," says Villiers.

Yeah, I want to curse too.

Mr Harrow's lips twitch.

Villiers makes a face at me and I realize he wasn't swearing, he was giving us the answer.

"Urine!" I say too loudly.

Everyone stares at me.

"I see." Turning back to the counter, Mr Harrow tidies away the leftover fillings. "In that case I'll be sure to acquire a new stockpot."

As the sound of Mr Harrow's steps echo down the marble stairwell, Leonie starts to laugh. "Living history? There is no way he bought that."

"I panicked," says Sam, covering his face with his hands. "He doesn't really care what we're doing, though, honestly. Give him ten minutes and he'll forget we're up here. His work is all-consuming."

Heading to the stove, I pretend to check on the paint because I need a moment of calm. With Mr Harrow gone, the stress of everything else is suddenly overwhelming.

We might already be too late to save anyone. They might not exist anymore.

The idea of anything like that happening to Audrey, or any of the missing ghosts, makes me feel sick, although that could be the smell of the paint. Mr Harrow was right, it stinks: a dank odour that takes me back to the ruins of Saint-Lô, and my nightmares about a cold-eyed man leaning over mud-streaked corpses. The bodies didn't look any different after the man moved on, but something about them seemed diminished, like he'd violated them worse than bombs and bullets ever could. And always there's a sense of disgust and anger and, worst of all, guilt.

"Nothing is forever."

The glint of light on glass.

A bottle. There had been a bottle trap in his hands.

He was collecting souls.

A soul catcher bottling the ghosts of dead soldiers in the Second World War. I didn't realize it because I was looking at it through her eyes, not mine, and she wasn't a seer.

It can't be the same man ghostnapping souls in York, he'd be long dead. But Audrey wanted me to remember something about Saint-Lô and the woman whose deathloop I fell into there. Is there really a connection?

Think, Frith. Think.

"Remember the Capital of Ruins."

Remember what? Everything I lost? My mind. My mates. My chance with Mitch.

He's beside me, sending worrisome glances my way. "You

242

doing all right? You look kinda sick."

I'm gripping the counter, staring into the pot. Little bubbles rise and break on the surface of the paint. "Just the smell."

"Yeah, bloody stinks." He laughs, then sneaks a glance behind us at Sam, Leonie and Villiers, who are debating how a ghost battery might be used to power advanced theorems. "I told her, by the way." Mitch keeps his voice low. "When we first got together."

I pull my focus back to reality. "What?"

He clears his throat. "Leonie. I told her about when we, you know, when we kissed. I didn't say it was you, because I know you're not out at school, but she's kind of guessed and she's cool with it. Just so you know."

"She's cool with it?"

"Yeah, I mean, no big deal."

No big deal? It was a pretty big deal to me.

"So, it was just an experiment?" I say coolly.

"Everything's an experiment." He gives me a sideways smile and his cheeks flush. "But, truth is, I'd wanted to kiss you for weeks before the France trip."

"Are you … bi then?"

Mitch shrugs. "People are just people. And I guess I'm a people person, but … I'm not out yet. My parents wouldn't get it, and I don't want to be labelled before I know myself. Honestly, I'm still figuring it out." He takes a deep breath. "I liked you a lot. You're a really good bloke and I…" He swallows slowly, then he looks at me. There's hope in his face. "I really miss us being mates."

All those times he asked me to sit with him at lunch, he wasn't just having a laugh. When he let me know a lad was looking for me, it was an excuse to talk, not wind me up. Something else clicks into place.

"Did you tell Girshaw to leave me be?"

Mitch's nostrils flare. "Josh is a knob."

That's a yes, then.

Just before Josh stopped beating the shite out of me, I'd seen them together and assumed my old best friend was now mates with the lad making my life hell, when really Mitch was warning him off.

Leonie was right. I cut them out. Saint-Lô was the worst day of my life – screaming in the middle of a French pharmacy all covered in blood, arms burning, my class staring at me in horror. I pushed everyone away, refused to talk about it, and blocked the details out to keep myself safe.

Now, I need to remember it again. Somehow, what happened back then matters. I don't know why, but it does.

"Mitch, I've been an absolute bellend."

He hands me a wooden spoon and gestures to the pot. "Does that seem thick enough to you?"

Like he needs my opinion, but I give it a stir anyway and the surface rucks up. Mitch nods. "Yeah, that's ready. Oi, Sam, got a blender?"

"Bottom cupboard to your left."

I fetch it up for him and when Mitch says "thanks, Charlie", I reckon he means, "you're welcome for everything, mate."

It's been almost a week since we met Rawley. We've not warded a single crossroads in York against the Shadow Man and Miri can't find any record of Caleb Gates in the Yorkshire police service. Maybe he's using a fake name, or maybe he's not even a real rozzer. We've no way of knowing.

At least the paint is almost ready. Mitch is stood at the stove scrolling through TikTok with one hand and stirring the paint with the other. It's got to be kept in constant motion until the colour changes. We've been taking it in shifts. Leonie is snoozing in the armchair Sam dragged in from the living room, my tracksuit top rolled up under her head, her cryptolenses slightly askew.

I haven't told them what I remembered about Saint-Lô and the soul catcher yet because I don't understand it, and I can't handle too many questions. Missing pieces are starting to worm their way back. Remembering feels like sticking my tongue in the soft iron hole of a lost tooth, something I can't leave alone now I've noticed it.

I'm back on the online research, scrolling through census records to cross reference with a book about the history of York Cemetery I ordered. It arrived this morning and I've been reading up on the history of the place. Whoever the Hanged Man was, I reckon he had to have a link to the cemetery. How else do you build a whole soul catcher lair beneath the chapel without it being on the architectural plans?

So far, it's not proving a fruitful search. That chapel was finished in 1838, long before the Hanged Man would have been born. The ration book in the underground chamber was dated 1944, so he can't have been involved in designing or building the crypt. But whoever he was, he had to be someone with easy access to the cemetery.

A dog's bark echoes through the house, waking Leonie just as Ollie stomps through the kitchen door, Dante barrelling after him.

"Door!" I motion to the solid wood he just ghosted through.

"Sorry." He looks sullen. "Bad news. The coroner just told the investigation team that there's no hope of identifying the body. Seems there's not enough of him left after the fire, and they don't have dental records that far back."

"They're packing it in," says a voice in the hall. I open the door to Heather and her frown. "They're no longer treating the death as suspicious, case closed."

"We won't get a name from the police then," says Sam, reaching down to scratch the top of Dante's head.

"Bollocks," I huff, sliding back into the breakfast booth and leafing through the history book. I turn the page, and—

"That's him," I say, stunned.

"For real?" asks Mitch.

"Look at this." I hold up the book and they crowd round the grainy image dated 11th August 1940. It shows three men standing around the crater of one of the first bombs to fall on York. Apparently, one fell in the graveyard, and there's the Hanged Man, side on to the camera, standing in the crater holding a shovel. I scan through the caption, hoping for a name.

"Groundskeepers … hold on, Ruddock, Heath, Tussle… Simon Tussle." The name sinks into me like a pebble into a river, tumbling and bouncing off half-formed ideas.

Simon.

I flip through the open tabs on Sam's laptop to a short newspaper mention about a man from Fishergate, near the cemetery, who was reported missing in the summer of 1944. I'd kept going back to it, unsure why I felt it was significant.

"Neighbours reported him acting strangely before he vanished," I read. "There's no photo, but it says here he worked at the cemetery, and listen, he's recorded as Mr S. Tussle. It fits. It's him."

"Good work," Sam claps me on the shoulder.

But there's something else here, something I'm not connecting.

"How did Audrey know him?" asks Ollie, "She was all the way in France when he died, right? They can't have met."

Heather bites her lip, thinking. "Unless they knew each other from before the war."

"What, like, she was a soul catcher too?" asks Leonie.

"Audrey wouldn't—" Ollie starts, then falls silent.

"It's … possible," says Heather, though she clearly doesn't like the idea. "I mean, we really don't know much about her, she's so secretive. But what I don't get is how she knew Simon Tussle's deathloop was beneath the – what's wrong, Charlie?"

I must be making a face. "Simon, the name, I've heard it recently." The answer's dancing a jig at the edge of my memory, but I can't place it. Bollocks. I'm useless.

I think back to the deathloop, Simon's weathered face twisted by grief and worry. I remember the hollowness he felt, the agonizing sorrow. He'd lost something. And there was a feeling of inevitability too, the pain and panic of being backed into a corner. He genuinely thought taking his life was his only option, the last act of a desperate man. But *why*?

I know that I don't just experience the memories of the souls I meet inside a deathloop, I can feel what they felt and know what they know, and I take some of that with me when I leave. The answer has got to be rattling about inside my head someplace, but I can't focus on it. My thoughts slip sideways and I realize there's a question we should have asked right from the off.

Why York?

It's said to be the most haunted city in Europe, but that doesn't mean there aren't rich pickings in London or Bath or Edinburgh. Sam is right. Gates broke into Simon Tussle's lab looking for something specific. Problem is, I don't have Sam's sharp memory. I can't recall all the details of the deathloop to work out what's missing.

"No," says Heather firmly.

I raise my hands. "I haven't said anything—"

"Oh, I know you, Charles Frith, and I know that look. You're fixed to do something stupid."

She's right.

I need to go back into Simon Tussle's deathloop.

26

AN UN~~TE~~THERING

It takes us twenty minutes to get to the school, me standing on the pegs of Leonie's bike as Sam pedals, Mitch behind us on his old BMX. Dante runs alongside, with Heather and Villiers following on foot.

Ollie stayed on as a lookout for Leonie, who is taking the finished paint and our research back to her place. We didn't want to leave them at Sam's after that chat with his dad, but I'd feel better if we were all together.

I reckoned on some teachers being in school to prepare for the start of term on Monday. Instead, the gates are locked. Dumping the bikes behind a hedge, we pick our way along the chain-link fence around the playing field to the tangle of hawthorn. Behind it is a hole. Grabbing the links, Mitch hauls the metal up and out, rolling it back like opening a tin of fish.

Sam scrambles through and I follow, wiggling on my belly.

The scent of cut grass and earth fills my nose. After Mitch is through, he pulls the chain link down so the breach isn't obvious. I scan the playing field, cursing the damp and the mud. Dante's off, loping towards the storage pavilion and Tussle's deathloop.

The old chestnut tree shifts in the breeze, branches creaking. From here the shadowed spot beneath the canopy is empty, but if I get any closer…

I falter, remembering the dreaded cold, the weight against my throat, my tight lungs. A hand on my back – Sam.

"You're all right," he says.

His touch triggers the flight of ten thousand winged things through my veins, distracting me from the crushing numbness. My face is burning from being so close to him but he seems calm, like there's no storm raging inside his head. I figure he doesn't want me, not in that way, but he's here for me as a mate. He's got my back.

I make myself look up. I force myself forwards.

This was my idea. But kitchen bravado is different from being here, the threat of a hanging just metres away. Right, I'm going to walk back into it. *On purpose*. I'm going to keep my wits and take a good look around to find what Gates was searching for and why Simon Tussle is connected to the missing ghosts. Maybe I'll remember more of how he felt and what he knew. Maybe I'll find something pointing to who Gates's mystery client is.

As I near the tree, something taps against my shoe. I nudge it out of my way and keep walking. Where's the loop? I reckon

I might feel better if I could see it. The problem is, by the time I'm close enough, I won't be able to stop myself from sliding inside. If I go in when I'm not expecting it—

No, that won't happen. But knowing Sam, Heather, Mitch and Villiers are here to pull me out before I'm strangled to death isn't enough to stop the panicked pounding in my skull.

I'm dangerously close now. Turning slowly on the spot, I expect Simon's boot to whack the back of my head, but there's nothing.

Dante barks. He's focused on something in the damp grass under the tree. I go to see what is getting him all worked up.

It's the thing I kicked – a dark, round stone like a small fortune-teller's crystal ball that's flatter on one side. There's a big crack running through it and something is scratched into its surface. It's heavier than it looks and slightly warm to touch.

"That's black tourmaline," says Heather. "My ex was really into her crystals, used to keep a lump of this by the bed to ward off bad dreams."

"It can also be used to ground ghostly energy," says Sam. I offer him the stone. He picks mud off the surface, and swears. "See that symbol there? That's identical to one of the wards beneath the chapel. Remember the red markings on the walls? This was used by a soul catcher."

"To do what?"

"Master Frith!" Villiers is standing under the chestnut tree, looking up. "There is no trapped soul beneath these branches."

As it starts to rain, I realize two things.

One. Simon Tussle's deathloop is gone.

Two. I know where I've heard his name before.

The Snickleway Inn is crammed with people. They've got a live band in, the fiddle player working up a sweat as patrons whoop and holler. In the front room Roderick the Elizabethan barman flings Mrs Tulliver in a circle, their spectral bodies sliding through the people around them. It makes my head swim. Even Sam looks a little nauseous.

"That's a sight," he shouts over the din as we inch our way towards the stairs.

We squeeze around the end of the bar and the black tourmaline ball in my pocket jars against my leg. We sent a video of the stone to Leonie, who found a reference in Rawley's little book about black tourmaline and a mirror being used to anchor and displace intact deathloops.

This has been about the Hanged Man all along.

Sam reckons Gates broke into the chapel to trap Tussle's ghost, disturbing the wards, which set off some kind of defence mechanism, dislocating Simon's loop. He ended up on the playing field, of all places. Meaning, Simon died knowing there was a chance he could become a deathloop and that someone might come for him one day. He prepared for it.

But why does Gates want Tussle's loop in the first place, especially when he can create artificial loops using ghost bottles? And how did he even find out where Simon's deathloop ended up? York's a sizable place; he wouldn't have stumbled upon it by accident.

We need answers.

I bloody hope I'm right about my hunch.

Upstairs is just as busy as down. The windowpanes have steamed up from the press of warm bodies damp from a heavy dousing. Me and Sam look like an advance party sent to nab a table for our group. A man shifts a jacket on to the back of the only free chair in the place, claiming it, but I'm already looking past him, searching for a mass of crinkled hair.

When I was last here Ophelia mentioned someone called Simon, and I was so focused on Millie I just assumed it was the pillock who'd broken her heart centuries ago and left her tethered. But Mrs Tulliver said Ophelia had been unable to leave this room for eighty odd years. Ophelia is much older than that, four centuries deceased – give or take a decade – so something happened eighty years ago to tether her here. Eighty years takes us back to the early 1940s. Simon Tussle went missing in the summer of 1944.

It's guesswork and a long shot all in one.

Ophelia is curled up on the floor, half hidden between two tables near the window. I push towards her. A bloke shuffles his chair over so I can get by, though he's flummoxed, which is fair enough. Ophelia looks up and recognizes me. She unfurls, legs sliding down beneath heavy skirts, back straightening. I offer my hand. She takes it and I pull her to standing. Her cheeks are flushed, eyes puffy.

"You came back." Her speech is slow and languid. "Have

you found Millie?"

"Not yet, but we're close." I don't bother lowering my voice and people are staring. I don't look at them, focusing on her hands in mine. It feels important somehow that I hold on to her for this. "I need to ask about Simon."

"He was supposed to meet me here and he never came."

"I'm sorry for that, and I'm sorry to ask and all, but his last name, was it Tussle?"

Her eyes widen, then her expression hardens and she fixes me with a level stare. "Where is he?"

"Umm." Is this terrible, guilty ache what Heather felt every time she had to tell a relative their loved one hadn't made it? "The city morgue. Probably."

"No, not his empty husk. I need *him*. Where is he?"

The grief and remorse Tussle felt before he died comes back in a wave, like his loop still has a claim on me somehow. It makes looking at her hurt. "He was trapped in a deathloop at York Secondary, down in Acomb—"

In a sweep of skirts, she spins me towards the door. "Then you will release him."

"I can't," I gasp, stumbling for footing and almost tripping over a chair leg.

Sam steps into her path. "Deathloops don't work like that, and Simon isn't—"

Ophelia shoves him aside with an unnatural strength I've only seen from the Mouldy Oldies. He clatters into a table, smacking a bloke around the head with his arm, spilling pints and scattering crisps.

"Wait!" I call. But Ophelia doesn't stop, disappearing through the wall beyond.

I help pick up Sam, who is trying to apologize to the man, gathering up fallen glasses and brushing salt and vinegar crisps off the tabletop.

"I thought she was tethered!" he says to me.

"Not anymore," says Heather. "She's a free soul now."

"Where will she go?"

"After Simon," I say, turning to Heather. "Can you catch up and slow her down, maybe talk to her?"

Heather levels her gaze at me. "I'll need to be quick."

I understand what she's getting at and I don't like it. I've taken little steps, trying not to turn away when they're forced to break my rules, but this? Right now, I don't see how we have a choice.

"Do it," I say.

She nods back, a smile flickering over her lips and then—

She's gone.

The spot in front of me is empty and I look beyond to the curious faces of an entire room of people staring at us, silent and confused.

I couldn't give a flying fuck.

27

THE GHOSTS OF WAR

It's pissing it down. Puddles of light slicked by the downpour leave the narrow pavements gleaming. Zipping my jacket closed, I squint down Goodramgate. No sign of Heather or Ophelia.

Mitch whistles. Me and Sam duck in the dry ginnel where he's sheltering.

"I was right," I tell Mitch. "But Ophelia just took off to find Simon. You see her leave?"

He didn't. *Bollocks*. He was looking for Dante because the daft mutt got a whiff of something and disappeared. Ophelia could be halfway across town by now. Even if Heather manages to catch her up she's got no way of telling us where they are, and we've little hope of finding them in the maze of streets.

Sometimes I do wish seeing the dead came with a kind of

257

sixth sense. *Oh yeah, I know where they are; we've a psychic link Heather and me.* Not that I'd want anyone in my head like that, but it'd be useful right about now.

"Where's Villiers?" I ask.

Mitch rubs a spattering of rain off his cryptolenses. "Took off when I was looking for Dante."

It's possible he followed Heather and Ophelia. We've no choice but to get soaked, again. Unchaining the bikes, we head west on foot in the direction of the school.

By the time we reach St Sampson's Square I'm piss-wet, rain dripping off my cap and down my neck. I wish we could cycle, it'd be faster, but we might miss Heather and Ophelia huddling in some dark corner. Although the streets are almost empty of the living, there are loads of dead about – priests, Roman soldiers, Vikings, all carrying on their usual business. What's a storm to them? The rain just goes right through them, striking stone.

The bluster fusses the trees lining Parliament. We keep our heads down against the wind and turn on to smaller streets, trying to make it look like our not bumping into any of the dead is sheer luck. Sam and me do an alright job of it, weaving this way and that like we're mucking about. Likely anyone watching thinks we've been on a bender.

"Master Frith!"

The shout is almost stolen by the wind, but when it comes again I turn to see Villiers flying towards us, waving frantically. A few of the ghosts stop and stare at him, then look at me, their brows going up when they realize I can see them. Two women in vintage skirt suits point at us, followed by a butcher in a blood-stained apron. My heart speeds as the growing crowd quickly becomes a wall of the dead, all watching us, silent as the grave.

Calm yourself, Frith.

Mitch adjusts his cryptolenses. "If that lot attack, what can I do to help you?"

"Not much," I whisper.

Sam pulls the BMX to his side like a shield. "Why are they so still?"

There's a flash of silver and the face is gone as quickly as it came. I tense. The silver-eyed ghost is here somewhere.

Villiers reaches us, pushing through the crowd. "Heather hath halted the sorrowful lady at the bridge, though I know not how long she might be persuaded to remain."

Keeping a wary eye on our ghostly audience, he ushers us along the road. More dead have clotted up the end of Market Street, blocking our path. As we near them I half-expect dead hands to grab us, but they step aside. There could be whispering and angry mutters, but I can't tell over the roaring wind.

Ophelia and Heather are on King's Landing, just outside the pub. I hate going down to the river. The cobbles are slippery and the waters, thick with ghosts. Some lurk under the surface, pale faces in the dark. Others wander the banks, still dripping after a century or more – the loser of a drunken brawl, a child swept away by floodwaters, a desperate woman jilted by her lover, souls drowned when the old bridge collapsed, pitching the shops and homes along its length into icy waters.

All of them are tethered. The river keeps what it takes.

Heather gives us a sharp wave, as if to say "get yourself down here". Mitch hesitates, hand on the railing as he scans the water. Does he see a shimmering wash of ghostly light through the cryptolenses, or can he see their individual faces? Even Sam seems wary of heading to the waterfront. I end up going first.

Ophelia rushes me, face pinched with rage, and I realize Heather's wave was a warning. She tries to pull Ophelia back, but Ophelia is old and strong and she flicks Heather off with a sharp jab of her arm.

The stink of the river fills my nose as I stumble against the wall. Ophelia gets right in my face. She looks different, her shift and gown tidy, long hair covered with a coif. She's remembering herself differently and it's changing her. This isn't the confused tethered soul I'm familiar with. This is a free spirit burning with hate.

The kind that comes after me looking for blood.

"You walked in his loop, but you *left* him there," she spits.

Sam elbows in front of me and I'm caught between the cold stone at my back and his warmth. "We can't free souls from loops, that's not how it works."

"Speaks the child green to his gift. I told him" – she glowers at me – "to help them remember."

"Help them remember *what*?" I ask, frustrated. I look at Heather, but she seems as confused as I am.

Ophelia throws up her arms. "To remember death! Then they might be free."

"Of … the loop?" asks Heather.

"Not in all my wanderings have I ever heard of such a feat," says Villiers.

Ophelia groans. "This is what we – the death-touched, the seers – are for!"

It sounds a lot like the Mouldy Oldies favourite "seers serve the dead" bullshit to me. But if it is possible to free looped ghosts then I could help the boy on the Shambles and that Ragged lad at Bedern.

"You were like us?" asks Sam.

"I was killed because of the sight," Ophelia goes on. "Accused of 'conjuring the devil' by fearful men with secrets to keep. I did not become a looped soul, but I was angry and lost until I met Simon. Catchers are often our enemy, but he is different." She smiles. "We fell in love."

Ophelia explains that the Mouldy Oldies discovered her relationship with Simon and forced them apart. The broken girl is now fully put aside for this woman, wiser than her age, calm and clear.

"We met in secret in the upstairs parlour for years until he disappeared." She points at me. "Make Simon remember. Free him."

"I can't. Simon is gone," I say.

"Gone?"

Scrambling in my pocket, I hold up the black tourmaline ball. "We found this where his deathloop used to be."

261

Her eyes widen. "A grounding stone?" Then her face crumples. "Now he is a prisoner of a soul catcher, as well as of his loop."

"Yeah, Caleb Gates," says Mitch.

Ophelia starts, as if she's only just registering he's there. "Who?"

"The catcher we're calling the Shadow Man," I explain. "He's been stealing ghosts in York for a mystery client. We think he took Simon's deathloop."

"Why?"

A blustery gust sprays rain in my face. I'm soaked through, my trackies clinging to me. "We were hoping you could tell us."

Ophelia shakes her head. "I don't know, unless … the restoration theorem, if Rachel succeeded then that might be why…"

Rachel.

The name I whispered into the granite beneath the chapel. Grief. The acrid wash of smoke. A single photograph of a man and a girl amongst the flaming bundle of—

"Letters," I mumble. "I've been a right idiot … they want her letters."

Everyone looks at me, expressions caught between surprise and confusion.

"What letters?" asks Heather. "Who's Rachel?"

"Simon's daughter," says Ophelia. "She became obsessed with developing a spell to give me a permanent physical presence. She called it a restoration theorem. There were scattered rumours that it could be done. Rachel started experimenting with a blend of mathemagics and phantasmic engineering based on the known side effects of the bottle trap. She had some success, but neither she nor her father had the financial resources to move forward. With the advent of war, the military recruited her. They offered money and resources to develop her work, shipped her out to the continent to implement her theorem on subjects in the field."

Ophelia's words pick a lock inside my mind. It's like opening a door with a long, deep darkness on the other side, the kind of dark that's going to swallow me whole. Rain drips down my nose and over my lips. There's a burning in my belly and at the back of my throat. Rank air. Cold. It's in my bones, humming through my marrow, wiggling into my skull.

I know things: the souls of soldiers were trapped in bottles, brought to Rachel to be looped together and sent out to fight and die again and again. And they'd made it feel like the right sacrifice to make because we were fighting to protect our people.

Sixteen souls linked together in an artificial deathloop can win the war … but the cost … the cost is more than I – than she – can live with.

I blink. Churned earth and broken stone. They're coming after her and she's shit scared. Rachel tries to back away into the bombed house in Saint-Lô, taking me with her. I smell blood.

"What is the solution to the theorem? Tell us how to stabilize it."

The letters. She's not a daft lass, so why'd she take that risk?

Ophelia, it was all for her, the ghost she loved as much as her own mother, the woman who made her father happy. Rachel had written home about her progress on the theorem, spilling secrets. If they could find an alternative formula then her dad and Ophelia could truly be together.

As she died, Rachel burnt with fear. I feel it as my own. Once Saunders was done with her, he would go after the letters. She'd prayed her father would get out of York before he came knocking.

28

RESTORATION

Stumbling, I heave on to the cobbles but nothing comes up. Heather leans over me, one hand on my back.

"Remember the Capital of Ruins."

"The deathloop I fell into in Saint-Lô," I gasp between tears. "It was Rachel Tussle's. I've been carrying her secrets around for two years, I just … I couldn't remember."

"Saint-Lô. As in Normandy?" asks Sam, offering me his hand. He pulls me up and passes me a handkerchief. It's monogrammed, of course. I wipe my lips and clear my throat. Mitch offers me gum. I chew on it a moment, letting the spearmint wash round my mouth before spitting it into a nearby bin.

"The Capital of Ruins," I say. "It's where the military caught up with her. They were taking the ghosts of allied soldiers, right? Bottling them, like the Shadow Man is now, and then they got Rachel to combine them into something monstrous so they could send them out to fight again."

"So, restoration is like legit *resurrection*?" asks Mitch.

Sam looks dubious. "I don't remember learning about unstoppable Second World War zombie soldiers in history class."

"Maybe they only teach that at A-level."

"I am doing A-levels, including history. So far, no zombies."

"Not zombies," I say. "The theorem doesn't rebuild their bodies; they were more like super-powered poltergeists."

I close my eyes again, trying to sort through the memories Rachel's soul shared in the panicked, painful moments I was inside her loop. This is part magic, part science and I'm shite at both. I can't help thinking of Audrey and wondering if she and Rachel were mates, and how much of all this she knows.

"First, Rachel paired the ghosts up, looping them into each other to stop the energy leaking out. They feed energy into each other, so they can just keep going, never turning back to normal. But the bosses didn't want Rachel to stop at looping two souls. They wanted the theorem to make something well powerful, a beefed-up weapon made of sixteen souls. But trying to link more than two ghosts made the system unstable." I shake my head. "Rachel found the solution. It was going to win them the war. It was going to save thousands of lives, until she sabotaged it."

Raindrops smash at my feet. The river ripples and swells. Restless ghosts clutch at the bank and sink back into the waters. No one hurries me; they're silent, waiting.

"She didn't want to use the soldiers, not after they'd given their lives for their country, but that wasn't what made her run. It was the solution itself. Whatever it was, I dunno, it … it's *evil*. The military went after her, caught her and tried to bleed the answers out of her. Rachel died rather than tell them the solution to stabilize the loops."

"Mate, I had no idea," Mitch whispers, shaking his head. "You lived that. I'm sorry."

Sam's face is flushed with anger. "How could we do something like that to our own soldiers? To *anyone*?"

"Because it was supposed to end the war, right?" says Heather darkly. "They wouldn't be the first to justify atrocities in the name of a greater good."

Villiers scowls. 'War turns all men into devils."

"What does it do, this weapon?" asks Ollie. "Is it a bomb?"

I shake my head. "Worse. It's like an unstoppable tornado made up of looped poltergeists that fucks up everything in its path. It could rip armies apart, or obliterate a city, way more effective and easier to control than air strikes. They were never going to stop looking for the solution Rachel hid from them. It's somewhere in the letters she sent to her dad. She was afraid they'd go after him too."

Ophelia nods. "They did. A man called Saunders came looking for him. Simon was afraid and heartbroken. He knew it meant his daughter was dead."

"Saunders?" Sam's gaze is intense, focused. "You're sure?"

"Yeah, that's him. He was a catcher too," I say, nodding as

more puzzle pieces start falling into place. "Rachel saw him bottling souls. When Saunders started sniffing around York, Simon warded himself a prison, burnt all of her letters and hung himself to keep the details she'd sent to him out of their hands. The wall wards and ghost line around the chapel were to keep his ghost trapped and undiscovered in case his restless spirit stayed earthbound."

"Audrey was watching the chapel," says Heather. "She must have had some idea of what was below it."

"I met Audrey in Saint-Lô," I explain to the others. "She saved me from Rachel's deathloop, so maybe they worked on the project together, maybe Audrey was part of helping her escape and was killed too. I dunno, but they must have a connection and that's why Gates took her."

"Now he has my Simon," says Ophelia, clenching her hands.

"And the letters because the memory of them is preserved in his loop. So, Gates has the solution to stabilizing the restoration theorem."

Heather shudders. "Meaning whoever is paying him knows how to make a phantasmic weapon from the souls Gates has been bottling."

"Yeah, except they *don't* have the solution," says Mitch. "Because no one can get inside the loop, right? Except for you two." He motions to Sam and me.

Sam blinks slowly. He looks shocked, lost and very afraid. Can't say I blame him. Suddenly, he turns and strides away.

I catch up with him at the steps, grabbing his hand. It's ice cold from the rain, but I hold on. He swings around to meet me, his eyes red rimmed and glistening.

"This is so fucked up." He shakes his head. "I'm sorry I brought you into all this."

"You kinda didn't."

"I rather did."

"You didn't push me into Rachel Tussle's deathloop in Normandy and you actually pulled me out of Simon's loop so, no, you didn't. And I probably never even said thanks for that, so, thanks, yeah?"

His lips tug into a half-smile. I want to kiss him so badly it burns somewhere inside. But this isn't the moment, right? Like, maybe when all this is over we can talk and—

He leans down, pausing too close to my face to seem casual. There's a question in his eyes. Wait? Is he thinking … no, no because a dangerous occultist is after us and we might die and, wow, it's hard to breathe. I'm scared to move in case I break the moment. Is this a moment?

"Sam, can I ki—"

A breath, barely, and his lips are on mine. He's kissing me, and a second later I'm kissing him back. This is *actually happening*. I can't feel the rain anymore. There's just him pulled close, my thumb along his jawline, his hand on the back of my neck, fingers in my hair. He's shaking. I'm shaking. There is an orchestra playing somewhere in my heart, and fireworks, and a compilation TikTok of cute couple moments, none of which have happened yet, but this kiss feels like a promise.

He pulls away, stretching the space between us.

"Where are you going?" I ask, lips still tingling.

We should talk about this, because I'd really like to do that again.

"There's something I've got to do." He takes another step. "Tell Mitch I'm going to borrow Leonie's bike." One more step. Our fingers break apart. "I'll call you later. Please, stay safe."

He grabs Leonie's bike from where he leant it against the wall and pedals off.

"Sam!" I hurry up the steps after him. "They'll be coming for us both, you pillock."

I follow him until I reach the end of the bridge. He's gone. Rain stings my face, but I don't turn away, not yet. What the hell is going on with him?

He kissed me. He *kissed* me.

And then he ran away.

Did I bugger this up?

"You would do well to mind yourself more keenly, seer."

I pivot so fast I catch myself on the sidewall of the bridge. Earl Henry Percy – trussed up in his usual blue velvet – floats closer. His smile is nasty. I search for an escape, but there's nowhere to go except into the water where the river ghosts would straight up drown me. Maybe that's his plan.

"If the Emperor knew you had breached the accord and entered the Minster he would enact his claim upon you, and mayhap your friend also."

My alarm mixes with something sharper. If any of them

ever tries to touch Sam I'll tear them apart. "He's not a seer, so let him alone."

Percy raises his hand and I brace myself. "Make not a mockery of me, boy!" Instead of striking me, he turns his palm out in a gesture of reassurance. "Your attempts at deceit are insulting. However, I've not come to make claims this e'en. I offer a warning. Your ignorance, once amusing, grows troublesome. I thought you wouldst have the truth from your doctor friend by now."

He comes closer. Taking a chance on the river is looking more and more appealing. I'm petrified of him, but I'm also soaked through, freezing and exhausted. He's about two seconds away from me just telling him to sod off, damn the consequences.

Keep him talking, buy time until Heather can fend him off. He's just trying to stir things up.

"What truth?" I ask.

Percy's smile is thin. "She hath knowledge of the creation of your kind."

"Of seers? Nay-fuckin'-way, mate," I scoff. "She'd tell me."

A distant shout tears through the sound of the wind and the traffic. Heather has spotted Percy. I've just got to hold out a few more seconds.

"Your unsubtle loathing of earthbound souls is a poison between you and, as Doctor Noble hath more than a hand in your present condition, I doubt she will share her knowledge freely."

"How does Heather have a hand in my present condition?" I ask.

"She made you the way you are." Percy's voice is so soft I can barely hear him over the wind. "A seer of souls."

I've always known Heather has secrets. Like how she didn't tell me she was tethered to York until I was leaving for France. But this? Seeing ghosts, having to lie to my family every day, getting attacked – is it all because of her?

"Bollocks," I say. Because she's one of my best friends and she's never, not once, done something to hurt me. Percy's just muck stirring for kicks.

Lifting off the pavement, he hovers a metre in the air, looking down at me with disdain and pity just as Heather appears between us. "Ask her yourself."

29

SECRETS FOR KEEPS

I'm really sorry." The guilt in Heather's voice throws my world off its axis. Everything feels tight and very sharp. I'm still in my wet clothes. I need to change into something warm, but everything is too much.

Heather is standing by my bedroom window, hands clasped in front of her. The walk home was awkward. She urged me to talk about my feelings or whatever. I ignored her until she lapsed into silence, wanting space to think but then not really knowing how to process what Percy revealed, or Heather's pained admission that it's true. If Villiers were here he'd distract us both with stories about the Stuart court or something, but he went with Mitch to update Leonie on what we've learned, and to watch over them.

Now we're back home, Heather won't leave me be. I can't look at her as I ask, "Was it an accident?"

Her answer is slow to come. "Making you a seer is the most deliberate choice I've ever made."

"But, *why*? You hardly knew me; I was just some kid—"

"Because I killed you!" A sob escapes her. I wait, trying not to cry. Slowly, she starts to talk. "A&E was packed, we were understaffed and I was running on four hours sleep. It's not an excuse, I just … I thought you had flu. I told your parents they were overreacting and I sent you home. By the time your nan brought you back in presenting severe meningococcal septicaemia, well … the infection was too established to respond to treatment. I wasn't even allowed to try and save you myself; they sent me home, and then in the car park—" She draws her arms around herself. "This isn't about that, I just … you died because I made the wrong diagnosis."

"She hath more than a hand in your present condition."

Numb horror bleeds into anger, into sadness. It hurts too much. "Why didn't you tell me?"

"I thought you'd hate me and you're all I have. It was a deliberate choice to bring you back, yes, but how it happened took me a long time to process and I didn't want to complicate things by explaining it badly. I still can't fully explain it, and you have so much to deal with already. After Normandy, every time I tried to bring it up you changed the subject."

"You still should have told me."

"How? When you don't want to talk about something you just shut the conversation down. You'd stopped talking to your living friends and your parents, and if you knew the truth I was afraid you'd push me out too."

"Yeah, because you lied to me for *years*, Heather."

I flinch when Ollie steps through the wall. He grimaces when he sees my face. "Sorry, I thought it was all right for us to ghost in now – Jesus, who died?" When no one speaks his eyes go wide. "Seriously, who died?"

"Me," I say, voice sore.

"Oh." And from the look he gives me I know he's always known, and he never said anything either. Not even after the ghosts of Clifford's Tower chased me, howling demands. Not on the nights he had to shake me awake because I was screaming in my sleep, or when I told him lying to my family was destroying me.

He knew Heather did this to me and he didn't say shite.

Ollie winces. "Charlie—"

"Save it." Spinning my wheelchair, I start taking down the Hellboy comic page by page.

Heather steps closer. "I'm sorry this happened to you. I'm sorry you didn't have a choice in any of this. I'm sorry I didn't tell you the truth sooner."

I'm silent because I can't express what I'm feeling. It's too much.

She killed me. It was her mistake.

"Charlie, please say something."

"I need you to go."

A breath. "I understand."

"I'll watch out for him," Ollie promises her.

I shake my head. "You too."

He looks up, confused. "But—"

"Seriously. I need you both to piss off. Right now." The words come out as a harsh hiss, harsher than I mean, but I don't take them back.

Ollie's eyes flash with hurt. I wait for Heather to argue. Instead, they both look at me for another long moment, and then Heather vanishes. Ollie is only a heartbeat behind.

For the first time in years I'm completely alone.

It's getting late and there's still no sign of Dante. I want to bury my face in his fur and curl up in bed. I could sleep for a week, but Rachel and Simon's memories are swimming about in my thoughts and I feel scraped raw. There's only so much I can handle and I know I'm right at the edge.

Even though the house is full of my family, it feels empty. I can't stop thinking about Heather's face and the look in Ollie's eyes when I told them to go.

Even if I wanted to find them now, I couldn't, not this late. I've no idea where they'd go anyway.

I'm worrying about Sam too – that kiss was … *wow*. His heart was going ten thousand miles an hour against mine. He's safe, right? Rich people have lots of locks and alarms keeping them and their homes and stuff secure. I doubt Gates will be able to break in easily.

I message Sam and he replies straight away:

Still alive.

Which isn't the same as being all right, or fine or OK, but yeah, he's still with me. I want to ask why he ran off, but it feels like a daft question. We're probable targets for a murderer who'll try and force us into a deathloop to question a spirit consumed by grief and regret. He's got the jitters.

Or, what if he's realized this thing between us is stupid and probably doomed and that I'm a disaster?

That kiss though. *That kiss*.

I wish he was here right now, but I just have to trust him on this.

Avoiding sleep, I make myself a sandwich and clean the kitchen. Mum comes out, bleary eyed, and tells me to stop fussing and get to bed. Instead I do some crunches, counting the reps in my head so I can't think about anything else, especially not Heather and Ollie. Afterwards, I take a long, hot shower.

Stepping back into my room feels both familiar and strange, like the space doesn't belong to me anymore. I want life back to normal. Not *normal* normal. My normal. Revising for school with Ollie, the twins sticking glitter gems on to my prostheses, walking Dante with Heather.

I'd give anything for that right now.

I slump into bed.

The quiet rushes in. There's a prickly static in my ears and everything feels broken. I'm crying, coughing and shaking into my pillow, and the tears just keep coming, rolling down my nose in hot drops.

If I fall asleep I don't dream.

30

KILL HIM KINDLY

The house smells like burnt toast. My sisters are thundering up and down the hallway and I can hear the deep rumble of Dad's voice. It must be later than I thought. After the nightshift he isn't normally awake before ten unless something's got him up.

I wonder why Ollie's not in his hammock. Then I remember and I want to cry again. Everything about yesterday was too much – Rachel's letters, Simon's missing deathloop, the resurrection theorem, Heather's confession.

I feel bruised inside, so I just lie there for a while staring at nothing, trying to feel nothing. Whoever said boys shouldn't cry can fuck right off. I need to, so I do, and afterwards I feel like maybe I can move again. I sit up.

Yeah, Heather should have told me the truth earlier. But she's right, I didn't make it easy and I don't face things head on. Feelings are too big sometimes. They don't fit inside me and I don't know how to talk about them. She didn't just make me a seer, she saved my life. I can't hate her for that. Whatever she's done or not done, whatever my life is or isn't now, I'm lucky to be here.

I am such a dick.

I pick up my phone, but there's no message from Leonie telling me that Heather and Ollie are at hers, heartbroken and angry, and how I'd better get my act together. Instead, there's a message from Sam. I go to open it, then hesitate.

What if he regrets kissing me? Maybe it's all too much and he doesn't want to see me again. If he wants out then I'm on my own.

Audrey and Heather would both tell me to stop being such a pessimist. Maybe Sam's messaging to say he's well into me and that no matter what happens it'll be me and him against the world.

Hope lifting, I open it.

Miri will probably call. Tell her I'm going to make it all OK. If I survive I want to take you on a proper date. Please don't hate me Xx

I read it again, the elation of hearing from him fading. "*If I survive.*" What the hell does that mean? I call Sam but it goes straight to voicemail. I hang up and try again. No luck.

What if Gates got to him? What if he's in trouble?

My phone flashes. It's Miri. I answer, but before I can speak she asks, "Is Sam with you?"

"I haven't seen him since last night but he messaged me, said you would call."

I can almost sense Miri frowning. "What else did he say?"

"Something about how he's going to make it all OK, whatever 'it' is."

A sharp explosion of words in a language I don't understand.

"What? What's he going on about?" I ask. "You find who sent that email?"

"I need to speak to Sam first."

"Why?"

Silence.

"Miri?"

"I'm sure there's an explanation."

"MIRI!"

Another pause. My pulse quickens with every second.

"I don't have time for this," I say, about to hang up. "He's obviously in trouble—"

"It's not a person," she says. "The client that hired Gates, and tried to hire Rawley is a company."

I swear that if she draws this out any longer I'm going to scream.

Finally, she tells me.

And everything falls apart.

"Charlie? You there?"

I am and I'm not. There's me way down there, fist clenched at my side like I've been stabbed. And then there's me up here watching it all from someplace far off, not feeling much at all except light-headed and twisted up inside.

S & H Systems

Saunders & Harrow

I look at the long white scars on my forearms and think of the curly haired man who put them there when I fell into Rachel's deathloop in Saint-Lô. I didn't give him Sam's face in my nightmares because Sam was on my mind, but because they look so alike. I've *seen* both men's faces before, in a photo, not just in my nightmares – *August with Henry S before deployment, 1943*.

Mr Harrow said his grandfather worked on weapons development. It was them all along, Saunders and Harrow, trapping souls to use in Rachel's experiments, forcing her to solve the restoration theorem, chasing her, torturing her.

Mr Harrow's special project, the one he had a recent breakthrough for – he's trying to replicate Rachel's theorem and finish his grandfather's work. *"It won't be long until I can start tests on the prototype"* – I bet that breakthrough was finding Simon Tussle's deathloop.

The strange blue sheen in Mr Harrow's eyes is the same as the blue tinge of the cryptolenses. Has he got magical contact lenses or something? God, we were cooking up the paint to ward the city right in his own kitchen and he could see Villiers *the whole time*.

"S & H systems is an Advanced Technological Solutions

company that mostly works with the military and private security contractors," says Miri, forcing me to focus on her voice again. "But they're struggling, lost a big military contract three years ago and almost went under."

I bet a phantasmic weapon that takes angry and powerful ghosts off the battlefield and merges them into a super-powered poltergeist capable of extreme destruction would be enough to secure a new contract. Mr Harrow told me himself how important his family business is to him.

Was Sam in on this from the beginning?

My eyes sting with angry tears. Google, my arse, this occult stuff probably runs in the family. No wonder Audrey was afraid of him. He looks so much like his great-grandfather she must have recognized him from when she was helping Rachel escape him and Saunders in Saint-Lô. That's why she tried to stop us meeting. She knew who was behind this all along.

Maybe Sam only befriended me to get me to go into Simon's deathloop and find the theorem, but that doesn't add up. Although he claims he's never been inside one, there's nothing I can do that he can't do better. So, maybe he got close to me because he needed to learn how to survive a deathloop.

I'm pissed more than anything. Yeah, it's not like I'm in love with the lad, that's daft, we've only known each other a few weeks. And last night, that kiss, his fingers in my hair, it doesn't mean we're…

It doesn't mean I…

Shite.

If Sam went back to his dad last night, then he could have already gone into Simon Tussle's deathloop, read the letters before they were burnt, and come out with the formula to stabilize the theorem.

Or he could be dead.

I swipe at the sting in my eyes. Sam's tough, clever and much better at this seeing-the-dead-thing than me. He'll make it.

But it's not that simple, right? I hardly got more than a glance at the letters before they burnt, not enough time to memorize them. Sam's memory is well good, but Ollie once told me a true photographic memory is a myth. No one is *that* good. Sam will have to go into the deathloop more than once.

"Charlie, are you listening?" asks Miri. "We're talking about military contracts here. That's serious money."

"Yeah," I lie. I'd forgotten I still have my phone pressed to my ear.

I should feel angrier. I should hate Sam for using me, and I do. But the thought of him going into Tussle's loop again and again in search of answers, dragged out after the rope snaps around his throat, only to have to go back in, kills me.

Then it clicks.

He'll go into that loop so that I don't have to.

Sam Harrow, you absolute pillock.

"What are you going to do?" asks Miri.

I hesitate. Can I trust her?

"Charlie, I'm scared for my friend and I'm an eight hour flight away."

All the ghosts taken by Gates were either old and strong or fresh and angry. If Sam does find the final solution to stabilize Rachel's restoration theorem, either from the letters in the loop or directly from Tussle's ghost, then Mr Harrow is going to turn them into something monstrous.

The theorem calculates for sixteen souls, which means Gates will be going hunting again soon.

I need to find Heather and Ollie, then check in with Mitch and Leonie. If we can ward certain streets then we might be able to focus Mr Harrow's target areas and set a trap for him and Gates. And if Sam is with them…

"I'll try and help him," I promise Miri.

And I mean it.

Raised voices bounce down the hall. My Dad is arguing with someone in the kitchen. I hear my name. The bedroom door clatters open. Poppy, Lorna and our cousin Danielle tumble inside, still in their pyjamas.

"You're in trouble," says Lorna.

Poppy is trembling. "There's a policeman here!"

"Did you kill someone?" asks Danielle.

31

CHASING SHADOWS

My compression socks make a shushing sound on the hallway carpet as I shuffle along the wall and glance around the kitchen door frame. Mum's back is to me, her shoulders hunched up and shaking.

"—witness placed a teenager matching Charlie's description in the area shortly before the body was discovered. Have you noticed any changes in his behaviour? Has he been unusually withdrawn lately?"

I can't get eyes on the speaker, but I know that voice. Last time I heard it, he was sitting on a bar stool in The Fleece warning me off looking for the missing ghosts. I was right, Crew-Cut, the bloke with the creepy hand-holding-a-torch tattoo *is* Caleb Gates. Why else would he be here?

Then it hits me. The Shadow Man is in my home with my family.

"I need to speak to your son," he says.

"Then I'll bring him down the station later." Dad is around the corner so I can't see him, but his tone is hard.

Gates and Harrow have Sam, so why are they still coming after me? I picture Rawley's head caved in — murdered because he stood in their way.

They're tying up loose ends, getting rid of witnesses.

I slip back into my bedroom, struggling to think.

"Is he going to take you away?" asks Lorna. I motion for her to hush, sliding on my socks and liners and settling into my prostheses. She's still glowering at me, waiting for me to answer her, so I nod.

My folks don't know I'm up yet, which buys me a couple of minutes, but they'll be knocking before long.

Poppy chucks me some trackies. I pull them on, then dig out a fresh tee and trackie top, stuff a fiver in my pocket alongside my phone, and put on my puffer and my second favourite cap.

"He's scary." Poppy's little face is serious. "I don't want you to go with him."

"I'm not going to, Pops, I promise. I don't reckon he's real police." I kneel down to hug her. She seems so small all of a sudden, just a scrap of a kid. "I need to get him away from here so everyone is safe, all right? It's me he wants."

"Why?" asks Lorna.

"Because you killed someone?" says Danielle.

"Course not," I say. She looks genuinely disappointed.

Poppy's eyes widen. "Is this because of the invisible people."

Does she mean…?

"They're not real!" says Danielle. "Jamie says you're just messing with us."

"They are real," protests Lorna.

"Can you … see people around me?" I half whisper.

"No, but sometimes we can feel them there."

My sisters stand there like they haven't just changed everything I thought I knew about being a seer. I want to ask how long they've known, what they even know and what they mean by "feel", but now is not the time.

"I've got to run."

Poppy is tearful. "You can't run very fast, Charlie."

"Yeah, Pops, I know—"

"You have a plan, right?" Danielle folds her arms.

"Kind of, yeah."

I'll figure something out.

The girls huddle together, a quick conference, then fan out again, looking at me with big, innocent eyes.

Lorna's smile twists with mischief. "We'll distract him. You slash his tyres."

Fine rain fizzes the air as I drop out my window and sneak around the side of our bungalow, ducking behind Dad's taxi. Nan's sharp awl – a tapered metal spike as long as my hand – is clutched in my palm.

I'm still reeling at how devious my little sisters are. I'd

forgotten Nan was into leatherworking when I was a kid. And as far as party tricks go, Danielle's ability to chuck up on demand is actually dead impressive. She got it all over her brother too, quite the ruckus.

The Shadow Man's car – not an official police vehicle – is sat on the road blocking Dad's taxi into our drive. Pressing the tip of the awl to the back wheel, I shove my weight into the handle. It resists, and then slides in with a soft pop. I wiggle it about, creaking the rubber until I hear a sharp hiss of air.

"That'll take hours to deflate, that will."

I pivot too fast, ending up on my arse. Mr Broomwood towers over me. "I'd do his front tyre too, just in case." When I gawp at him he raises his brows. "Hurry up, lad, before he comes out."

I do as I'm told.

Moments later I hurry down our road. Broomwood follows, yammering all the rumours he's heard about me this week – that I'm trying to save York's ghosts, that *I'm* the Shadow Man, or in league with soul catchers, or working for the Mouldy Oldies.

I'd hoped Heather and Ollie would be about somewhere, but of course they're not here, else they'd have warned me about Gates.

There's nowhere to duck under cover, just rows of wide-open lawns and daffodils and snowdrops in pots along the boundaries. Mrs Ginty watches me from beside her car, Tesco bags clutched in either hand, eager for fresh gossip.

My front door opens. I glance back. Dad is in the doorway,

arguing with Gates.

The eager curiosity in Mrs Ginty's eyes shifts to wariness. She gives a little squeak of alarm and disappears into her car. Half sliding over her bonnet I yank open the passenger door and clamber inside.

"What are you—?" she gasps.

Gates is past Dad and striding this way. Dad hurries after him, hollering something down the road.

"Drive!" I gasp. "Go!"

"Get out!" orders Mrs Ginty.

"Stubborn, that one."

I spin to find Mr Broomwood in the back seat.

"When Norman wanted to chop down his apple tree she made a right fuss over the boundaries—"

Blocking Broomwood out, I turn back to Mrs Ginty. She flinches. I'm scaring her and I'm sorry for it. "I'm not going to hurt you. Please just drive."

Gates is getting closer. He's scarier than I remember from the bar. Behind him is Silvereyes, his intense gaze fixed on me like I'm some kind of prize.

Fuck.

Mrs Ginty grapples for her door, popping the latch. I reach over and pull the door shut. Her elbow connects with my chest and I fall back.

"Mr Broomwood is in the back seat bitching on about Norman's apple tree," I say.

That makes her pause. She glances nervously into the back.

"He's a ghost, and that bloke there isn't a real rozzer. He's after me, right. He's not a good person, like, he's been stealing ghosts from York because my sort-of-boyfriend's dad is trying to rebuild a Second World War theorem that turns phantasmic energy into a super poltergeist thing, and I'm sorry to bring you into this but you need to drive, like, *right now* because he killed this other bloke who was in his way. *For real!* My mates and me found the body and I think he's going to kill me too."

Mrs Ginty is staring at me like I've lost all good sense.

Arms reach through the side of the car and pull me back against the passenger window. Red nails scrape against my puffer. I try to haul myself away, but Silvereyes is strong. With a battle cry, Broomwood lobs himself through the car frame, tackling him to the pavement. As they fall, sharp nails catch my skin, leaving my cheek stinging.

"Your ... your face," gasps Mrs Ginty.

"Get goin', you old bat!" Broomwood shouts, dragging himself through the door and into the back seat again.

"Please drive," I repeat.

Maybe it's the desperation in my voice, the impossible scratch to my cheek, or the gleam of anger in Gates's eyes as he reaches the car and shouts my name, but Mrs Ginty turns the ignition and jams her foot on the accelerator, speeding off her driveway in a squeal of tires. I look out the rear window to see Gates holding Silvereyes back, a hand on his shoulder, stopping him from giving chase.

Caleb Gates is a seer.

I don't know what to think of that so I lean back in the seat, shaking with relief.

"They'll have her licence plate," warns Broomwood.

Right, of course they will. That means I can't get dropped off at Leonie's. I ask Mrs Ginty to head into town instead, interrupting the flow of questions I don't have time to answer right now. She takes a sudden left without indicating and I'm slammed to the side of the car.

No one is wearing seat belts. We should be wearing seat belts. Why am I thinking about seat belts? Broomwood doesn't even need one.

"I always knew there was something after death," Mrs Ginty says, glancing at my cheek again as if to reassure herself she didn't imagine it.

Ignoring her, I take out my phone. Seven missed calls from Mitch. I ring him back.

"Charlie, thank God – I'm at the hospital. The Shadow Man was at Leonie's last night."

"What? Is she all right?"

"No, concussion, a busted lip and nose, bruises. Villiers warned her just in time, but Gates used his shadow thing, darkness everywhere and he…" Mitch's breathing is short and sharp. "He threw Leonie against a wall when she tried to stop him destroying the paint. It's gone, Rawley's book too and all our notes and maps—"

"What about Villiers?"

"He's here. Leonie's dad and brothers are in a state, they think the shadows were some kind of smoke bomb. The police are asking questions and I don't know what to tell them. I mean, I know Miri says Gates isn't really on the force, but what if they're wrong, what if the police are in on it?"

When your prey goes to ground, don't leave them any ground to go to. I don't remember where the line is from, some film about cowboys in space that Ollie made me watch, but it makes sense.

"Stay with Leonie. Keep the cryptolenses hidden until we know who, if anyone, we can trust. Gates just came after me."

Mitch swears. "You hurt?"

"I'm all right."

"What about Sam?"

It's my turn to go quiet. "Mr Harrow is the client." I swallow. "We can't trust Sam right now."

"Nah, I mean … really?" Silence as Mitch thinks it through. "Mate, that's so shit, I know you two—"

"Yeah." I blink rapidly.

"What you gonna do?"

I don't know. Because I don't have a plan anymore. First, I've got to find Heather and Ollie. I can't do this without them.

"Wait, Leonie wants a word. Hold on."

There's a scuffling sound of fabric against the microphone, then, "Charlie?" Her voice is strained, as if it's painful to talk.

"Leonie, I'm so sorry—"

"He took them."

"What?"

She coughs, a clotted, hacking sound. "I never even saw his face … too dark but he said … he told me … to tell you … Heather and Ollie, he took them."

I can't even hear what I'm yelling. Everything is tight panic and despair. The car swerves. Mrs Ginty begs me to calm down. I'm scaring her, and that isn't all right. I ask her to stop. She does. I spill into traffic, hitting the tarmac, shouting an apology as I scramble off the road.

We're at Lendal Tower. I take the iron steps down to the river walk, rough brick snagging my jacket as the sloshing echoes sound against the bridge. It's dirty down here and stinks of piss and the cloying tang of weed, but I'm out of sight, at least from the living.

Leonie is in hospital. Heather is gone. Ollie is gone. It's all my fucking fault. I never got to tell Heather that I forgive her for everything, because I do, *of course I do*. I'll side with her and Ollie over anything or anyone because they're family.

Gates wanted me to know he has them, which means he needs something from me. He was probably over at mine to make his offer – me for them. Well, they can have me. I'll go over to Sam's place right now and hand myself over.

Broomwood offers me his arm. "Bad idea."

"You don't know what I'm thinking." I twist away and pain shoots through my ribs from where I landed on the road. I need Heather to take a look at me. I need Ollie to crack a joke.

"You're planning to hand yourself over for your mates, fair swap. Well, let me tell you, lad, I've seen enough CSI reruns to know that ain't how it works. You hand yourself over, what's going to stop him keeping them too, eh?"

He's right. I slump against the wall.

I need an actual plan, but I can't stop shaking.

My friends have been bottled, which means they're in an artificial loop, forced to repeat their deaths over and over, a hell no one should have to experience.

I'm alone.

I must have said that out loud because Mr Broomwood snorts and says, "What am I, a bloody mirage?"

Sam said we came back changed for a reason.

He said a gift like ours is meant to be used.

He said a lot of stuff, and I reckon that most of it was bollocks. But he wasn't wrong about that.

"Mr Broomwood, that night Heather couldn't get the Emperor to call a moot, you said it's because he tried to strike a deal and she wouldn't sell."

"Aye."

"What did he want to buy?"

Broomwood tilts his head. "I think we both know the answer to that one, eh, lad."

Yeah. We do.

I could hand myself over to Gates, but Broomwood's right, I don't like my odds. I need allies, someone stronger and more ruthless than the soul catchers, someone who is a real danger to Gates. Like me, he's a seer. And that makes him vulnerable.

It's not like I've got big plans for my life. I've not got an apprenticeship in a fancy restaurant like Mitch. Or the marks to reach a top university one day like Leonie. I'm not much good at anything, so I'll get good at being a whipping boy for the dead if it makes things right.

When I head up the road towards the Minster, Broomwood scampers after me as far as the top of the slope. "Oi, Charlie! Now where you going?"

I spin around and stick my hands in my pockets. "To sell my soul."

32

SACRIFICE

The ghost in the powdered wig is still lying on the Minster floor, humming a jaunty tune. I lean over him, blocking his view of the crossing tower ceiling. He blinks and sits up.

I take a step back. "Where's the Emperor?"

Powdered-wig stares at me, mouth falling open.

"Kind of in a hurry here, mate," I say, my body singing with adrenaline.

A group of nuns stop and stare. The problem with nuns is they're kind of timeless and I've no idea if this lot are dead or alive until one of them says, "The Old Souls have gathered in the Chapter House at the behest of Earl Percy."

Rubbing sweating palms on my trackies, I mutter my thanks and hurry past the giant astronomical clock to the broad L-shaped antechamber. I enter it like I'm walking to my own funeral.

I hear the Mouldy Oldies before I see them. And I *feel* them before I hear them, which is new. Somehow, the air is thicker and prickling with static. Every nerve in my body is on alert. I don't realize I'm clenching my hands until my nails bite into my palm.

Heather.

Ollie.

Audrey.

Mad Alice.

Ragged Peter.

Little Beth.

Millie.

Reid the Piper.

Peter Rawley.

Simon Tussle.

A mantra of the taken I'm here to save.

And Sam.

Sam too.

From the outside, the Chapter House is a gigantic circular jewel box with a witch hat for a roof. Inside it's all pale fancy stonework supporting vast stained-glass windows that join high above my head in a star of vaulted stone. Gathered below are the seven Old Souls of York. As I enter, Earl Percy swivels, followed by the others, their expressions twisting to shock, anger and one to quiet triumph.

They're on me in a swell of silk and gristle-hands, reaching through my clothes to grasp at my skin. My first instinct is to bite and scratch back as fingers rake across my scalp and pinch my flesh. I'm dragged, lifted up and spun like a puppet.

Exhausted, I stop struggling. The ghosts have me held fast, well off the ground, air breezing below us. Anyone coming in now for a peek at the famed Chapter House ceiling will get the shock of their lives.

"He hath come alone," says Inge of Jorvik.

Sir Danville's laugh is nasty. "What displeasure he shall face when Mistress Noble discovers his duplicity."

The Emperor leans in. He's an imposing man: round faced with a beard and tightly curled hair. "Why hast thou broken the accord?"

"I-I've come to make a deal." Heart thundering, I tell them about Simon and Rachel and the restoration theorem. I explain what I know about Caleb Gates and Mr Harrow. I'm as honest as I can be without mentioning Sam. When I'm done, the Mouldy Oldies exchange glances heavy with judgement.

The Emperor glowers at Percy. "It seems you make little advancement in your task when a mere boy is privy to such a conspiracy."

The Earl sniffs. "I am astonished of these falsehoods, Your Imperial Majesty."

"This simpleton hath no accomplishment in falsehood," says Sir Danville, gesturing to me.

I mean, technically he's speaking in my defence but he doesn't have to be such a dick about it.

King Aelle looks worried. "We ought to take heed and protect ourselves against this fiend, flee this very hour."

Hot anger pulses through me. "So that's it then? You run scared while Gates snaps up whoever he likes? If I can get off my arse and do something about this, then so can you lot."

Muttering flutters through the room. The Emperor gestures, a simple flick of his fingers, and they release me. I drop, letting out a sharp cry as I crumple on to the hard tiles. I suck my breath as the worst of the pain passes, and then glower up at the ghosts surrounding me.

"Look, Gates has Heather and Ollie." I try not to choke on my words. "I can't beat him alone. I need your help. He's a seer like me so you can hurt him, right?"

"If we assist you in this matter, what wouldst thou offer in return?" asks the Emperor.

"I'll be yours for ten years. I'll work for you, carry messages to the living, be your hands and voice in the world, whatever you want."

There's another flurry of muttering through the group and then I realize it's not disapproval, but laughter. They're *laughing* at me.

"What?" I struggle to my feet. My face is flaming. "That's what you want, right? A servant?"

King Aelle starts cackling, a proper belly laugh.

"Twenty years, then," I throw at them.

Inge swoops down to ground level. "His Imperial Majesty desires not your service seer, but your flesh."

Oh, shit.

The Mouldy Oldies are Hungry Ones. That or Septimus Severus wants to date me, and honestly, I don't know which prospect is more horrific.

"Eating me won't bring you back to life," I say. "That's bollocks, and you know it."

The Emperor smiles cruelly. "I shall not consume your flesh, but wear it. Other living men art like vapours to us, we pass through them. But you, who have known death and been returned at the sake of another, offer purchase. Damaged as you are, you can eat, breathe, fuck, fight. All that shall be mine to enjoy."

It's not that I didn't hear what he was saying: he's going to try and wear me like a Charlie suit. And if I could process anything past what I think *"returned at the sake of another"* means I'd be freaking out more, because there's no way possession is possible without me ending up looking like a victim of Freddie Krueger. But all I have in my head is the sound of Heather's voice breaking...

"The most deliberate choice I have ever made."

It hits me at once, a blow so painful I clutch my stomach. We were in surgery at the same time, our operating rooms side by side, doctors fighting for both our lives. Heather's colleagues weren't too late to save her. She should have come back. I was the one past hope. She swapped places with me because she blames herself for my death. Heather gave up her life for mine.

Oh my God. Sam. The lake. His friend Luci.

Two people die in the same time and place. One sacrifices their life for the other. The saved soul wakes up changed – a seer.

Sir Danville blocks my escape.

"It will be a pretty experiment and an improvement on the last." Lady Peckitt clasps her hands.

The fear of what they're about to do to me reaches through the fog in my brain. "Y-you've done this before?"

"Not with success," Inge admits. "Failure does make for a mean and messy end."

I urge adrenaline to flood my body and help me fight them off. But there's just paralysis and painful terror.

"Doctor Noble is not present and, as you trespass of your own volition you are, what do they call it?" asks The Emperor, slipping into more modern speech. "Ah, yes" – he lunges at me, grabbing my throat and pulling my face to his – "fair game."

I bellow for help. I don't care who comes, living or dead so long as someone comes. Then the Emperor's palm clasps over my mouth and Sir Danville and Inge take my arms. I thrash uselessly. Sweat prickles down my forehead. The Emperor is going to try to possess me right now, and it isn't going to work because I'm solid flesh and bone to him and this is sodding madness.

Sharp pain in my chest as he claws at me, trying force his way inside my skin. I scream through the hand over my mouth.

"Enough!"

Someone tears the Emperor away. He goes flying, falling through the wall of the Chapter House. Gasps of shock. The pain in my chest recedes to a dull throb. I look over to catch sight of my saviour.

Of the ghosts in York I'd ever expect to stand up for me, Earl Henry Percy isn't top of the list, but I'll take what I can get. He's sneering at the lot of them. Distracted, Sir Danville and Inge release me as the Old Souls turn on one of their own.

I keep low, adjusting my weight on my prostheses, finding grip, ready to run when I've got the best chance at escape. My fingers are splayed on the tiles. I feel like a sprinter before the starting gun.

"YOU DARE!" the Emperor thunders at Percy as he re-emerges through the wall.

Inge lunges, but the Earl darts out of reach of her clawing hands.

"Like you, Septimus, I desire to live again, to touch the world and make my mark," he says. "Force not your hand without first preparing thy vessel. You have suffered centuries of failure, yet you do not think to use the occult theorems of our enemies to further your design."

Something moves under my fingers and a slight tug hooks in my sternum. Ash on the air, and a sharper scent. Salt.

"Heresy and falsehood. The dead cannot command such vile arts," says the Emperor.

"Mayhap." Percy's smile is sinister. "But unlike you, my pride does not prevent me befriending those who can."

Patterns flare along the floor, criss-crossing lines encircling the large room to form a vast ghost trap. It snaps into place, wrenching the dead away from each other as if they are iron filings moved by a magnet. It settles them at even points around the centre where I'm still crouched. The Mouldy Oldies slash at the air, bellowing with rage, but the magic keeps them in check.

Percy isn't fighting. He's grinning like he's won the lottery. "I will be the first soul to be restored to flesh. My allies have the restoration theorem, all they need is additional fuel and you, my old friends, will serve that purpose well."

Dark smoke coils across the floor as the Shadow Man strides into the Chapter House.

It isn't who I was expecting, in fact, it takes me a moment to recognize the bull-necked bloke from the Fleece, the one who ran off the student trying to drum up customers for a ghost tour. For a moment I'm befuddled – half hopeful, half terrified. Why is he here?

And then I see what he's wearing. His dark coat is open to reveal a double bandolier full of bottle traps. His hands are gloved.

"All seven as requested, Mr Gates," says Earl Percy. "The additional seer I'll throw in for free."

Mr Gates?

I got it wrong. Bull-Neck is Caleb "Shadow Man" Gates. Then who the hell is Crew-Cut and his silver-eyed ghost? Is he real police after all, or are they both working for the Shadow Man?

Gates fixes on me. "Run if you like, lad. But I'll destroy

your pet ghosties if you do."

I clench my fists and stay put. What can I do? I eye his bandolier, hoping he has Heather and Ollie with him. If he does I might be able to wrestle their bottles free and smash them open. Then he'll be in trouble. Heather would make one hell of a poltergeist. But all the bottles I can see look empty.

Gates releases one from the leather loops of his bandolier and fishes in his pockets for a stick of wax. He's not wearing cryptolenses, so how can he see the dead? Is he another seer like the mysterious rozzer?

Seers are like buses; none around and then three come along at once.

Gates is a fair way into the trap now. The stained light from the windows glances off his face. My hope dies as his eyes flash with a pearlescent sheen. It's the same blue shine to the glass in the cryptolenses and in Mr Harrow's eyes – he's just wearing special contact lenses or something.

Gates sets a bottle at the feet of each Old Soul. When he gets to the Earl, Percy's face falls. "What are you doing? I gathered them here as instructed. They will fuel my restoration." He puffs himself up. "Release me as promised."

At first, I think Gates is replying. The Earl does too because he tries to lean closer, eager for an answer, but Gates is chanting something under his breath. I've no clue what he's doing, but I can feel the results – a dizzy tugging sensation in my chest.

The Mouldy Oldies start to scream, pulling at sleeves and hair as blood flows from their cracking skin. Sinew splits.

Their bones shatter into fragments, the unstoppable magic drawing them down into the bottles at their feet.

The pain has me groaning. Why does it hurt?

My soul. The trap is trying to tear it out of me even though I'm still alive.

I run as fast as I can. The magic lets me go, a privilege of not being dead yet. Earl Percy's wild broken howl bounces down the vestibule after me. The metal gate at the end has been pulled across and locked, a sign put up on the other side. The grille is cold on my hands as I rattle it, fumbling with the lock. I've no time to pick it. Gates is already rounding the corner after me.

My bellow for help is swallowed up by the vastness of the Minster and drowned by the hammering of the restoration works. But the ghosts of York hear me. The man in the powdered wig, two wimpled nuns and the gents with large ruffs come in a rush of hands. Mr Broomwood is with them, "Behind you, lad, he's comin'."

The dead reach through the metal, but they can't hurt the Shadow Man and they can't bring the cavalry. There is no cavalry.

I scramble for my phone. A rough palm covers my face, smothering me with a burst of inky shadow. The phone slips from my fingers and a second later there is a crunch as it is smashed underfoot.

"Stop pissing about," Gates hisses in my ear. He has my arms pinned. I blink hard, but I'm still blind. "I'm a fair man. You cooperate and I'll let your ghosties go. You can come with me and do what needs to be done, or you can fight. But if you fight, I will win. And for the trouble I will kill your family and I will bottle them one by one. It's your choice."

There is nothing left. I give up, give in and let the darkness take me.

33

S & H SYSTEMS

Except I don't pass out, not even for a few minutes of blessed relief. There's a rattling as the gate is unlocked and I stumble forward at Gates's command. He's holding my arms so I don't fall. My chest aches. My eyes burn. Voices.

"No, no, my lad just had a funny turn is all."

Cool damp air on my face. A vehicle door opens – engine oil and grease and a pungent herbal stink that makes me think of Sam, which makes me want to cry. I lie in the back of what I reckon is a van, smothered and sweating, feeling every bump and turn. There's a thrumming in my skull and my chest aches. I cough and the pain flares to a sharp knife-inside stabbing. Cracked rib, maybe. Heather will know.

If I ever see her again.

I blink hard. The ashy shadows are starting to wear off. I reckon I'd be able to see if it wasn't so dark in here. He used zip ties or something on my wrists.

My final exams start tomorrow.

It's a daft thought to have because I have bigger problems right now.

I curse myself. I curse Gates. I curse my stupidity. If I weren't such a coward I'd have had a proper look at him coming up the path to Rawley's and I'd have seen his face and known he was our enemy, not Crew-Cut.

Who is that bloke anyway? If he's not working with Gates and Harrow then what do he and Silvereyes want with me?

I pick apart my memories but no solutions offer themselves up. Nothing to do but sweat and wait, my muscles cramping and heart hammering.

I know where we are as soon as the door slides open: smart townhouse, polished steps and gleaming glass. Gates hauls me out of his van, peering this way and that up a street that doesn't welcome lads like me or crooks like him. People in this postcode like their crime white-collar. Or occult, apparently.

Inside, we pass the dresser in the big entrance hall and Gates pulls me to a rough stop. Picking up the photo of Harrow and Saunders as young men, his nostrils flare as he looks it over, then he smashes it on the wall until he can free it from its broken frame, folding it inside his coat without a word.

We head down a level where a long dining table leads to a

wall of glass, giving a princely view of a small but neat back garden of box trimmed hedges and stepped patios. Gates turns me the other way. There's a glow there, lamplight reflecting off a large golden mirror.

Mr Harrow is sat on a wide armchair like it's a throne. The white lab coat over his suit might as well be a smoking jacket for the way he's lounging, apparently unbothered that a bruised teenager is being hauled towards him.

"Ah, good work." Mr Harrow puts the book he's reading on the coffee table and I see its Sam's notebook, open to a sketch of Simon Tussle's deathloop. If my arms were free I'd lunge for it. What right does he have to go pawing through his son's secrets?

I swallow a hollow laugh. I don't know what I'm on about. Sam probably gave it him. "*Here, Dad, look at the fun I've been having with the locals. No, they've no idea, sad gits.*"

He wouldn't though, would he?

"Do you have them?" Mr Harrow asks Gates.

"All seven."

"Good. Though, you'll have to go out again. I'm short. The old woman and the child were corrupted, a disruption in the secondary coterminous bond. I've remedied it but it destabilized enough to shred what was left of both entities."

Shred.

You'd think he just lost some old paperwork, but those are people he's talking about. Souls.

"I need two more." Mr Harrow glances at me. "Today. The Frith boy will be missed."

"Already done." Gates pats his bandolier. "Took two extra last night to keep this one in line."

Heather and Ollie.

Mr Harrow makes a face. "Strong?"

"Stronger than Rawley and you accepted him. The red-haired lad is a century gone, and the doctor carries enough guilt to fuel the whole set-up on her own."

It seems Mr Harrow trusts Gates's opinion of Heather and Ollie's usefulness because he dips his head. "We'll still need a sixteenth."

NO. I have to stop this. I struggle, kicking up a fuss that can probably be heard all the way to The Shambles, or it would if that big glass window wasn't triple bloody paned. A meaty arm crushes my chest. I'm a big lad, but Gates is bigger and he has me firm. I'm breathing heavily with the effort. My cheeks are wet, nose all snotted up.

"Charlie?"

Sam is at the bottom of the stairs. Seeing him steals my breath and blows it back without oxygen. He can barely hold himself up. His neck is patched with a big piece of gauze. Someone has cut the sleeves off his shirt and his forearms are thickly bandaged. Both of his shadowed eyes are bloodshot and wet.

"Go back upstairs," says Mr Harrow. "You should rest."

"You don't need him." Sam is staring at me with heartbreak and horror. "I said I'd do it."

Mr Harrow strides over to his son. "I'll not let my only child—"

"I survived the first splice."

"You won't survive this."

"I'm stronger than you think."

"Be reasonable. The restoration theorem calls for a siphon—" Mr Harrow tries to usher him back upstairs, but Sam shakes him off.

"It's you or him, kid," says Gates, shaking me. "Got to be a seer."

"Then just stop!" cries Sam. "No legacy is worth this, Dad."

Mr Harrow's fists tighten. "This is *everything*. If we lose the bid the company folds."

"So what? It's just money."

Mr Harrow shakes his head. "You've never had to struggle, Sam."

"Yes, because being me is obviously one big party."

"I've given you everything you've wanted—"

"No, you haven't." Every word from Sam's lips is sharp. "I want you to take a fucking interest, maybe ask how my appointments at the gender clinic are going, ask if I'm doing OK – which I'm not, by the way – but you *don't care*. You'll pay for private treatment, but you won't actually talk to me. You never have time. If you cared you wouldn't steal my journal and lie to me, or threaten my friends to get what you want, or keep me in the dark."

"This is all for you and for your mother. Now, thanks to you, we can save the company. Everything is set up and the calculations are complete. I should have been more forthcoming, but there were hard choices to be made and you've always had a big heart. It wasn't something I wanted you to have on your conscience."

"But this is?" Sam gestures to me. "You think I'll just forget we had to kill my friend to keep mum's pseudo-spiritual yacht parties going? Is he why we came to York? You wanted me to find Charlie. This was always the plan."

"No, he was … unexpected."

Sam looks at me and my world shrinks, tunnelling until there is only him and his expression of pained resolve. "Then pretend we never met."

Mr Harrow shakes his head. "I can't let you do that."

"But you would have," says Sam. "If I'd not tracked down Charlie, you would have had to let me fix each splice."

"I would have found someone else."

Sam's laugh is hollow. "Yes, because seers just grow on trees."

"Mr Harrow—" says Gates.

Sam's dad holds up a hand. "Not now."

"This project is too vital to piss yourself like a coward because your kid has a crush."

Mr Harrow goes dangerously quiet. "That is not how my people speak to me if they wish to remain employed."

"Yeah, about my contract." Gates pulls down, forcing me to lean as he reaches for something low, then he springs up, shifting to my right. "I think it's time I renegotiated my terms."

Metal slides past my face, a crack so loud it sends me

crumpling. My wrists burn as I automatically jerk my hands, trying to cover my ears.

Mr Harrow's jaw splinters in a shower of bone fragments and torn skin.

A high-pitched alarm is screaming in my skull. Mr Harrow stares at Gates, disbelief on what remains of his face, tongue working in the hollow of his throat. Blood splatters from him in fine mist. He falls, crumpling at Sam's feet.

Sam stumbles backwards in horror, tripping into the bottom of the stairs where he sinks to the floor and clutches his stomach with shaking hands.

Look away, look away, I urge silently. But he doesn't. Maybe he can't.

Gates lowers the gun, strapping it back into the hidden holster at his ankle, like he knows he doesn't need it to control us. Or perhaps he just needs both hands for what comes next.

The soul rises out of the body like vapour, sinuous and twisted, joints clicking at unnatural angles. The face forms last, the jaw hanging off, cheek split. Mr Harrow's ghost tries to talk but only a gurgling sound comes out.

Suddenly he's whole again, handsome silver hair, face intact. "Sam," he croaks. His jaw breaks open and he staggers.

I reckon he's remembering himself, trying to understand what happened. If he can't, he'll become a loop. If that happens then Sam's way too close.

I'm on my knees, wrists burning from where I jerked against the cable ties. I try to lever myself up but the floor is slippery.

Gates has a bottle out, identical to the ones he used on the Mouldy Oldies. He spits out an incantation. Mr Harrow's bloodless flesh starts to unpeel, fragments flaking off and disappearing into the bottle in Gates's hands. I can see the shape of his shattered skull, jawbone swinging. Then he's gone, the echo of his moan evaporating until all that's left of his spirit is the painful ringing in my ears.

Sam's staring like his mind has clocked off and gone elsewhere, not crying, not saying anything. Then he moves all at once, clawing at Gates, desperately trying to knock the bottle trap out of his hands.

Gates jerks his fist. A single strike. Bone crunches. Sam goes down, gasping, hands to his nose. More blood. I holler a wordless sound and fight against my restraints. Using a lighter, Gates seals the ghost bottle with red wax, trapping Mr Harrow's soul inside. Pulling a knife from the base of his bandolier, Gates cuts through the zip ties on my wrists, then juts his chin towards Sam.

"Get him up and follow me."

34

HEIR AND SPARE

Gates ushers us into a lift tucked in a niche at the back of the room. Shining chrome doors close like a trap. He puts his back to us. He knows we're no threat. Sam is shaking. I try wiping the blood from his cheeks and chin but it just smears.

If I can get one of the ghost bottles off Gates's bandolier and release a poltergeist then we might stand a chance of escape.

The problem is, I'd have to let Sam go and I don't reckon he can hold himself up right now.

Also, Gates could spin and crush my skull against the wall in a heartbeat.

Oh, and releasing an angry poltergeist in a confined space would probably kill us too.

I stare at my blurred reflection in the shining walls, trying to calm my heart, trying to think things through. All I can focus on is the rattling sound of Sam's breathing and the fact that his dad was just murdered in front of him. He's got an arm around my waist, a bunch of my top clenched in his fist. I grip him tighter.

The lift settles. The doors glide open to a lab – clean tile walls, shining steel and a long whiteboard with equations and magical symbols scrawled across it. There are cupboards down either side, and a table covered in racks of empty bottles so dense I can't see through the layers of glass to the other side. There must be enough bottles here to trap half the souls in York.

The lift doors whir shut behind us with a heavy kind of finality.

It's cold, our breath misting. Sweat pricks on my skin as it dries. But the cold is more than that, it's in my bones, waves of ache that grind me down. This is the kind of cold that only comes from being in a deathloop. There is a cracking electric hum in the air. I can taste it on my tongue, sour and brittle.

Sam leans into me. "Charlie, I didn't know. I promise, not until the river. When I confronted him, my father swore he'd leave you alone if I helped—"

Turning, Gates presses a finger to his lips. "Boys who speak when they shouldn't get their boyfriends shot."

Sam shuts up fast.

We should have fought rather than let the Shadow Man march us down here, but Mr Harrow's body is still warm upstairs and Gates has that gun. He clicks his tongue, rubbing thumb and forefinger together, and we follow him like good dogs.

As we round the racks I glance about the lab, searching for an advantage. It's a deep, boxy room with a circular hollow at its centre. Four steps down there is a broad flat area surrounded by a frame of copper arcs braced with what look like spheres of black tourmaline. The whole thing is huge, the openings between each section wide enough to walk through. At the base, just outside of the cage, is a ring of catcher marks. Shards of broken mirror litter the floor inside the ring. Welded to the frame, equally spaced halfway down the arcs, are copper cups, the perfect fit for a ghost bottle. A collection of wires dangle from the core of each arc, dropping into the central space where something is moving.

Simon Tussle's deathloop twitches and shakes inside the structure, his body suspended by an invisible rope. The electric sound pops and crackles. Simon's body vanishes, replaced by a woman in a filthy dress, arms behind her back.

Blood drips from her bruised mouth—

A humming fizzle of light. The air crackles. She shifts and vanishes.

—Simon swinging, still and lifeless, piss dripping to the floor—

The woman, mouth wide, head thrown back, blood blooming along her arms—

The buzzing pales and changes octave. Another pop.

—Simon, alive, tying the rope—

—the woman sobs with the wild relief of someone close

to the end—

Rachel Tussle.

They have her deathloop. How? Did Gates collect Rachel's loop in Saint-Lô and bring her back to York? The two ghosts – father and daughter – are in the same loop, overlapping. No, it's more than that. They're joined together, their loops twisting into each other, cycling energy – a multiloop. Rachel's restoration theorem in action.

I remember what Sam said upstairs: "*I survived the first splice.*"

Saint-Lô. The cuts on Rachel's arms. My long pale scars. Sam's bandages. He went into a double deathloop to learn how to stabilize the theorem from the letters Rachel sent to her father. This is the beginning of the phantasmic weapon Saunders and Harrow dreamed of. And, thanks to Sam, Gates now knows how to complete it.

"You," he snaps, shoving Sam back towards the table with the bottles on it. "Wait there."

Sam's face creases and he almost falls, but he steadies himself.

"You. Here." Gates pinches his fingers deep into my shoulder. I grit my jaw, trying to resist him, but he's way stronger than me. He pulls a fresh zip tie from his coat pocket.

I don't know how I get my aching limbs to move, but I do. A last burst of adrenaline and I twist out of Gates's grasp and drop, slamming the point of my elbow into the back of his knee. It's a daft move, but it works. He goes down with a bellow, reaching out and pulling me with him.

"Run!" I scream at Sam, trying to crawl away from Gates.

His weight comes down on my spine. I'm crushed to the floor, pain dancing up my back and through my injured chest. Sam hollers my name. I curse him for not getting the hell away from this mess. Gates is yelling at him, at me. My hoody jerks against my throat as I'm hauled backwards. Gates dumps me against the table leg, jarring my bruised back.

"You bas—" My curses are smacked out of me. Blood fills my mouth. Plastic jerks against my left wrist – NO! I kick out, but my prostheses are too heavy for my exhausted muscles. Still, I catch Gates in the ankle. I get a boot in the side for my trouble, sharp pain blooming through my ribs. Doubling over, I close my eyes. Gates kicks me again, knocking the breath from my lungs. He says something, but I don't hear the words, just the nasty anger in his voice as another kick sends stars through my skull.

My mouth is full of copper and my bones are on fire. I spit blood and drag myself up. My right wrist is zip-tied to the table leg. I give the plastic a sharp pull, but the leg is firmly bolted to the floor.

Sam is curled against the stainless-steel cabinets to my left, one hand above his head where he's been zip-tied to a cabinet handle. Gates squats in front of him, nose wrinkling like he smells something nasty.

"You didn't have to kill my father," Sam whispers.

Gates unfolds the photo he took from upstairs. "Your great grandpa knew nothing about entities or the occult. He was just a hanger on, following Henry about, picking up his scraps and following his orders. *Our* family built up S&H systems, until your dad duped my mam out of her fair share, took the company and ran it into the ground." He lets the photograph fall. "I might have my old man's last name, but I'm a Saunders through and through. No, I didn't have to kill your dad. I wanted to."

"All this for … revenge?" Sam's voice breaks.

"Ah no, that would be petty wouldn't it? And we Saunders are not petty folk. Let's call it a bonus. All I had to do was show Harrow the research and let him imagine how weaponizing ghosties could save the company. He was too close-minded to see how this" – Gates motions to the copper cage with the flickering deathloops inside – "is much more than a weapon; it's the next step in an ancient mathemagical theorem. Most so-called occultists are just collectors, wasting the phantasmic energy taken from trapped ghosts on petty, arrogant glamours. They're too afraid to put grand theory into practice. I'll be the one who pushes the boundaries of possibility. Magic is in my blood. It's my right."

Sam stares at the photo at his feet. "You're going to kill me too."

"Aye." Gates runs thick fingers through Sam's curls and

grips hard, lifting his head back. "Unavoidable. See, I'm not death-touched like you. I can't make myself into a cosy nest for wandering souls and that's the kind of power that opens up all kinds of mathemagical possibilities. I need you to seal the deal."

Sam's glare softens. "Then let Charlie go. He's got nothing to do with this."

"Afraid not. He knows too much, and if something goes wrong with you, I'm going to need a spare." Gates grins a nasty, happy grin. "But if this works then he'll be a witness to the most important advancement in mathemagics for two centuries." He looks at me and winks. "Lucky sod, eh?"

Gates draws his knife. I bellow a warning, thinking Sam's going to get slashed up, but Gates cuts his own hand, clenching his fist as blood splatters the floor. Next, he paces around the copper structure, squatting to redraw the catcher marks on the floor with his blood. When they're complete, he places the bottle traps from his bandolier into the cups in the frame, their stems sitting against the metal arches. One of the cups already has the remains of a broken bottle in it. There's space in the frame for fifteen bottles in total, sixteen including Simon's deathloop.

Panic tightens my throat. Everything Sam said to his dad, and Gates's words – *"I need you to seal the deal"* – start to make sense. I finally understand why Rachel ran.

Seers, like me and Sam, we're the solution to the theorem.

We walk a strange line between life and death. Like the

Emperor told me, normal people are like air to ghosts, but seer bodies are fixed and physical. That same stability means our flesh and blood can settle the bonds between multiple deathloops, giving them substance, something to hold on to so that they don't break apart.

I'm definitely not making it to my exams tomorrow. Two years of lessons and GCSE revision, all preparing me for a future that I don't get to have.

Raising the handle of his knife above one of the bottles, Gates pauses, whispers something, and strikes. The bottle shatters.

I smell the change – sharp electric ozone and an iron tang, like licking a cut inside my mouth. Something gross and mangled slides up the copper arc. The spliced deathloops lurch as Saint Margaret appears inside the multiloop, spread-eagled, her body a crushed mess of broken limbs.

Gates is grinning with an eager, zealous certainty. I realize he won't ever listen to reason, won't stop, won't slow, because he knows what he wants and he doesn't care who has to pay the price for him to get it.

The circles of catcher magic on the floor flare with red light. The multiloop deforms. Rachel, Simon and Saint Margaret flit inside the frame, screaming. I can't cover both of my ears with my wrist still linked to the table. Sam's face scrunches up and, like me, he tries to stifle the sound of agony echoing through the lab. It chases all else out of my mind. I just want it to stop.

It does. An electric buzz takes its place, rises in pitch,

falls, settles.

Gates looks over at me. "Are you watching, lad? One down, thirteen to go."

35

SIXTEEN SOULS

Each splintering crack of the knife on glass makes me wince. One by one the dead are caught by the copper frame, pulled along the wires down into the centre of the multiloop, building the weapon soul by soul.

Simon drops, rope taut, body swinging.

Blood flows down Rachel's arms.

Saint Margaret gasps beneath a heavy wooden door.

A handsome young man screams as he is cut open and his intestines are drawn out.

Earl Percy falls to his knees, an arrow in his shoulder.

Peter Rawley's head caves in, his skull crumpling.

A young woman is crushed beneath the wheel of a cart.

Lady Peckitt lies on her back, convulsing.

Inge of Jorvik cries as whips tear into her back.

A girl, more skeleton than child, is too weak to move.

Sir Danville is strung up, neck broken by the drop.

King Aelle's mouth twists in a silent scream as his back is peeled, his ribs cracked open and spread wide.

Emperor Septimus Severus clutches his chest, face screwed up in agony.

Foam bubbles from the sides of Ollie's blue-lipped grimace.

Heather presses her hand to her belly as blood trails through her fingers.

A bullet destroys Mr Harrow's face.

Sixteen souls flicker in a looping stream of death and despair, breaking up and reforming. The cold deepens. The electric crackle is high-pitched and frantic, like the whine of an engine pushed too far. Fissures charged bright with sparks pierce the looped ghosts, adding sudden heat to the icy air.

Sixteen souls.

Terror slices through my nerves. I realize there is still one stolen ghost missing. Where's Audrey? Grief bleeds into my fear. She was taken, but Gates hasn't added her to the multiloop yet. What if she's already been destroyed like Mad Alice and Ragged Peter? She can't be just … gone.

Gates strips off his coat, bandolier and shirt, then presses the tip of the knife to his chest. Blood drips down his bare torso. God, he's *carving* a ghost trap into his skin. The rust glow from the deathloops lights up his eager face. There's wildness in his eyes now, like he's high on something.

Bulk outlined by the bright multiloop, he slowly spreads his arms. The catcher marks etched into the floor are moving in spirals like giant cogs. His muttered chanting is stolen by the hiss of electric sparks. The ghost trap carved into his chest begins to glow red-hot, like the tip of a ciggie.

The whine in the air drops in pitch as a huge lightning bolt rips across the multiloop. Gates isn't smiling now. His brow is furrowed. Pain thins his lips. Raising his hand, he snaps his fingers at Sam.

The zip tie pings from Sam's wrist, freeing him.

What the...? My thoughts scramble to make sense of it. Telekinesis, like Scarlet Witch or Jean Grey. How?

What he said earlier – *"cosy nest for wandering souls"* – he was talking about some kind of possession. He cut a ghost trap mark into his own flesh, so is he trying to trap the souls inside himself?

No, not directly. Somehow his chanting, the symbols on the floor and the ghost trap on his chest let him absorb the phantasmic energy that the looped souls generate, dragging it right out of the system. And it's turning him into some kind of super-powered, telekinetic X-man.

That's the advance in mathemagics he was going on about. He doesn't want to sell the multiloop as a weapon, he wants to *become* the weapon, a super-powered human fuelled by the dead. If he can already snap plastic zip ties with a wave of his fingers, what will he become when the energy of all sixteen souls are inside him?

A living bomb with the power to rip through cities? He could destroy York in a heartbeat. He could extinguish hundreds of thousands of lives on a whim. He could hold governments ransom.

The Emperor made it sound like if he managed to possess me then he'd be the one in control, but this is different, these ghosts are trapped, reduced to batteries. They're powerless to stop what's happening to them.

"Get over here," Gates orders Sam.

Sam stands shakily, rubbing his wrists. God, his face is a mess, but his eyes are blazing.

"Don't do it!" I shout.

"I don't have a choice." Sam's eyes flutter closed, then open. "One of us *has* to stabilize the multiloop or the coterminous bonds will shred and all of the souls in there will be destroyed."

I don't know what a coterminous bond is, but I get the idea. If one of us doesn't walk into the heart of the multiloop, adding our flesh and blood to steady the links between the different ghosts, then the whole multiloop will tear itself apart. Bad news for Gates, but worse news for the souls trapped in the system.

I'm minutes away from losing Heather and Ollie forever. Ragged Peter and Mad Alice are already gone. Shredded. I can't let that happen to anyone else.

Whichever one of us steps in the multiloop is going to die. Mr Harrow made that clear. Sam survived two spliced deathloops, but sixteen ghosts one after the other? No way.

I don't want to die. I *really* want to live. Whoever is left behind will have to stop the weapon Gates becomes when he's got sixteen amped-up poltergeists trapped inside of him.

Sam is smarter than me and better at magic. He might actually stand a chance.

My skin tears against the zip tie as I pull at it. "I'll go in! Sam, stop, you pillock, I'll do it."

Sam lets out a sharp sob. Ignoring my shout, he walks towards Gates and the loop. Will he be torn to pieces straight off? Or will it be slow, facing each of the deaths in turn, his own end held back until the last possible moment?

Even with my wrist slick with blood, my scrunched-up hand won't slide through the plastic loop. I can't get free. I can't stop him. I'm crying, tears blurring my vision. Sam is about to die.

He steps on to the ring of symbols at the base of the copper frame and pauses. For a second, I think he's going to turn and look at me, say a final goodbye. But he doesn't.

36

THE MIRRORED WAY

Sam is falling backwards, away from the copper arches and the cracking multiloop. How? Silvereyes stands over him, fingers bent like claws. Where did he bloody come from? He grabs Sam, dragging him by his shirt, hauling him away from Gates and the multiloop.

A bark. Dante shoots past me, diving towards Sam. Mr Broomwood hurries after the dog, his dressing gown cord trailing. On his heels is Ophelia and behind her comes Mrs Tulliver, puffed up and pissed off.

Silvereyes vanishes and reappears beside me. I flinch, I can't help it, but he just motions at the zip tie on my wrist with a lazy wave. It snaps. I stare at him, bemused and afraid. He's not a poltergeist. Like them, he can touch physical things, but he seems to be able to control it – which should be impossible. And how is he so strong?

He motions for me to stand, but I can't. Not on my own. My skull is agony and I feel sick.

"Master Frith! Thank the Lord, we feared we would arrive too late." Villiers scoops me into his arms and plants a scratchy kiss on my forehead.

Done checking Sam over, Dante licks my face, whining with excitement. Villiers is petting him too, telling him he's a good dog, how they never would have found us without him.

Mrs Tulliver and Broomwood carry Sam to where I'm crouched. I fall into him, feeling his hair on my forehead, his heartbeat against mine.

"You're a prick, you know that?" My voice breaks.

His arms settle around me and my tears leak into his shirt. "The worst."

"Escape first, embrace anon," Villiers hisses, helping us both up.

The lift is opening. Someone else is here. Someone living. I think it's going to be Mitch and wish he hadn't come because he'll get hurt, but when the door is fully open Crew-Cut steps out. He's holding a nasty looking baton like the rozzers carry, but instead of police uniform he's dressed in dark clothes and a long coat, just like Gates. Apparently, creepy blokes into occult shit have their own dress code.

Silvereyes flits to his side.

I've never seen a ghost move quite like that. Disappear and reappear yes, but never that fast. *What is he?*

"Caleb Gates, you will stop this aberration," says Crew-Cut.

The energy in the air thickens and the trap mark on Gates's chest glows brighter. "You're from The Hand," he says.

"Jan Liska." Liska shows Gates the tattoo on his left wrist, then motions to Silvereyes. "This is Dusan."

"Dusan?" Gates sneers.

"He could not remember his name and so he chose another to suit him."

Dusan moves his hands, and I realize he's speaking in sign language. Liska interprets. "He says we may be few, but we are well connected. Meryem knew you'd try another path."

"Meryem can fuck off. *My* family started all this." The multiloop crackles and a bolt of lightning darts from the copper to strike Gates. He doesn't flinch.

"This atrocity is built on whispers we could not silence. Rachel Tussle started this." Liska nods at Ophelia. "And however noble her intentions, The Hand's secrets are not for occultists to toy with."

"You can't let someone better your piss-poor theorems, that it?"

"The mirrored way is sacred to the death-touched."

Dusan signs something and Liska nods. "He says you wish to enslave the dead rather than pay the price for symbiosis and true unity."

"Oh, my bleeding heart!" Gates roars. "It's just like The Hand to care about the pissing lot of humanity when only we matter, those with power. We should be their masters not their servants."

"I'm not a servant," says Liska. "We have a partnership."

"How romantic."

"Do this and you will become monstrous, Caleb. Some steps, though possible, are not meant to be taken." Liska looks over at me and Sam, but when he speaks he's talking to Villiers. "Get them both out, now. Whatever you do, keep them away from the aperture."

Aperture? He must mean the lightning-riddled copper-cage multiloop thing. The phantasmic weapon.

The trapped ghosts are a swirling horror now. Ollie's pale face twists, mouth open wide, then he fragments, replaced by Heather, then The Emperor, then Reid the Piper—

I don't reckon we've much time before the multiloop shreds. Not that I'm an expert or anything, but the whining sputter in the air is higher pitched, like the system is already straining.

Squaring his shoulders, Liska flicks his wrist. The collapsible baton in his hand expands to its full length. Gates moves – a sharp twist of his wrist and the baton tears itself from Liska's grip, spinning high above their heads and clattering into the counter.

Gates lunges, teeth barred, fist raised. Liska doesn't move. But Dusan does, shifting towards Liska until they're so close they're touching. Then, he steps *into* him, his body swallowed whole by Liska, who takes the full heft of Gates's fist to his face. His head snaps back with a crack like a brick being broken, but he doesn't fall. Gates throws another punch – but this time Liska slides to the right in a fast, slick movement that I swear down is quicker than is humanly possible, then turns, catching Gates off balance with a strike to the chest.

Villiers pulls Sam and me out of the way as Gates falls against the racks, sending empty bottle traps crashing around him. I can sense the ghost inside Liska, like a shadow under his skin. Their eyes are silver.

Possession is possible. And I realize *this* is what Gates wanted for himself: inhuman speed, strength and power, but he's taken it too far.

Who is in control when Dusan is possessing Liska? I can't know, but one thing I'm sure of, they're stronger together and they work as equals.

Air swells, magic screams. The few remaining bottles start to rattle in the racks, a tinkling uproar joined by shards of broken glass. There's a strange smell in the air, chemical, sharp. Liska goes down, apparently struggling for breath, then leaps up and the glass shards fly at Gates, who deflects them.

What if the strength Gates is pulling out of the aperture to fight Dusan and Liska is making the deathloops inside fragment faster?

That's the point, I realize. They're forcing him on the defence while Sam and me escape. Not because they care about us, or because they plan on saving the trapped ghosts, but to stop Gates from absorbing the phantasmic energy and becoming a living weapon. They're trying to use up the multiloop's energy quickly, forcing it to fragment. Heather, Ollie and the others will be shredded out of existence.

Not today.

Somehow, I need to break apart the multiloop and wind down the system without hurting the souls inside. There must be a solution that won't stabilize the theorem or channel the power to Gates. Ophelia said it was possible to free a soul from a deathloop by reminding them that they're dead. But *how*? Inside a deathloop I can hardly remember myself, let alone save anyone.

I look past Liska and Gates locked in battle and the shards of glass whirling in the air. Ophelia is standing beside the flickering loop, reaching out to her lost family. Behind the copper arches Rachel's face settles for a few seconds and I swear she's looking right at me.

Except she's not Rachel anymore.

For a half-breath I'm staring at the ghost of someone I know isn't trapped in the multiloop. Is it a trick or something, my mind making stuff up? But now I've seen the familiarity, I can't un-see it. No matter that her hair is different, her clothes, hell everything about her.

But it is her. It's always been her.

And it changes everything.

"I know how to stop this," I holler to Sam over the crackling hum of the multiloop.

He grips my hands and I think he's going to argue. Instead he nods. "What do we do?"

"We", like we're a team.

335

I could kiss him.

"We need to go inside the multiloop to free the souls." I try to sound confident. "I can do it, but I'll forget myself. It always happens. So, when we're in there, I need you to help me remember who I am."

"OK," says Sam, like it's really that simple. He squeezes my hand harder. Shite, he's brave.

Villiers grimaces. "Master Liska was very clear that you must not enter the aperture."

"You will die," says Mrs Tulliver at the same time Broomwood yells something about me being an idiot lad.

We risk giving Gates the advantage, but if I'm right, that won't matter.

"Trust me," I say.

Villiers looks at the multiloop like his heart is breaking, then he nods. "Our Lord bless and protect you both."

Sam and me don't so much run as duck and scramble, keeping to the edges of the room. He gasps as a flying piece of glass slices his forehead, wipes away the blood, and we push on.

A shout bursts from Liska. Dusan moves inside his skin. They yell at us again, their silver eyes panicked and angry. Gates knocks them back. We're seconds away from the aperture. Electricity riddles my limbs, but I feel only the faintest static. It's the cold that aches. Our breath comes out as thick white billows.

Something hits my chest and I can't move forward. Sam stumbles too. The air feels thick and hard to move through.

What's doing this?

Liska and Dusan. One of their hands is outstretched, fingers bent like they have hold of us. Gates gestures sharply. Pressure rolls into a broiling heat that makes the air around them simmer. They block the attack well enough, but they're sweating, blood runs down their face, and their teeth are gritted in concentration.

Something metallic slams into them – the twisted remains of the racking. Sam and I tumble forward as Dusan lunges at us, his body breaking from Liska's. I push Sam ahead of me. My stinging palms smack to the floor, cushioning my fall.

I look up for Sam. I'm a metre from the copper arches, but Sam has landed on the ring of catcher marks around the base of the multiloop. Dusan has me by my left prosthesis. I kick out, but I can't dislodge him.

Behind him Liska is getting the shite pummelled out of him. Without Dusan's strength and speed, he's no match for Gates, and I realize he'll give his life to stop this if he has to. That weighs on me, but there's no time to explain my plan.

Dusan pulls on my leg and I slide away from the multiloop. NO!

Suddenly Villiers is there, lacing a bicep around Dusan's neck and hauling him off me. Dusan flickers and vanishes, reappearing behind Villiers and sending him flying. But Broomwood, Ophelia and Mrs Tulliver take Villiers' place, throwing themselves on to Dusan.

"Go!" Broomwood shouts.

Sam pulls me up. Our bodies break the surface of the

aperture. As we fall into fragments of lives lived and lost the last thing I hear is Gates's bellow of triumph before the whole world starts screaming.

37

†HE NIGH†INGALE

The cold is sharp, ice shards straight to my marrow, aching teeth and cracking lips. Hands claw at my face and hair. I roll over and stand up.

I'm on a street, alone. This is York, familiar buildings stripped of modern shopfronts, no adverts or flashing lights, no cars. The air smells like autumn and manure. A young woman with a world-weary face watches me. Millie. I step into the road towards her. The sound of a cart on cobbles. I'm thrown back.

No, pulled.

A man with sour breath rips my woollen dress. I know him and I hate him. He calls me traitor, whore, witch. Inge presses her hand to mine, gritting her teeth against the first lash of the whip.

I scramble forward. The earth under my fingers becomes

fine linen, damp with sweat. The air is sour with sickness and age, the stink of a body wasting away. My lungs are heavy, rattling with every breath, and with the tightness comes fear and sadness.

I tear off the covers. I'm here to find someone.

Rope chafes my face as the hangman slips the noose over my head.

No! Their deaths aren't mine. I drop into darkness, landing in a hospital car park. I'm exhausted and crying because that kid is going to die and it's my fault. I don't notice the man step out of the bushes beside the walkway until he lashes out. My palm stings. There's something warm and wet seeping through my clothes. I can hear him screaming, or is that me?

Hands press me down. I'm in a wood beside an open field filled with rotting bodies. A murder of crows circles overhead, landing to pick at the dead. I'm slick with fear, tied up at wrist and ankle, no shirt, skin bare and raw. The cuts are done slowly, sharp agony either side of my spine. Next, they'll peel the skin back, break my ribs open one by one... I'll never survive.

The breeze licks my sweaty face. I smell fire and I know all hope is burning. I shouldn't have come here. I'm not strong enough. I've never been strong enough.

A mouth on mine, crushing my lips hard enough to draw blood. Salt and iron. The rope slides off my wrists. My feet are free and I step into the woods, clinging to Sam, a drowning lad seeking dry land. His hands are hot through my clothes.

"Charlie," he whispers, catching a tear from my cheek with

the pad of his thumb.

I am not a king called Aelle, or a man called Simon. I am not a woman called Heather, or a girl called Millie.

I am Charlie and it is not my time to die.

"You have to help them, remember."

I take Sam's hand. "We need to find Rachel."

Time twists in on itself, but I'm in control now. The multiloop shifts at my command. Smoky trees and the sodden battlefield turn into the crumbling ruins of Saint-Lô. Rachel, slumped forward, looks up at us through red-rimmed eyes. Is it really her? I fall to my knees, pushing back her hair and see another face in the bones of the first.

"Audrey!" I hiss, shaking her as gently as I can. "Audrey, it's Charlie."

She coughs. "My name is Rachel—"

"I know, I know, but you call yourself Audrey now." I'm kneeling in a pool of blood. Mine? Hers? It doesn't matter. "You were running from these blokes, right, changing identity all the time and when you died, well, I guess the instinct to hide was still there. You became someone else for a while, in case they were still looking for you."

Ghosts remember themselves. Their clothes and the way they look is all modelled off how they were in life. If they have enough control and self-awareness they can change appearance, like Ophelia did when she broke her tether. It's rare to change as dramatically as Rachel did, but I don't know of a soul more aware of the painful details of being human than her.

"Charlie!" Sam's voice is sharp with panic. Dark shadows gather in the corner, clagging together into the shape of two men. Saunders and Harrow.

"They're not really here," I say, not sure if I'm speaking to Sam or Rachel, or trying to stop myself panicking. "This is all a memory."

Sam's arms begin to bleed again. I'm only half aware of the wet heat running down my ruined back.

"You died here," I tell her. "Those men murdered you."

"No," says Rachel, scrunching her eyes closed.

"Yes! Listen, please. We've done this already but I was just a kid. I fell into your loop in Saint-Lô. I was scared, remember?"

"You screamed at me."

"Yeah, do you remember what I said?"

She opens her eyes. They're puffy with tears. "Dead, you're dead, you're dead, you're dead!"

"You. Are. Dead." I sound out each word. "I thought Audrey pulled me out of your loop, but you *are* Audrey. *I* saved *you*, but I was so scared I pushed the memories of what happened away. You came back to York with me, remember, probably to guard your dad's lab—"

"I wanted to tell you everything, to warn you and ask you to go into the chapel," Rachel says, and I think I see a hint of Audrey in her face and in her voice. "Then I would finally know what happened to him. But you weren't ready, Charlie, and maybe I wasn't either. It wasn't safe. The restoration theorem can't be used, not ever—"

"It *has* been used; we're inside a multiloop right now. You knew this might happen and you left me a message asking me to remember Saint-Lô, to remember this moment and how I freed you. Well, I do, so here I am again, telling you what I told you before, that you're dead, Rachel Tussle, you're dead and that means you're free."

"I'm free," she whispers. "We're all free."

I stand as she does. Other figures step into the cellar, gathering as shadows, their faces stretched and distant. Ollie and Heather are here, side by side with Little Beth. Mr Harrow stands beside his son wearing a complicated look of mixed-up pride and regret. Sam stares at him, tears welling, then he reaches for my hand. I take it and I feel stronger.

"You're dead," I tell them all. "This is a trap built to steal and use your energy. The man taking it will hurt people, but none of you have to stay here."

"I must," says Mr Harrow. "This is my project, my legacy."

The other souls mill about, confused and frightened. Little Beth begins to cry as the loops shift around us, brick walls falling away to reveal piles of rags on wooden floorboards, blood dripping on wet leaves, a cobbled street, a canopied bed with heavy drapes, a brightly-tiled chamber, the colours of each place swirling into one.

"Charlie, I can see the lab," says Sam.

He's right. The limits of this place are flexing. I'm dimly

aware of the room around us, figures moving beyond the outline of the copper arches.

Rachel's torn clothing shifts into a tailored skirt suit, her face filling out, lips reddening. Her hair is blonder now, curling into perfect waves.

Rachel smiles Audrey's smile. "Charlie, you remembered."

I nod. "So did you."

"Thank you."

"Next time, don't be so bloody cryptic, yeah?"

"I have no more secrets." She turns to the little group around us. "Hold on to the seers."

Hands reach for us. Heather is on one side of me, Ollie on the other. Seeing her father, Audrey shifts her appearance to look like Rachel again. She's in total control of how she looks, more than any spirit I've ever known. She and Simon take Sam's hands. Ollie clutches Millie, who grips Reid the Piper, who is embracing Little Beth. Rawley's palm is on my shoulder. Earl Percy grabs my sleeve with tight fists, his expression desperate. I let him. The remaining Mouldy Oldies mutter and argue amongst themselves.

"Take hold!" I tell them.

Light criss-crosses my vision. Behind it are the white tiles and shining chrome of the lab. I look to Sam, checking he's ready, and side-by-side we walk out of the multiloop, leading the dead behind us.

Not all of them follow.

38

ALL FALL DOWN

Everything happens at once.

We leave the aperture in a surge of phantasmic energy as the multiloop fragments. Snatches of other-worldly voices cry out as the dead stream past me and Sam, twisting rope-like into Gates. His body lifts off the ground from where he was lying motionless. His eyes and mouth stretch wide like he's screaming.

Copper splinters, sparks, crackling heat and light and a pulse that knocks me forward, head over arse, tumbling into Sam. Gates is upright now, floating a metre off the ground. Lost souls writhe inside his skin, flickers of phantasmic energy scenting the air like metal and brine. His eyes glow silver. It ripples through his flesh.

No! This shouldn't happen. We didn't die. We freed the ghosts instead, breaking the multiloop open. Heather is here, so is Ollie, Rawley, Millie, Earl Percy, Little Beth and Reid the Piper. Villiers and Reid are locked in each other's arms, kissing passionately. Ophelia hugs Rachel and Simon close.

But we didn't save them all.

Sam is shaking, his clothes soaked in blood. I look down. So are mine. My back is sticky with it. *We bled inside the multiloop.* That must have been enough seer flesh to stabilize the theorem, and the system still had fuel. Mr Harrow chose his project over freedom, and most of the Mouldy Oldies were too stubborn and set in their ways to follow us.

Now they've become something terrible.

Gates is looking at his hands like he's a newborn seeing the world for the first time. Teeth gritting into a frantic grin, he presses his palms together and the air pressure changes. My ears threaten to pop. He throws his arms wide and a shockwave rips through the room, the pressure keeping Sam and me flattened to the floor as the cabinets beside us fracture, handles wrenching off and doors exploding into sharp fragments.

Where are Liska and Dusan? I can't see them.

A metal handle flies at my face. Heather throws herself forward. The stainless steel rebounds off her arm and imbeds itself in the wall, cracking the tiles.

"Bloody hell," she gasps, and laughs.

She's a poltergeist – all the ghosts we freed from the aperture are poltergeists, at least for a short time.

Gates is shaking, maybe struggling to contain the ghostly energy inside him. Tiles tear from the walls. Cracks zigzag across the ceiling. The whole building groans.

"Heather, get the boys out," shouts Rachel.

"What about you?" I ask.

"Dad and I have to end this."

Ophelia laces her fingers through Simon's. "When you run empty, take from me until it is done."

Simon cups her face. "Not you, sweetheart."

"We are a family," she replies simply. "We do this together."

Rachel takes her other hand, her smile sad, but determined. Brave.

"Count me in," Rawley's heavy glare is fixed on Gates. "I trained him up as a lad. I reckon that makes him my responsibility."

As four poltergeists stalk towards Gates, hand in hand, the floor ripples under their feet. The air pressure surges. The table wrenches and groans. Above us the ceiling creaks.

A cry comes from the far right of the lab, near the lift. Dusan is helping Liska up from … oh, shit. Liska's corpse lies broken inside the contorted metal racking. His ghost clings to Dusan.

"Oi!" I bellow at them.

Dusan signs something to us. I don't know exactly what he's saying, but I do understand what all the pointing means. He's telling us to get out.

I want to say I'm sorry that Liska's dead, but they're striding past us to face Gates. Liska is fully upright now, looking less shocked and more in control, and I get that going into battle is something he knows so well not even death will stop him.

Ollie shouts a warning. I throw myself over Sam, trying to shelter him from the sharp tiles swirling our way. But Ollie flings up his arms and the currents change, compressing the tile until it explodes into a fine powder.

"Did you see that?" he cheers. "I'm basically an Avenger."

"We should not linger," says Millie.

"You heard the woman. Out!" shouts Heather.

Sam and me stagger towards the lift, leaning on each other. If the electrics are out, we're buggered. I never thought I'd say it, but I wish there were stairs. Debris is hurtling all over the place but Heather, Ollie and the others protect us from the worst of it. Flying lumps of copper, wood and stone splinter into harmless fragments or change direction mid-air, giving us a clear path.

I glance back towards the broken aperture and catch sight of the six ghosts surrounding Gates. Strange smoke drifts up from their joined hands. The air around them shimmers blinding white.

Brick crunches. Concrete churns. Dust in my mouth, raining on to my face. Agony in my back. I cough. Sam rolls against me, coughing too. There's hardly any air. The ground shifts. Bellowing, we slide over brick and stone, then settle, gasping.

I think Sam's house just fell on us.

"Heather?" I splutter and spit as dust coats my tongue.

She's above us, hands over her head like she's holding up

the earth. "Push up!" she shouts. "Keep that air gap open!"

Ollie, Millie, Reid the Piper and Little Beth are all beside her. Brick moves. The light dims, but I can still just make out their faces, all straining their newfound power to keep us from being crushed.

"Can't … hold … it … for long," gasps Reid.

"Charlie," Sam sobs. "My shoulder, it's … I can't feel my fingers."

His short breaths warm my neck. Something is wedged into the cuts on my back and its agony. I try to shift slightly and Sam cries out.

OK, no moving. "Just hold on," I tell him. "We'll be all right."

A lie, blatant and daft. The rubble shifts to block the last of the light. In the new darkness no one says what we all know, but I can hear Leonie in my thoughts laying it out for us: *"the amplification of phantasmic energy doesn't last long once the poltergeist is released from the bottle trap."*

At some point soon, their borrowed strength will fail and Heather, Ollie and the other poltergeists will go back to being regular souls, their ghostly bodies passing straight through the material world. The hollow we're stuck in will collapse, crushing us.

"Take from me, Master Reid." Villiers speaks into the dusty dark.

"And me." That's Broomwood, I recognize his dulcet tones from his many evening rants.

"Too much and you'll be used up," warns Ollie. "It could

349

take you centuries to recover."

"We care not," says Mrs Tulliver.

"It will hurt." There's an edge to Heather's voice and I realize she knows that pain. I knew ghosts could injure each other, but I didn't understand that one could give their energy or essence to another. Or have it taken by force. Is this what the Mouldy Oldies did to her when they thought she'd overstepped and needed punishing? Is that why she'd disappear for days or even weeks at a time, because she wasn't strong enough to hold herself together?

"Take a little from many," says a voice above us. I don't know who is speaking; I recognize the voice, but can't place it.

There are more voices now, ten, twenty, or more, all crying pledges of support and invitations to take from them. I feel them. It's a tingling down my spine and in my hands. At least, I hope that's something like sixth sense and not a sign of serious injury.

I imagine ghostly hands reaching through the brick and concrete around us, lending Heather and the others strength to keep the ceiling up and the small air hole open, all to keep Sam and me alive.

Tears mix with the dust and blood on my cheeks. The ghosts of York are here for us.

39

A ROOM OF ONE'S GHOST

"Muuuum!" a high-pitched voice hollers in my ear. "He's waking up!"

I'm in ward seventeen with a drip in the back of my hand – fluids, antibiotics, maybe painkillers by the feel of it. Poppy's on a chair beside my bed. I snag her for a hug. Feet patter and a weight presses against my side as Lorna clambers on to the bed beside her sister, her mouth running a thousand miles a minute.

I don't answer. I can't. I just need to ignore the pain and hold my sisters close for a second, because I've never been this thankful to see the little brats in all my life.

"Gis a hand, eh," I say. "Help me sit up." They have fun playing with the control buttons and the top half of my bed slowly rises. I'm so stiff I can hardly move. When I try, everything from neck to hips feels crusted and taut.

"Careful, they sutured the wounds on your back, you'll be very tender." Heather steps through the curtains around my bed. The fabric doesn't move – no more poltergeist powers.

I open my hand and she laces her fingers with mine. Are her lips touched by a smile that somehow encompasses pride and love and the history of everything we've been through. "Can you forgive me, Charlie?"

I blink back tears. "If you can forgive me."

Lorna is frowning at me. "Are your invisible people here?"

I hesitate. Heather raises her brow. I remember how the girls said they could *feel the ghosts there*, but I don't have the brainpower to process what that means right now.

"Only one," I say, not breaking eye contact with Heather. "Her name is Doctor Heather Noble and she saved my life. She's basically a superhero."

Lorna grins. "Cool."

"There are lots more outside," whispers Poppy.

"More ghosts?" I ask.

"You know Broomwood." Heather shrugs. "He already rounded up a good few souls to bring to your rescue. After all that, word got out and now almost every ghost in York knows about what you and Sam did for them. There's interest, obviously. Free souls have been flocking to the hospital for hours. Ollie and Dante are out front reminding the hordes to keep off the ward and give you space."

"Where's Sam?"

"His mam got him a private room down the hall. Villiers and Reid are keeping watch outside."

"Is he hurt, though?" I ask, worried. "His shoulder—"

She adjusts the lanyard that holds her hospital ID. When she speaks it's with the experience and authority of a medical professional. "On top of injuries to his neck suggestive of a partial hanging, a broken nose, and deep lacerations to both arms, he suffered an anterior dislocation of his right shoulder and a serious compound fracture to his right forearm. He had surgery yesterday to relocate the bone and close the skin. No complications. He's stable."

I shift in the bed, wincing as pain flares up my back. "Can I see him?"

Her face falls. "He's … he needs a bit of time. He just lost his dad. Twice. And he's on strong painkillers; it's all a bit much."

I get it. A thing like that, what he's seen, what he's done, what's been done to him, that doesn't just go away. But … what if it always feels like too much for him? What if he needs to go away and never see me again? I'm ready to tear myself out of bed and get down the hall, no matter how many ghosts are out there, but I can't force him to see me if he doesn't want to. We all have our limits and boundaries and I have to respect his, no matter how much it hurts.

The curtain around my bed is ripped back. Mum. She kisses my forehead.

"Thank God, thank God." She kisses me again. "Dad is on his way, he's just dropping your cousins with Chrissie. Yes, yes, she's back home again, responding well. How are you feeling? Should I call a nurse?" Worry has deepened the crow's feet beside her eyes. She'll be thinking of how close they came to losing me again.

"I love you, Mum, and I'm sorry."

"Oh, Charlie, I love you so much it's stupid. And don't be sorry, it's not your fault. Thank God they dug you out before—" A sob and she presses her forehead to my hand for a long moment, then shakes her head. "The police handled it badly. It was all a misunderstanding, you're not a suspect at all. They're now claiming they never sent an officer over."

Makes sense. Jan Liska used the uniform to gain access and trust but he was never with the police. He and Dusan were sent by The Hand, whoever they are.

"Hey, look who's awake." It's Dad. Two strides and he's ruffling my hair and kissing the top of my head. Tears shine in his eyes. I put my arms around him as best I can without pulling on my stitches and we huddle a while.

"Does anyone have a pen and paper," I ask when we break apart.

"What for?" asks Mum.

"I need to write a very stern letter about the proper care of garden roses."

"You sure about this?" asks Mitch.

I lay an arm over his shoulders, being careful not to knock his cryptolenses askew, and ease myself to the edge of the mattress. "Yeah, mate. Let's do it."

The curtain around my bed is semi-drawn so I put my other arm around Ollie and together they help me stand. I wince as my stitches pull.

"Feeling steady?" asks Leonie. She seems a lot better today, but there's a new wariness in her. She flinches at loud noises and Mitch says she's sleeping with the lights on, when she sleeps at all.

When I grimace and nod, they let me go. I take a trial step. It hurts all through my torso, but walking in my prostheses is manageable.

The official word, no matter how daft it sounds, is that I sustained my injuries when Sam's house landed on us. The collapse was the result of a slow gas leak meeting a flame, destabilizing the foundations and bringing down the Harrow house and part of the neighbouring property.

It's utter bollocks, so I reckon another member of The Hand is behind the cover up. Ollie thinks someone official will be round to talk to us soon, but so far there's been no sign of anyone with any answers, living or dead.

And I'm bloody keen on getting some answers. The papers reported three casualties: millionaire business owner Francis Lish Harrow, his employee Caleb Gates and a John Doe, still unidentified. Liska.

We lost people. Good, brave people. Liska, Dusan, Peter Rawley, Rachel, Simon and Ophelia are all gone. They're not *shredded*, according to Heather, but *dissolved*, their consciousness, or whatever ghosts are made of, spread thin over the whole city. They'll come back, piecing themselves together, but it could take a lifetime.

Gates is dead. But in my world dead doesn't mean gone. If there's a chance his ghost is out there then I need to know.

But first I want to see Sam.

He might not even want me as a friend now, let alone anything more. I don't mean to push things, but my nightmares haven't stopped, if anything they're worse. I need to see for myself that he's all right. Then I'll leave him be.

Mitch opens the ward door for me. As soon as I make it into the hallway I stop in my tracks like I've been punched.

Sodding hell. Heather wasn't kidding. The corridor is still packed with the dead, the newly deceased and long timers alike – several cyclists, a man covered in brick dust, a woman in a smart suit. Roderick from The Snickleway Inn chats to a clique of nuns. There's a contingency of ruffed noblemen, a man in full armour, tangle-haired women with rouged cheeks, deceased patients in dressing gowns, a nurse with an old-fashioned watch pinned to her apron, teenagers wearing ripped jeans and Converse, and more, all the way down the hallway.

As one, they all turn and stare at me, mutters dropping into silence. I clench my fists, willing myself steady.

"Make some room," Ollie bellows. "Noble protector of the corporeally-challenged coming through."

I'd laugh if I weren't so flummoxed. As the ghosts step back to let me pass, living doctors, orderlies and patients walk through them, but I don't feel so unsettled watching both worlds – life and afterlife – meet anymore.

Ghostly hands reach out to brush against me as we pass, but they're gentle, not grasping. Tentatively, I reach back. Murmurs of thanks become hearty cheers. An old man clasps my hands in his. Women dip into curtseys, silk and wool rustling. Some bow, hands over their hearts.

I'm somewhere between numbness and on fire. *Don't cry. Don't cry.* It's all too much to take in at once. I'm trying not to shake.

Mrs Tulliver is just up ahead. I stop and greet her. She flushes with pleasure. I nod to Roderick the Elizabethan barman, whispering my thanks to the other ghosts I know gave part of themselves to keep Sam and me safe until the fire crews and ambulance personnel could dig us out. There is a bubble of hope lodged somewhere around my diaphragm, that maybe, just maybe, I don't need to be so afraid anymore.

A living nurse stops us from going into Sam's room. "Excuse me, that's a private room. Who are you?"

My chest feels tight. "Charlie. I'm a mate of Sam's."

"Sorry, family only."

"He is family," a voice calls from behind the door.

The nurse pushes it open. Sam is awake, half sitting up against the pillows, with Mrs Tulliver's cat Seamus curled up on his feet. "He's my secret boyfriend."

I almost choke with happy laughter. A warm, soft feeling sparks inside me, like dying embers given a blast of oxygen.

My friends leave me at the door. It closes behind me, hiding the eager press of the dead, and suddenly I'm alone with Sam. His nose is swollen and there are dark bruises under

357

his eyes. One arm is in bandages. The other is in a thick cast with metal pins sticking out and joining to a metal bracket along his forearm.

He's staring at me, like maybe he doesn't ever want to look away again.

"I hope it's all right I'm here," I mumble. "I know you wanted space—"

"Get up here." He pats the bed and grimaces a little as he slides over to give me room.

I settle in beside him, tucking my body carefully against his, my head on his uninjured shoulder so I don't have to lie on my sore back. Seamus opens one eye to glare at us, turns over and goes back to sleep.

"So, you're a cat person then," I say.

"He kind of adopted me," says Sam.

"Dante won't like that."

Silence. And I let it be for a long while, the two of us just existing, together.

I think I hear him whisper and I tilt my head up. He's crying, silent tears drifting down puffy cheeks. I don't tell him that everything is going to be fine and that he's going to come out of this stronger at the end of it, because that's not how grief works. All I can be is here with him, if he wants me. He's quiet for a while longer. I give him the space.

"My mother wants us to move to Italy as soon as I'm strong enough." His voice hums through his ribcage. "She's looking at apartments in Florence. There's a private gender clinic who will take me on, and a college I can go to."

"Oh." I struggle to keep my face impassive, because if he wants to go then I can't stop him – I *won't* stop him. I want him to be wherever he needs to be.

"What will you do now?" he asks.

That's it then. He's decided to leave.

When I think I can talk without crumbling I sit up and face him. "Heal. Study, try and scrape some passes during my GCSE re-sits, because I kinda missed all of my exams, and then…" I hesitate slightly.

The Charlie of a month ago wouldn't say what comes next. I've lain awake thinking about it these past few nights, and it doesn't matter that Sam's not going to be here, because it doesn't change what I need. My mind is set on what to do with the life Heather gave me.

"I'm going to make another batch of that paint and ward the streets," I say. "No matter how long it takes. I'm going to hunt down books on theorems and learn to use them, even if it's hard. I'm going to find Meryem and the rest of The Hand, whoever they are, wherever they are, and learn what I can about being death-touched, or a seer, or whatever you want to call it. I know how to free ghosts from deathloops now, and there are still plenty of trapped souls all over the city. I'm going to do what I can for them. And if another soul catcher like Caleb Gates comes around I'm going to stand between him and the ghosts of York."

"Even if it's dangerous?" asks Sam.

"Yeah. What you said about this being a gift. It's not. I'll always say that it's not. But it is my reality and I'm in control of what to do with it. All this has made me realize that at the end of the day, people are what really matter. If I can make a difference to their lives, or afterlives, then I want to try."

Sam is watching me with an intense look. The furrow in his brow lifts. "Well, if we're warding the whole city we're going to need to get hold of a bigger stockpot."

I look up sharply.

"I'm not leaving York, Charlie. How could I?"

Oh.

I burst with a relieved laugh, and start to cry at the same time, leaning into him. He's kissing my cheekbone, and I move so that my lips meet his. He's soft and warm. He smells of citrus and sleep. I'm committing it all to memory, taking in every second of him because we're so bloody lucky to be here.

Sam swallows, his chin trembling. "I'm not OK, Charlie, and … I don't know if I will be, maybe not for a very long time." His fingers meet mine. "But I've been talking to Miri and she's helped me realize that moving to Florence feels like running away. York was my big fresh start. It was the place I came to be my true self, and I am myself here, with you and our ghosts." His lips quirk. "Plus, I still need to take you on that date."

"Oh, yeah," I smile as something warm unfurls in my chest: the promise of orchestral music and fireworks. "Where do you want to go?"

"Anywhere that doesn't involve breaking into ecclesiastical property."

I laugh again. Kiss him again, because I can, because I'm not alone.

I never was.

Acknowledgements

They say it takes a village to raise a child. A book is a lot like a baby: it's an expensive undertaking that consumes your attention but is incredibly rewarding. It's certainly taken an entire community, and some impressive plot twists, to get Charlie and his ghosts into the hands of readers.

Thank you first and foremost to Palomi Kotecha for your unending support and friendship. Without you I'd probably be lost in the woods wondering how old I am. If I achieve anything it's because you steadfastly remind me that I can. Also, thanks for making me buy a smartphone that one time.

Thank you to those who took the first look at this novel: the Prologue Preservation Society, Laura Bartlett, and everyone at Curtis Brown Creative. Sorry I took out the kecks.

Thank you to Tash McAdams, whose belief in this story came when I needed it most, and to Cynthia Murphy, the best Write Mentor mentor ever! Thank you to Lee Newbury for being a wonderful friend and a great inspiration.

I am eternally grateful to my amazing sensitivity readers: Reuben Thomas for affirming this story's quiet kind of thunder, and to Amber Sidbury and Dan Sidbury for their advice and guidance regarding Charlie's disability. Any mistakes or inaccuracies are entirely my own.

To my wonderful editor Leonie Lock. Thank you for your passion for *Sixteen Souls* and for Oodie clad zoom meetings, amazing publishing advice, and (most importantly) for your friendship.

Thank you to Becka Moor, my lovely typesetter, for your unceasing patience and beautiful layouts.

Can I get a bit of commotion for the cover! To my incredible and talented cover designer Andrew Davis, I am in awe. IN AWE!!! Thank you for saying yes.

My endless gratitude to the wonderful Yasmin Morrissey who believed in *Sixteen Souls*, took a chance on an about-to-be-indie novel and made my author dream come true. To Harriet Dunlea, Hannah Griffiths, Ellen Thomson, Claire Yeo, Sarah Dutton and the whole Scholastic team for being so incredible. It is an honour to be one of your authors!

I am profoundly grateful for the amazing support of my fellow Waterstones Booksellers. To Lydia, who has read this story more times than anyone should have to. To Kurde, the best manager in the world and for believing in me as an author. To Tabitha, for all the writing chat. To Gemma for the home-baked goodies. To the Cheltenham Festival crew for screaming the loudest. See you at Bentley's, my friends! Thank you to so many others across the company for featuring and uplifting my queer little story, I wish I could name you all individually.

To authors Lee Newbury (yes, I'm thanking you again!), Amy McCaw, Brianna Bourne, Marisa Noelle, K.D Edwards, Erik J Brown, Menna van Pragg, Kathryn Foxfield, Rory Michelson, H.M Long, Bex Hogan, Kat Ellis, Dawn Kurtagich, Phil Stamper and Adam Sass for writing such amazing books and for championing mine.

A very special thank you to the BookTok community and all of my online friends. I could quite literally never have launched *Sixteen Souls* into the world without you. To every single one of you who posted about this book, who pre-ordered, who left reviews and organized read-a-longs, you've transformed my life, thank you!

To Jacob Demlow for being the best book friend. London is lonely without you.

To Becky Albertalli. Words fail to encapsulate my immense gratitude for everything you have done for me as a bisexual woman and author who was afraid to share my writing with the world.

Thank you to Dad, who will never read this book but believes in it anyway. To Mum, for being my best friend (even though you think that's kind of sad). To my sisters, Helly and Emma, for being so supportive of my dreams.

To Ed. My ghost will haunt your ghost.

And lastly, to you, dear reader. Thank you for taking a chance on a strange little book about chaotic ghosts in York. I appreciate it more than *you* can ever know.

About the Author

A lover of dark and tightly woven stories,
Rosie is inspired by creepy things in junk shops,
haunted houses and strange magic. She is a graduate
of Curtis Brown Creative and Write Mentor. By day
she works as a bookseller. By night, she spends time
sewing big skirts with outrageously large pockets and
wondering why her family has a suspiciously large
collection of cauldrons. She currently resides in a
mysterious pocket of the Sussex countryside with her
very patient spouse and two cats called Tinkerfluff
and Captain Haddock.

You can connect with Rosie via TikTok and
Instagram (**@merrowchild**) or on her website
www.rosietalbot.co.uk where you can sign up to
her scintillating newsletter and gain access to free
stories and artwork.